THE BLOOD HEIR

THE TETHERING, BOOK FOUR

MEGAN O'RUSSELL

Ink Worlds Press

To the boy waiting in the window who started it all

THE BLOOD HEIR

WALLS

"*Volavertus* Aunt Iz." Emilia's voice trembled. "*Volavertus* Isadora Gray."

The mirror in her hands shimmered for a moment before fading in the dim light.

"*Volavertus* Molly Wright." The mirror shook in Emilia's hand. "*Volavertus* Larkin Gardner."

Emilia brushed the tears from her cheeks with her sleeve. The fabric was rough with soot and scented with smoke.

Fire. Thousands of people turned to ash. The Pendragon flying away, leaving Rosalie—

"*Volavertus* Dexter Wayland!"

But the mirror didn't care how desperate Emilia sounded. No face appeared in the glass. Emilia pressed her forehead to the cold concrete wall. The florescent lights made the grey walls look sickly and filthy. Like the whole Academy was rotting from within.

Emilia lowered herself to the hall floor. She wanted to run away, to find Jacob and Connor. The Academy nurse wouldn't let Emilia go into the infirmary with her to try and heal Claire. The headmistress had taken Jacob and Connor to the boys' wing.

Emilia had been left alone and helpless in the shadowy corridor.

The pull in Emilia's chest told her Jacob was still nearby. He was angry, frightened, and tired. But so was she.

"He's fine," Emilia whispered to herself. "Jacob is fine."

Footsteps carried down the hall. Emilia leaped back to her feet. Her legs screamed in protest at being asked to move again.

"I want to see—" Emilia began, but it wasn't the headmistress who ran down the hall toward her. It was only a girl, the same age as Emilia, wearing the grey and black uniform of an Academy student.

The girl slowed as she reached Emilia, eyeing her up and down before shrugging and opening the door to the infirmary that Emilia had been forbidden from entering.

"Wait! Let me see"—the girl slammed the door—"Claire."

Emilia shut her eyes tight, forcing herself not to scream or pound on the door. They needed help. They needed the nurse to heal Claire.

Images flew unbidden through Emilia's mind. The Pendragon shooting spells at them. The spell missing Connor and hitting Claire.

Panic rose in Emilia's chest. The Pendragon was still out there. Emilia was pacing in front of the infirmary door before she even realized her feet were moving.

She needed to do something. She had to help.

"*Volavertus* Isadora Gray," Emilia said to the mirror again.

Aunt Iz wasn't answering. She had been rescuing Samuel with Larkin, Dexter, and Molly. Dexter had collapsed the tunnel. The Pendragon had known they were coming.

Stone. It all went back to the traitor MAGI Jeremy Stone.

"*Volavertus* Proteus." Emilia's voice echoed down the long hall.

The mirror shimmered again, but this time the light didn't fade into nothing. Instead, a face appeared. The man had long hair that was greyer than the last time Emilia had seen him only a week before. The creases on his face seemed deeper, and they shifted to lines of worry as he looked out of the mirror at Emilia.

"Emilia Gray," Proteus said, his deep voice resonating from the depths of the mirror, "I had not expected to hear from you. Isadora said you had been taken to safety."

"We had," Emilia said, trying to hide her fear, "but the Pendragon found us. He found Rosalie. He took her. Proteus, she's dead." Tears burned in the corners of Emilia's eyes, but now wasn't the time to cry, not when so many people were still in danger.

"It was Stone." Emilia's voice grew fierce. "He betrayed all of us to the Pendragon. Stone told him where we were hiding. He told them Aunt Iz and the others were going after Samuel."

Proteus's shoulders tightened, and his eyes flashed with anger. Even if Emilia hadn't known Proteus was a centaur with the enormous body of a powerful horse, his look would have been terrifying. "The MAGI scum betrayed the Gray Clan."

"Yes, and if he can, he'll send people to attack the Green Mountain Preserve. He'll send them after all of you." Emilia took a deep breath. "You need to move. You need to find a safer place for the Tribe."

"We will be prepared for the Dragons, and if Stone shows his face, I will kill him myself," Proteus growled.

"Good." For a moment, the fact that she had said *good* to a person promising to kill someone seemed absurd. But Rosalie was dead. Claire was unconscious. Aunt Iz and the others were missing. "Kill him."

Proteus nodded.

"Contact the Wrights at the High Peaks Preserve," Emilia said. "I don't know how much Stone knows about their settlement."

"I will contact the Wrights and make sure they are safe."

"Thank you, Proteus."

"Do you want me to send the fighters of the Tribe to Graylock to search for Isadora?"

Emilia's heart leaped to her throat just before a terrible sickness settled into her stomach. "No." Her voice cracked as she said the simple word. "We have no idea where they are. And we can't send anyone else to Graylock."

We can't lose anyone else.

Proteus bowed, and the mirror shimmered again before leaving Emilia staring at her own reflection.

Tears cut pale tracks through the dirt, ash, and blood that covered her face. Her grey eyes were bloodshot and looked much older than seventeen.

"This is what war does," Emilia murmured.

It had been coming for a long time, since before Emilia had really known it. Attacks on humans, disappearances, murder.

But Aunt Iz had been trapped at the Graylock Preserve. Rosalie was dead. Thousands of humans had been murdered. There was no mistaking it now.

The Gray Clan was at war.

⁓

"You'll need to sleep in the boys' dormitory," Mrs. Dellard said in a clipped tone as she led Connor and Jacob down the dark hall.

The dim light coming from the ceiling was only strong enough to cast strange shadows on the floor.

"What we need is to be in the infirmary with Claire," Connor said, his voice somewhere between a yell and a growl. "She needs us!"

"She needs nothing but medical attention." Mrs. Dellard rounded on the boys. She had a face that had probably been pretty before years of scowling had taken their toll. Her hair was pulled back in such a tight bun, Jacob was amazed she could move her mouth to speak at all. "I have seen to it that she is receiving the best care the Academy has to offer, despite the fact that none of you are students here."

"How—" Connor began, but Jacob cut him off, stepping between Connor and the headmistress.

"We're very grateful to you for taking us in," Jacob said as calmly as he could. His fingers were still frozen from standing at the gate for twenty minutes, begging to be let into the Academy so Claire could get help.

Mrs. Dellard had insisted they would have to follow the rules and not disrupt the order of the Academy if they wanted Claire to be taken care of. That meant the boys and girls would have to be separated, just like the students.

Jacob hated it. He hated letting Emilia out of his sight. He needed to hold her, to protect her. She had watched Rosalie die only a couple of hours ago. He could feel that she was safe, but after all they had been through, that didn't seem like enough. And Claire...

Emilia would be terrified if Claire was still in danger and heartbroken if she was...

Jacob couldn't bring himself to think the word *dead*.

"We'll stay wherever you want us to," Jacob said, looking into the steely blue eyes of Mrs. Dellard.

Mrs. Dellard's brow wrinkled as she considered them both. "It's a pity you were never sent to me." Her lips pinched together as though she could literally taste her dissatisfaction. "You might have learned proper manners and discipline."

"Yes ma'am," Jacob said, grabbing Connor's arm and half-dragging him to keep following Mrs. Dellard. "We're very grateful for your hospitality, but please don't tell anyone we're here. If they find out, your students could—"

"Young man," Mrs. Dellard said, not stopping her swift stride down the hall, "I do not know in what chaotic state Isadora Gray cares for her wards, but I can assure you the students of the Academy are perfectly well protected."

Connor gave an awkward laugh through his nose, which thankfully Mrs. Dellard didn't seem to notice.

She stopped at a big brown door made of heavy wood. "*Compuere.*" The lock clicked open, and the door swung forward.

Jacob squinted into the room. Two rows of bunk beds stood against either wall. The faint noises of dozens of people sleeping whispered through the shadows.

"*Proluxeo.*" A tiny shimmer of light crept from the tip of Mrs. Dellard's wand, hovering for a moment before gliding into the room and being swallowed by the darkness.

Jacob waited, expecting the light to reappear or, if the spell had failed, for Mrs. Dellard to try casting it again.

After a minute, something began to move in the darkness. It wasn't the shimmer of light but rather the distinctly slumping figure of someone who had just been woken up.

As the figure neared the door, Jacob could make out the pale face of a boy about the same age as himself. The boy was broader and taller than Jacob. He rubbed a hand over his freshly shaven head as he stopped in the doorway, his eyes squinted against the dim light of the hall.

"Good evening, Mrs. Dellard," the boy said, his voice raspy with sleep, "can I help you?"

"Lee," Mrs. Dellard said, "we have just received two new male students."

Lee looked at Jacob and Connor as though noticing them for the first time.

"Show them to the beds at the end of the hall, and make sure they have what they need for the night," Mrs. Dellard said. "In the morning, take them to the dining hall. I will collect them there."

"Yes, Mrs. Dellard." Lee gave a slight bow.

Without even a hint of acknowledgement, Mrs. Dellard turned and walked back down the hallway.

For a moment, Jacob wanted to scream after her that her students weren't safe.

No one anywhere was safe, especially not if they had Emilia Gray hiding with them. But Claire needed help, and what would they do if Mrs. Dellard kicked them back out into the snow?

"Coming or not?" Lee asked, pulling Jacob's attention away from the hallway.

"Sorry," Jacob muttered.

"Don't worry," Lee yawned. "The first night is always the worst. Once you get used to being abandoned, it's not too terrible."

"We haven't been—" Connor started, gasping when Jacob stepped on his toe to shut him up.

"This way." Lee led them into the darkness.

The sounds of slow breathing were peppered with occasional snores and sleepy murmurs. Lee didn't use a light to guide them, but there was no need for one. The row between the beds was perfectly straight, and the floor was clear without even a stray sock to get in their way.

"Lee," a small voice whispered as they neared the end of the row. "Lee."

"Shut up, Mikey," Lee hissed, "you'll wake the whole dorm."

"But why are you awake, Lee?" A face appeared at the foot of a bed, staring up at them. "And who are they?"

"New students," Lee said. "Just got here, and they want some sleep."

"Why'd they come in the middle of the night?" Mikey tipped his head to the side.

Claire used to do that when she was confused. A pang shot through Jacob's heart.

She's not gone.

"I don't know, just go back to bed," Lee said.

"Why'd you come in the middle of the night?" Mikey asked Connor.

"We were being chased by a Dragon, and it seemed like a good idea at the time." Jacob's voice sounded hollow in his own ears.

"If you really break it down, yeah." Connor shrugged.

"Come on." Lee waved for Jacob and Connor to follow him. "Get back to sleep, Mikey."

The last three bunks at the end of the row were empty. All had sheets and blankets waiting on them as though Mrs. Dellard had been expecting people to show up at the Academy gate in the middle of the night.

"You take these two." Lee pointed to the top and bottom bunk closest to the rest of the boys. "We aren't allowed to leave any blank spaces. Bed checks." Lee shrugged like Jacob should understand exactly what he was talking about. "You got a few hours before breakfast. Try and get some sleep."

Before Jacob could ask a question, Lee was gone.

Connor cursed under his breath.

"Yep." Jacob climbed up onto the top bunk.

"We shouldn't be here," Connor hissed. "We should be with Claire."

"I know, but she's fine. Emilia's fine." Jacob pulled up the blanket. The rough wool scratched his hands.

"Sometimes I envy you," Connor whispered. "You know Emilia's all right. I don't know anything."

The bed below Jacob creaked, and Connor fell silent.

Connor didn't know what being tethered was like. It had changed everything for Jacob and Emilia. Their souls were intertwined. He could feel what she felt. She was a part of him. And losing her…

Jacob shut his eyes tight against the darkness. It was impossible to think about. They hadn't chosen to be tethered. It was never meant to happen.

But Jacob loved Emilia, and she loved him. And lying in the darkness, he knew she was safe and alive, even though he couldn't see her.

He wouldn't have traded that for anything in the world.

THE ACADEMY

*T*he sun had just begun to turn the sky a pale, golden grey. Its light crept in through the high-barred windows of the hall. Emilia sat on the cold stone floor, trying to stay awake. Claire had been locked in the infirmary for hours. The last time the door had opened was when the Academy girl had gone in.

Emilia's eyes stung, and her lids sagged heavily. Blinking, she kept her eyes as wide as she could. Sleep threatened to take her, but she needed to be awake in case there was news of Claire. And sleep might bring dreams.

"Come on, Claire," Emilia murmured. "You've got to be okay."

As if in answer to her plea, the infirmary door swung open with a hollow *groan*. Emilia spun, her heart leaping as she half-expected to see Claire skip into the hall, her long, blond hair streaming behind her. But the girl who came through the door wasn't beaming with Claire's mischievous grin. It was the Academy student that had passed by earlier.

"Nurse Bracken says you can come in now," the girl said, not moving out of the doorway as Emilia sprang to her feet. "You'll have to be quiet, though. Your friend may be our only patient in here right now, but Bracken will toss you out if you make noise. She's gone back to sleep, and that woman is a damn bear if you wake her."

"What about Claire?" Emilia whispered as the girl stepped aside to let Emilia into the infirmary.

Curtains struggled valiantly to block out the light. Twelve beds lined the two long walls of the room. Each bed was perfectly made with pristine white sheets, which made the grey of the walls seem somehow crueler. All of the beds were empty except for the one farthest to the left.

"Claire," Emilia breathed, walking as quietly as she could toward her.

Claire looked like a doll lying on the stark white bed. Her bright blond hair framed her face like a halo. Her skin was even paler than usual, and her lips were a strange pinkish-blue.

"Is she okay?" Emilia asked, wanting to take Claire's hand but afraid even that gentle touch might break her.

"She's alive," the girl said, though her tone didn't bring Emilia any hope. "Whatever the spell was that hit her did plenty of damage. Bracken did her best, and she thinks she'll wake up."

"Thinks?"

"There's nothing else to do but let her rest. Claire, is it?"

Emilia nodded.

"Claire got hit by a nasty spell. We did what we could to help her. Now she's on her own." The girl turned to the bed next to Claire's and pulled the sheets down. "If Claire were a human, she'd be dead. But she's got magic inside of her and one hell of a will to survive. The only thing we can do is let Claire's magic fight against the nasty spell."

"But there has to be—"

"The only thing you can do right now is get some sleep so the infirmary doesn't gain a new patient." The girl pointed to the empty bed. "I convinced Bracken to let you stay in here. So play nice, and get some sleep."

Emilia stared at the girl, trying to sort through her heavy brain to think of another way to help Claire. The girl stared back at her with unblinking, deep brown eyes.

"I'll bring you food after breakfast."

"Thanks." Emilia kicked off her shoes and climbed into the white sheets with her coat still on.

"I'll show you where the showers are once you've slept." The girl glanced over to Claire. "I know it's impossible, but try not to worry. Other than being trapped in the Academy, you're safe."

Emilia swallowed the laugh that rose in her throat. "What's your name?" was the only thing she could think to say that didn't involve the imminent doom creeping toward them all.

"Maggie," the girl said as she headed toward the door. "Maggie Trent. Goodnight, Emilia Gray."

Emilia was asleep before she could bother to wonder how the girl knew her name.

～

"Come on." Someone was shaking Jacob's foot. "Breakfast is in ten minutes, and if you're late, you don't eat."

Jacob opened his eyes, blinking at the bright sunlight and wondering how he had managed to sleep through it.

"You'll have to stay in your clothes," Lee said, backing away to give Jacob room to jump from the top bunk. "Mrs. Dellard hasn't brought you uniforms yet."

"Whatever will we do?" Connor asked dryly as he stood up next to Jacob.

"Be grateful you get to keep your hair one more day." Lee rubbed his closely shaven head. "I've been here five years. I don't even remember what having hair feels like."

Lee paused for a moment, and Jacob searched for something to say.

But Lee spoke again before Jacob had to. "Let's get going."

Jacob wanted to shower, or at the very least brush his teeth. But Lee led them to the end of a line of boys filing out into the hallway. All of them were wearing black pants and grey shirts that matched the concrete walls. Each boy's head was shaved like Lee's, and none of them spoke to each other as they walked.

"This place is freaky," Connor whispered.

A small boy, not more than ten years old, had slowed his paced to fall behind in the line.

"Wow," the boy whispered. "It wasn't a dream. Did you really come here because you were running from a dragon?"

"Quiet, Mikey," Lee hissed.

"But if it was a real dragon—"

"It depends on what you call a *real dragon*," Connor said. His face was set and tired. He looked older than he had the morning before. When they had been getting ready to celebrate Christmas.

"Did it breathe fire?" Mikey gaped.

"It was the Pen—"

"Connor—" Jacob cut him off and gave him a warning glare. They couldn't afford to risk telling any of the students they were running from the Pendragon. "It was close enough to a real dragon. But it's over now."

Mikey gave a disappointed sigh. "Well, new students in the middle of the night is still exciting, I guess."

They walked down a long hall, back the way Mrs. Dellard had brought them the night before.

The group stopped at a door wide enough for a car to drive through. The boys all stood waiting, staring at the door. Jacob craned his neck to see over the heads of the crowd, searching for what they were so uniformly gazing at, but he couldn't find anything.

In less than a minute, the door swung open.

Jacob and Connor followed the boys as they marched forward in a mundane sort of way. As though being herded through doors that moved on their own was not only normal, but boring.

The room they entered looked like it belonged in Fairfield High. Well, Fairfield High before Jacob had accidently destroyed every piece of glass in the building.

Greenish-grey tables sat in rows around the room, bowls of food already laid out on them. Jacob took a deep breath, expecting the sweet smell of breakfast, but the scent coming from the food was more like that of old paste.

Jacob followed Lee to the row of tables closest to the center of the room. It wasn't until he was next to it that Jacob saw the rib-high wall running down the middle of the cafeteria.

"Why is there a wall?" Jacob asked, but he didn't need to hear Lee's answer.

A door directly opposite the one the boys had entered through had just swung open, and a pack of girls marched into the cafeteria. Their uniforms matched the boys', and their hair was pulled back into tight buns like the one Mrs. Dellard wore.

One girl at the front of the pack pointed to Jacob, and a flurry of whispers flew through the girls.

"Silence!" a booming voice shouted from the end of the room. "This is not the time for speaking!"

A man of about fifty stood at the end of the room, wearing a black uniform. His gaze swept over the students as they took their seats. No one seemed inclined to speak again.

Lee pointed for Jacob and Connor to sit at the table with him and silently began passing them food. It tasted as horrible as it smelled.

Connor gagged softly next to Jacob, and Jacob couldn't blame him. Connor was Molly's nephew. He had grown up on a solid diet of her amazing food. If the orange-ish slop was terrible to Jacob, who had spent years living off stale sandwiches, it would be unbearable to someone used to perfect, home cooked meals.

Lee looked at Jacob and Connor and tapped his wrist where a watch would sit, before miming shoveling food into his mouth.

Jacob picked up his spoon and tried not to breathe as he worked his way through the muck.

He hadn't even reached the bottom of his bowl when the big doors swung back open and everyone stood to leave.

"Should we go with you?" Jacob whispered, glancing at the man in black to make sure he wasn't watching.

"Mrs. Dellard should've come to get you," Lee said, "but it's time to go and I can't just leave you here."

"Can you take us to her office?" Jacob whispered.

"Or the infirmary," Connor said. "Our friends are in there."

"There are more of you?" Mikey asked.

Lee gave him a solid shove out of the way.

"I don't have permission to go anywhere but class," Lee said, speaking a touch louder once they were out in the hall, "and I definitely don't have permission to let you wander around the Academy without me."

"They can come to class with me!" Mikey bounced with excitement.

"Not a chance, Mikey," Lee said. "Now get out of here."

"See you at lunch," Mikey said before hurrying to catch up to a group of boys who seemed to be about his age.

"Don't blame Mikey," Lee whispered as though Jacob had just said something mean about the boy. "He's only been here a few months. Human-born, late in manifesting his magic. He still thinks a Clan will take him in as a ward and teach him. He hasn't figured out that once they ditch you in here the only way out is to age out."

"Age out?" Jacob asked.

"They kick you out when you hit eighteen." Lee's face broke into a brief grin. "I have fifty-two days left. I only have to survive fifty-two more days, and I'm free."

Lee and the group of the oldest boys all turned and walked into a room as one. Giving Connor a glance, Jacob followed.

Desks had been laid out in three long lines facing a chalkboard at the end of the room. It looked like a normal classroom, except all the classrooms Jacob had ever been in had at least made an attempt at cheerfulness. There were no motivational posters or colorful diagrams on the walls of this room. In fact, the grey walls were completely bare.

"Is this a school or a prison?" Connor whispered.

All the boys turned and glared at him as though he had just done something terribly wrong. Lee led them to the back of the row and pointed to two desks. Jacob nodded and slid into a seat. The boys all pulled books and papers from their desks. Connor opened his desk and looked inside before mouthing at Jacob, "No books for us."

Jacob lifted the top of his desk a crack and found he didn't have any books either. They weren't really there for class, but there was still a tiny bit of panic stirring in his stomach, shouting at him that he had come to school unprepared.

Jacob glanced around the room. Half the seats were still empty. The whole row closest to the windows, which were too high to look out of, and the front half of the middle row. Before Jacob could wonder why there were so many students missing, a woman wearing an all-black uniform entered followed by a silent flock of girls.

The woman couldn't have been more than thirty but had the haggard face of someone twice her age. She stood beside the large desk at the front of the room, watching carefully as the girls settled themselves into their seats.

Jacob searched for Emilia and Claire as each of the girls passed. But as the girls sat down, Emilia and Claire were nowhere to be seen.

When all but the very back desks were filled, Lee raised his hand.

"Yes," the woman said, nodding curtly to Lee.

"Ms. Tellner," Lee said, "Mrs. Dellard told me to escort these two to the cafeteria, but she didn't come to get them."

"Mrs. Dellard is busy with more important matters," Ms. Tellner said. "Though I doubt they will be able to understand the content of my class, they will have to wait here."

"But where are the girls?" Jacob asked, not faltering when every student in the room turned to stare at him. "We came here with two girls. Where are they? We need to see them."

"Young man," Ms. Tellner said, her voice growing colder, "we do not speak out of turn at the Academy. You will see your acquaintances when Mrs. Dellard says you may. For now, I suggest you respect the rules of the Academy, unless you wish to be put straight back into the snow where we found you."

Connor's shoulders tensed. For a moment, Jacob thought Connor might scream at Ms. Tellner, but instead he merely nodded. They would just have to be patient. At least for a little while.

3

WITHOUT A CLAN

*T*he sun was high before Maggie came to the infirmary to wake Emilia up, and by the time Emilia had eaten and showered, it was the middle of the afternoon. Emilia watched Nurse Bracken as she muttered words over Claire that Emilia couldn't hear, but nothing seemed to change. After fifteen minutes, the pointy-faced woman went back to her office without saying a word to Emilia.

"Don't be offended," Maggie said, coming in through the infirmary door, bearing another tray of food, just as Bracken shut her office door with a *snap*. "She's awful to everyone."

"I don't care how much she ignores me as long as she fixes Claire," Emilia said, staring at the sandwich Maggie had brought. It looked dry and plain. Molly would never have approved. Emilia's heart ached even thinking about Molly. She could have been captured. She could be dead.

"I know it doesn't look great," Maggie said, "but that's pretty standard around here. Eat fast, and try not to think about the taste too much."

"Thanks." Emilia took a bite of the cardboard-like sandwich as Maggie perched on the end of her bed.

"How did it happen?" Maggie asked after a few moments of silence. "I mean, your friend got in the way of some pretty bad magic. Something like that didn't happen by accident."

Emilia studied Maggie for a moment, the urge to keep the secret battling with her need for an ally. "It was the Pendragon. Claire got in the way of the Pendragon."

"The Pendragon?" Maggie asked. "Like the Pendragon who isn't supposed to exist even though the teachers whisper about him like he's the boogey man when they think none of us can hear? He's actually real?"

"Very real. Last night, he went to a concert. There were thousands of humans there. He killed them. We tried to stop him, but…" Emilia couldn't bear to finish.

"The Pendragon killed humans?" Maggie ran her hands over her slicked back hair as though she were trying to hold on to the concept of the Pendragon being a real murderer and not just some imagined terror.

"It's not the first time." Emilia took another bite of the sandwich.

"Then why hasn't the Council of Elders stopped him?" Maggie asked. "I mean, the Council likes to jump on wizards for humans even noticing magic. For a mass murder, why isn't half of MAGI arresting him right now."

"You don't know?" Emilia said. "You don't know what's been happening?"

"I live at the Academy." Maggie gave an angry laugh. "We don't know anything. They don't even let the kids with families on the outside talk to their relatives unsupervised."

Anger boiled in Emilia's chest. The world was falling apart, and the Academy hadn't even bothered to let their students know.

"There is no more Council," Emilia growled. "There is no more MAGI. The Pendragon destroyed all of it. All that's left are a few people trying to keep the Pendragon from killing everyone."

Emilia waited for Maggie to protest, to scream for help or shout at Emilia for being crazy.

"Well," Maggie said after a long moment, "makes sense."

"Makes sense?" Emilia asked, wondering if maybe Maggie was the crazy one.

"Well, it does." Maggie glanced toward Bracken's door before continuing. "We've had some kids with weird deaths in the family. More than normal. And the teachers have all been super tense, too."

"Your family didn't tell you anything?" Emilia asked.

"I don't have a family."

"Oh." Emilia set down her sandwich. "I'm so sorry. But your Clan—"

"I don't have a Clan, either." Maggie shrugged as though trying to make it clear she didn't think it was a thing to be worried about.

"Were your family humans?"

"No. We were all Virginia Clan." Maggie picked at the sheet that covered Emilia's bed. "My family always had a liking for blood feuds, but when I was about five they started a feud with a family that was stronger than ours. My mother sent me here, and within a week, everyone back home was dead."

"I'm so sorry."

"I thought the Clan might come and claim me." Maggie grimaced. "The first two years or so I woke up every morning expecting my Clan Elder to come get me. I was smart, great with spell work. I could have been an asset to my Clan even if I didn't have parents anymore. But no one ever came. And the school won't let you out until you're eighteen unless someone will claim you. No one on the outside cares that I'm stuck here, so why would anyone bother to tell me the magical world is falling apart?"

"I'm sorry," Emilia said again.

"Don't be." Maggie stood and walked toward the door. "If things are really as bad as you say out there, it's probably better if there's no one for me to care about."

$\sim$

They had spent the day in classes with the rest of the students from the Academy, Jacob pressing his hands to the top of his desk, trying not to scream at the teachers for being ridiculous. There was a war going on beyond the Academy walls. The Pendragon had killed thousands of humans, and the police knew it. Humans would start to wonder, and magic would be found out. At this very moment, the Pendragon could be turning another thousand people to ash.

But the teachers didn't mention anything about it. Ms. Tellner lectured on the structure of laws within the magical community. When she had finished, a little old man took her place. Jacob's heart had melted for a moment. The elderly gentleman was withered and toadish, seeming almost like Professor Eames.

Until he opened his mouth.

"I will have no foolishness," was the man's start to class. "Anyone who disobeys me will be sent immediately to Mrs. Dellard."

Jacob had to hiss, "Don't do it," to keep Connor from standing up.

The old man taught them about using magic to mobilize different objects. Books flew across the room, desks glided in circles. The shades on the high windows opened and shut on command. It should have been fun, but it was more like a military drill than a lesson in magic.

When the last desk had returned to its place, the old man escorted the boys back out into the hall for a silent walk to silent lunch. As soon as the last boy had left the room, a woman Jacob hadn't seen before entered. Jacob watched over his shoulder as she escorted the girls the other way down the hall.

The afternoon started with sparring practice. While Connor and Jacob had both stood aside and watched the desks fly around the room earlier, this time the teacher, Ms. Bildge, a large woman who looked strong enough to throw Jacob across the room with one hand, insisted both he and Connor take part in the lesson.

"You're Clan trained," Ms. Bildge sneered. "You think you know better than the Academy. You run around in your pretty gardens and find the *beauty* in magic. Magic is a skill to be used. It's not art. It's not candy. It's a muscle that has to be honed. Pair off!"

They were in a gymnasium large enough for all the boys to break off into pairs. Where the girls had gone, Jacob wasn't sure. But each boy seemed to know who they were supposed to spar, and they spread out in pairs around the room without speaking.

Connor shrugged and began leading Jacob to the far end of the room where there was a little open space.

"Oh no," Ms. Bildge said, "I don't think you two should skulk in the corner together. How will you ever know what you're made of if you just hide with your little friend? Johnson, Bonner." Ms. Bildge snapped her fingers, and the two biggest boys in the room came running forward. "You take the two Gray boys."

The boys nodded and took positions opposite Connor and Jacob.

Jacob didn't know if it was Johnson or Bonner who stood opposite him, but whatever the boy was called, he glared at Jacob for a moment before smiling and cracking his neck.

Jacob swallowed his laugh, and a dangerous glint flitted through the hulking boy's eyes.

"On my count!" Ms. Bildge bellowed.

"Wait!" Jacob raised his hand.

"What?" Ms. Bildge said. "Are you afraid of a little sparring? Has the Gray Clan spoiled its children that much?"

"No ma'am," Jacob said loudly, his voice ringing around the room. "I just want to know what's allowed in sparring here. I wouldn't want to break any rules."

"One rule—no killing spells." Ms. Bildge walked slowly over to Jacob, only stopping when she was mere inches from his face. "But I doubt Isadora Gray taught you any of those."

"Sounds fair," Connor said from his place six feet to Jacob's right. "I mean, it's been a while since we've sparred, but I think I can remember how it's done."

"On my count," Ms. Bildge roared at Connor who grinned cheerfully back at her.

"It'll be fun to spar inside—" Connor said.

"One."

"Just think of how much we can ruin this floor—"

"Two."

"And there are no hooves here to stomp on us."

"Three."

Before the word had fully left Ms. Blidge's mouth, Connor and Jacob had both shouted, "*Talahm delasc!*"

4

KNOWING THE DRAGONS

*I*t had been hours since Nurse Bracken had come back to look at Claire, mumbled a few spells, dripped a foul smelling liquid into Claire's mouth, and completely ignored Emilia's questions before disappearing back into her office, leaving Emilia alone again.

Emilia sat on the bed, alternating between staring down at Claire and trying to skry Aunt Iz, Molly, Larkin, and Dexter. But Claire didn't move, and the surface of the mirror remained a reflection.

Finally, the door to the hall creaked open, and Maggie entered with another tray.

"Have you seen Mrs. Dellard?" Emilia asked, standing as Maggie approached.

"Dellard?" Maggie shook her head. "She's been in her office all day. Didn't even come to collect the boys you came here with."

"What?" Emilia asked, her heart leaping at the mention of Jacob and Connor.

"The boys you came in with." Maggie unloaded the tray of food onto the little table between Emilia's and Claire's beds. "They were sitting in the back of class this morning. Two of them

—one with red hair and yours with the dark blond. Your one caused a fuss asking where you were." Maggie laughed. "I thought Ms. Tellner's head was going to explode when he started asking about you without permission."

"How did you know?" Emilia's neck tensed.

"That he was asking about you? You're the only girls who came in last night."

"No," Emilia said, her fingers tracing the blue pendant at her neck that was her talisman. "How did you know Jacob was my one?"

"You're tethered."

"How did you—"

"I saw the mark on your hand," Maggie sighed as though explaining centaurs weren't horses.

Emilia clenched her fist to hide the golden streak that marked her palm.

"I knew you were somebody's *coniunx*, so I stared at your friends' hands until I saw the gold on...Jacob, was it?" Maggie sat down on Claire's bed. "Don't worry, I'm not telling the entire Academy about it or anything."

"But how did you know what the gold streak means?" Emilia sat down on her bed, wishing she were the one sitting next to Claire. "They don't teach that sort of magic here, do they?"

"Oh no. That sort of thing would never be taught here. We're not even allowed to speak to the boys. I just remember the stories from when I was little. I didn't know tethering was even allowed anymore, but I guess people can make their own choices."

"We didn't really choose it." Emilia's mind dragged her back to the caves at Graylock. "It just sort of happened."

"Do you like him at least?"

"I love him." A trickle of joy bubbled in Emilia's chest just from saying the words. "He was my best friend before it happened. If it had to be anyone, I'm glad it was him."

"You're lucky," Maggie said, picking the crust off Emilia's

bread and eating it. "In all the stories from back home, the people hated the ones they got bonded to."

"What stories?" Emilia asked.

"Family stories. It was how my family won a blood feud when my grandmother was little. They kidnapped the daughter of the family they were feuding with, tethered her to their favorite son, my great uncle."

"That's terrible," Emilia whispered. Feeling the heartbeat of someone you hated in your own chest, feeling their every emotion. It had killed Rosalie.

"It was," Maggie said. "He got all moony for her, and they were keeping her locked up, so she was all tormented in the basement. But then her family came and killed my great uncle, and even though the kidnapped girl had hated him, she died from the pain of having him die. So it turned into a huge fight right on the front lawn. They say it was a bloodbath. The Trents lost a few people, but the girl's family was slaughtered. So my family won the feud."

Emilia stared open-mouthed.

"What can I say? I come from violent, nasty stock." Maggie pulled off another hunk of bread crust. "I mean, as far as I can remember from when I was little, there were no bloodbaths. But things like forced tethering are sort of common in blood feuds and Clan wars."

"Is that why you want to heal people?" Emilia asked, grasping for something hopeful to say. "To get away from all the fighting?"

Maggie tossed her head back and laughed so hard that, for a moment, Emilia was convinced Claire would wake up from the sound.

"Want to heal?" Maggie gasped between laughs. "Want to heal? Working in the infirmary is my punishment. Apparently, I lack proper respect for authority and have a disregard for the well-being of others. By which Mrs. Dellard means I can't take her crap anymore and find the occasional disruption of order to be highly entertaining."

"And they sent you here for that?" Emilia raised one dark eyebrow.

"Detention didn't really do the trick, and I've never done anything bad enough to get sent to the pits. I think Mrs. Dellard just ran out of ideas. But it's not terrible." Maggie waved a dismissive hand. "I have all sorts of cool healer training, and I get out of class when people show up half frozen. Not too bad a deal."

"Not too bad."

"Well, enjoy your dinner." Maggie headed for the door. "Try not to choke on the slop."

"I know you aren't supposed to talk to them," Emilia called after her, "but if you see Jacob, can you find out if they're okay?"

"Can't you feel him?" Maggie stopped with her hand on the doorknob.

"Yeah, but..." Emilia couldn't find the words.

"I'll do what I can." Maggie nodded and left.

Emilia picked up the bowl of creamy goo and took a bite, imagining what Claire would say if she had seen the slop.

Maggie was lucky. She was an orphan. She had no one on the outside left to lose.

Emilia choked on her tears, and the sound echoed through the empty room.

The Pendragon had destroyed her family. It was his fault Rosalie was dead. His fault Emilia had only had a few days with her mother.

Sobs wracked Emilia's chest. Rosalie was dead. Claire was unconscious, and there was nothing Emilia could do to help her. Half her family was missing, and the other half was locked in the Academy.

But the Pendragon was still alive. Alive, and free, and hurting people. The only way to protect her family would be to kill her father. Emilia had to make herself an orphan.

~

*J*acob sat on his bed in the dorm, watching the other boys mill around. It was the first time he had actually heard them talking to each other. The two boys Connor and Jacob had sparred were over in the corner, glowering and shooting angry glares in Jacob's direction. Not that Jacob could blame them. They had avoided being sent to the infirmary, but both boys looked terrible, and Bonner had entered the dorm with a pronounced limp.

The rest of the boys had been studiously ignoring Jacob and Connor all evening. From the hushed tones they were speaking in, and the surreptitious glancing in Connor and Jacob's direction, Jacob felt sure he knew what they were talking about.

Only Mikey seemed intent on speaking to them, inching closer to Jacob's bunk and sneaking peeks at him every few seconds.

"You all right?" Jacob finally asked when Mikey was only a few feet away.

"I'm fine," Mikey said casually, though the excitement in his eyes hinted he had been hoping Jacob would speak to him. "I'm not the one who got thrown around by a glowing whip."

"Nope, you're not," Connor growled from the bottom bunk.

"I just mean," Mikey said, "I've never heard of anybody sparring like that before. That was really fancy magic."

"It wasn't *fancy* magic," Connor said. "It was *centaur* magic."

"Centaurs!" Mikey said so loudly half the room stopped bothering to pretend they weren't listening. "Where did you learn centaur magic?"

"From centaurs," Connor said.

"When did you meet centaurs?" Lee asked, leading over a pack of boys.

"For the first time?" Connor asked. "When I was about two, but I don't really remem—"

"We were sent to live with them," Jacob cut Connor off before he could dig either of them into an even larger hole. "We were both living with the head of the Gray Clan. When the Bonforte Clan Elder was killed, they decided it wasn't safe for us anymore, so they sent us to train with the centaurs."

"You like, *lived* with them?" a boy Jacob didn't know asked.

"Wait. A Clan head was killed?" Lee asked.

"Yeah, but that was months ago," Jacob said. "The Pendragon sent Nandi into their home...they were slaughtered."

A murmur of shock and fear rippled through the boys. All of them were crowded around Jacob and Connor's bunk now. Even Bonner and Johnson had crept in to listen.

"You didn't know, did you?" Jacob asked.

"No," Lee said darkly, "we didn't."

"How could they not tell you a Clan head was murdered?" Connor stood up. "Aren't any of you from the Bonforte Clan?"

"I am," a tall, dark-skinned boy in the back said, "but Mrs. Dellard said Elder Bonforte died in her sleep."

"The Nandi got them in the night if that counts," Connor said.

"But didn't your family tell you?" Jacob jumped down from his bunk.

"I haven't heard from them in a while," the boy said. "Mrs. Dellard stopped allowing direct contact."

"What?" Something between fear and anger squirmed in Jacob's stomach.

"She won't let you talk to your families?" Connor asked. "What the hell kind of rule is that?"

"There's something going on out there," Bonner said from the back of the crowd. The boys standing in front of him split apart, giving Bonner a path to Jacob.

Jacob clenched his fist tightly, turning his knuckles white.

"It all started last summer," Bonner said. "My dad wrote some strange things in letters. About needing to be careful. He said he was coming soon to bring me home, 'cause we needed to stay in the Clan boundary. But he never showed."

"And then they stopped letting us into the Hall of Mirrors," Lee said. "Mrs. Dellard did something to the bathroom mirrors so we can't use them anymore either."

"And your parents haven't done anything?" Connor asked.

"Maybe they tried," the tall Bonforte Clan boy said. "How would we know?"

"Maybe Mrs. Dellard is trying to protect you from the Pendragon." Jacob grasped for a logical explanation.

"Who's the Pendragon?" Mikey asked.

Jacob looked Lee square in the eyes. "Tell me you know who the Pendragon is."

"Not a clue." Lee shook his head.

Connor cursed so badly Mikey began to giggle.

"Do you want to tell them or should I?" Connor asked, giving Jacob a look that he understood at once. The boys had a right to know what was happening if their families were in danger.

But they didn't need to know Emilia was the Pendragon's daughter.

"I can," Jacob said. "I'll tell them what they need to know."

5

SECRETS AND SNOW

*A*t 10 pm, a man in black came and turned out the lights. At 10:05, all the boys were crowded back around Jacob's bed. They had never heard about the exploding dam, the Council of Elders crumbling, MAGI falling apart, or the thousands of concertgoers being turned to dust.

Jacob talked for hours, trying to remember how everything had happened. He stared down at the faint, golden light that gleamed from his palm as he skipped the part of the story where he and Emilia were bound together deep within the tunnels of Graylock.

"We can't just stay in here," Lee whispered to the boys. "There is a mass murderer out there who is trying to ruin everything for all of us. If he keeps going, there won't be a Magickind left for us to join when Dellard finally lets us out of here. We need to get out there and fight him."

Murmurs of agreement swept through the darkness.

"Maybe that's why Mrs. Dellard hid all this from us," Mikey said, poking curiously at Jacob's glowing palm. Jacob quickly shoved his hand in his pocket. "Maybe she doesn't want us to try and fight and get hurt."

"Has anyone ever gotten out of here before they aged out?" Lee asked Mikey. "They haven't. Not unless a Clan or their family claims them, and she's made it so we can't even beg anyone to come get us out. Maybe Mrs. Dellard isn't telling us what's happening because she doesn't want us to break out of this grey, Hell-hole prison."

"Maybe she agrees with the Pendragon," a voice came from the shadows. "If he wants a world where magic reigns—"

"It's not the world you're thinking of," Jacob said more loudly than he should have.

The whole room froze for a moment as they waited to see if the man in black would swing the door open to yell at them.

"I've met the Pendragon. We've fought him," Jacob whispered. "He's crazy, he's psychotic. And the only thing he'll lead people to is death."

"We've got to get out of here," Lee said. "We can't stay locked in this damn school while people out there are dying."

"I agree," Jacob said, "but we can't go without Emilia and Claire."

"And we can't move Claire until she's better," Connor said.

"But once she is," Lee said, "we find a way out."

"We'll ask Isadora Gray," Connor said. "She's a Clan head. She'll claim all of you. Emilia has a mirror to skry with. At least she did."

"And if your Clan doesn't come to save you?" Bonner asked.

"Then we break out," Jacob said. "We break out, and we take the fight to the Pendragon."

"Good." Lee waved the others to bed. "We'll work on a plan tomorrow."

"Jacob," Connor whispered as everyone backed away. "Did we just start an Academy rebellion and promise to take a bunch of angry kids to fight the Pendragon?"

"Yep," Jacob whispered.

"Cool."

"Yep."

"Emilia's going to kill us."

"Yep."

⁓

*S*now drifted across the high windows of the classroom, piling up against the panes. It should have been beautiful, but it only made Jacob feel more trapped.

Lee had woken him up early that morning to talk about how to break all of them out. But none of the Academy students knew how to get past the gates. And since Connor and Jacob had only passed through them once, they had little advice to offer. The conversation hadn't gotten beyond that before the door had opened for them to be escorted to breakfast. They hadn't been allowed to talk since.

It made sense for the students not to know how to get through the gates. If they were meant to be kept in, why would you teach them to get out? But Emilia would know. Aunt Iz must have taught her about protective barriers. He just needed to see Emilia.

Jacob gripped his wand under his desk. He could make a run for it. Head straight for the infirmary. But Claire needed help. He and Connor had been allowed to keep their own clothes, and no one had tried to shave their heads. Maybe Mrs. Dellard would let them out. Then they could get help from Iz to break the students who wanted to fight the Pendragon out of the Academy.

But if Iz hadn't come for them yet…

Jacob gripped his wand so hard, his hand ached. A burning sensation drifted up onto his forearm, tingling and stinging like needles carving into his flesh. Jacob moved to itch his arm but stopped as words slowly appeared on his skin as though written by an invisible hand.

I've talked to Emilia. She's fine. Claire's still out. E's tried to contact Grays. Nothing.

Jacob read the words on his arm. Carefully, he touched the letters, but as soon as his fingers grazed the black marks, they disappeared.

Jacob glanced around the room, sure he had been hallucinating. A girl at the front of the class, who was hunched low as though taking notes, glanced back at Jacob and winked. But she returned to her notes so quickly, he wasn't really sure she had been looking at him.

E wants to see you. Meet her at 12:15 tonight in the grove. Tell Lee. He'll help.

Jacob nodded, not sure if the girl would see.

Lee told me you would help us get out of here.

Jacob nodded again.

Good, Gray boy. Don't let me get left behind.

Jacob stared down at his arm as the words disappeared, leaving his skin feeling prickly and hot.

"I will not have minds wandering in my class," Ms. Tellner barked.

Jacob sat up as straight as he could and stared at the blackboard.

That girl had spoken to Emilia. And if she wasn't lying, he would see Emilia tonight.

Jacob wanted to tell Connor and Lee about the message on his arm right away, but he didn't find an opportunity to speak again until after dinner.

"Lee," Jacob whispered as soon as the door had shut for the night. "Connor." He grabbed the two boys' arms and dragged them away.

"*H*ow exactly is this supposed to work," Emilia whispered to Maggie as she dabbed Claire's lips with sweet smelling goo. "Mrs. Dellard won't even let me see Jacob. If he can't get in here during the day, how am I supposed to meet him in the middle of the night?"

"I don't think I've ever fully appreciated the advantages of being raised in the Academy," Maggie sighed. "This place is run like a prison—there's a rule for everything. But the best thing about rules is finding a way to break them. Do you really think they'd be able to lock this many teenage boys and girls in a building and ban us from speaking to each other and not have us find a way around that?"

"So how does it work?" Emilia's heart raced at the mere thought of seeing Jacob's face. "Where can I meet him?"

"In the old orchard," Maggie said, her eyes gleaming. "It's out of sight, and they don't patrol back there."

"How do I get out?"

"Follow the grey cement road." Maggie winked.

It wasn't hard for Maggie to make an excuse to stay late in the infirmary. She spilled a tray of foul smelling vials that steamed and bubbled as they hit the floor. Nurse Bracken shouted and told her she couldn't leave for bed until the mess was cleared.

It was nearly midnight when Maggie led Emilia out into the dark hall, steering her quickly through the shadows and stopping right between two doors. One was large enough for a centaur to walk through, the other looked like a door to a pantry.

"Back corner of the closet," Maggie said in a hushed tone. "You'll feel the draft coming in. It's a tight squeeze but you can crawl through."

Emilia nodded.

"Once you're on the outside, run for the trees. Jacob will meet you out there." Maggie smiled. "But remember where you came out, because you can't see the hole from either side, and if you can't find it, you're stuck out there for the night. It happened to a girl once…it was awful."

"Did they kick her out?" Emilia asked.

"If you could get kicked out of the Academy for sneaking out, all of us would have been caught by now." Maggie grimaced. "They put her in solitary for two weeks. Poor thing suffered, but she never gave up the way out."

"Great," Emilia muttered, unsure of what to say.

"Good luck," Maggie whispered, "and if you get caught—"

"I won't let you take the fall." Emilia opened the closet door.

The tiny room was freezing and reeked of mildew and floor cleaner. Emilia pressed the sleeve of her coat to her nose, trying to block out the stench. As soon as the door was shut behind her, the room went black with only the faint gold glimmer from her left palm breaking through the darkness.

"*Inluesco*," Emilia murmured, and a sphere of blue light appeared in her palm.

Mops hung from the walls, and buckets were scattered pell-mell across the tiny floor. Emilia peered down into the corners of the room, but all she could see was solid cement.

Kneeling on the floor, Emilia kept the sphere of light balanced in one hand while she reached her other palm out, waiting. She held her breath, not wanting to disturb the air in the closet. Then she felt it. A faint breeze coming from behind an overturned bucket. Emilia touched the bucket to move it aside. The bottom was iced over as though it had been sitting in the snow.

Sliding forward, Emilia grazed her fingers against the wall. Or what should have been the wall, but there was nothing there. Her fingers disappeared into what seemed to be solid grey but felt like winter air. Letting go of the ball of light, Emilia lay on her stomach and crawled forward, eyes closed so she wouldn't have to see the wall coming closer.

She inched forward, bit by bit until her fingers met ice. She opened her eyes to find starlight glinting off the dazzling fresh snow. The air was crisp and cold and shot life into her lungs.

Leaping up, Emilia raced toward the woods, the snow crunching under her feet with every step. She didn't stop until she reached the tree line. Hiding behind a snow-laden pine, she carefully studied where she had come from before whispering, *"Sevossus."* With a cold swirl of wind, her footprints disappeared.

She could feel the pull of Jacob in her chest. Feel his heart pounding as he ran. Emilia stopped in a stand of trees that hid the Academy with their snow-covered branches. Emilia waited in the darkness, feeling Jacob coming closer.

She pressed her hand to the ground. *"Alavarus."* The snow melted away, leaving soft, green grass in its place. Emilia smiled. Such tiny, fragile life could survive harsh winter.

The heat of the ground flooded up into her feet. The air around her warmed. Soon the snowflakes that had been kissing her cheeks turned into a gentle rain. Emilia tipped her face up to the warmth as the rain grew stronger. Tears slid down her cheeks, but the rain washed them away as quickly as they formed.

Emilia pulled off her coat, letting the rain cleanse her of the stale scent of the Academy. A sob caught in her throat as she tried to push everything from her mind but the rain. If she started crying, she feared she might never stop. She knelt, threading her fingers through the warm, dry grass that remained untouched by the rain that soaked her.

"Emi," Jacob said from the edge of the grass. He stood bundled up in his winter coat, snow dusting his hair.

"Jacob." Emilia reached for him.

In a moment she was in his arms. She unzipped his coat, burying her head on his chest, relishing the sound of his heartbeat.

"Emi, I—"

Emilia pressed her lips to his, stopping his words with her kiss. Her heart raced as his warmth flooded through her.

All fear, pain, and worry slipped away until there was nothing left in the world but them. She could feel his heart racing as he touched her, feel his soul shouting that this was where they belonged.

Emilia gasped as his freezing fingers found her waist. Sparks of heat shot through her veins where their skin met as his hand traveled up her side. Her entire body hummed. She looked into Jacob's bright blue eyes as his heart kept time with hers.

Jacob raised her palm, kissing the golden streak that showed their bond. The air around them glowed with the golden light that shone from their skin, pushing back the night.

Emilia pulled Jacob closer, letting herself forget as she tumbled away from fear, entwined in his arms. Allowing them both a moment of peace.

6

LILACS

"They didn't know," Jacob said, still holding Emilia close, her head resting on his shoulder as they stared up into the snow-covered trees. "The students here, they didn't know about the Pendragon or the Council falling."

"I know."

"Lee, the one who helped me get out here"—Jacob kissed Emilia's forehead—"he said they cut off all communication. No skrying, nothing. Do you still have your mirror?"

Emilia found her coat on the grass and pulled the hand mirror out of her coat pocket. "But I can't get Aunt Iz or the others. I warned Proteus about Stone."

"Good." Jacob took a deep breath, inhaling Emilia's scent. Lilacs. Even in the middle of winter, lilacs. "I'm surprised Mrs. Dellard let you keep it."

"I didn't tell her I had it. And I think she's scared of me anyway." Emilia sat up, running her hands through her hair. "She hasn't come to the infirmary since we arrived. I've asked to talk to her, but nothing. If I weren't worried about her kicking us out without Claire, I'd march into her office tonight."

"Why would she be scared of you?" Jacob slid his fingers

through Emilia's, reveling in the warmth that spread up his arm and into his chest.

"Because of who I am." Emilia bit her bottom lip. "Because with Aunt Iz…" Emilia paused as tears began to shine in her eyes.

"Missing," Jacob finished for her.

"I'm in charge of the Gray Clan," Emilia said. "I outrank Mrs. Dellard."

"What?"

"I'm Aunt Iz's heir." Emilia looked fearfully into Jacob's eyes. "She's not here, so I'm supposed to take care of everything."

Jacob's mind raced, working through a dangerous but possible plan. "Does that mean you could take people to Gray-lock? We could get some of the centaurs and preserve folk to come with us. We could find Iz."

"Getting enough of them to fight our way in?" Emilia shook her head. "Aunt Iz tried to rally the preserve folk, and it didn't work. If they wouldn't fight for her, they won't do it for me."

"But the boys in the dorm," Jacob said, getting more excited by the second, "they want to fight. If we get them out of here, we could take them with us!"

"They're kids, Jacob."

"So are we!"

"No." Emilia took his face in her hands. "We aren't. You and me, even Claire and Connor. We've seen too much to be kids. I'm not saying life in the Academy is easy, but fighting, killing…it's different. We can't ask them to do that."

"No, we can't." Jacob pressed his forehead to Emilia's. "But we can't leave them in here either. Mrs. Dellard is insisting the Academy is safe, but how could it be? These kids don't even know if their families are alive or dead. We can't just leave them trapped. If the Pendragon decided to attack here, it would be a massacre."

Emilia drew Jacob back to the ground, nestling her head onto his shoulder. "I'll find a way to talk to Mrs. Dellard in the morning. Make sure the gates are safe. I'll make sure Maggie tells the girls what's going on out there."

"And when we leave?" Jacob asked.

"Anyone who wants to comes with us."

They stayed in the trees until the sky began to brighten. It would have been so easy to stay with Emilia, to follow her on her path back into the school.

But she whispered, "I love you," and ran through the snow to the high grey walls of the Academy.

Jacob cut through the trees, keeping far enough back he wouldn't be spotted if anyone climbed up to look out the high windows.

As he walked, Jacob studied the high stone wall that blocked out the world beyond the Academy gates. Lee, or whoever had made the hole in the wall at the back of the boys' bathroom, had found a way out of the school and onto the grounds.

Jacob spotted the corner of the Academy he was aiming for and sprinted through the snow, not slowing until he pressed himself to the wall, holding his breath as he slid sideways through the long, narrow crack.

If they could sneak onto the grounds, there had to be a way to break out of them. They just had to find it.

7

SLEEPING BEAUTY

*E*milia was halfway down the hall before she noticed the wet footprints she had left behind.

"Come on," Emilia growled to herself. *"Alavarus."* In an instant, her feet felt as warm as if she had just had her toes next to a fireplace. *"Sevossus."* The footprints on the floor vanished, leaving nothing but tiny wisps of steam rising into the air.

Dim light crept in through the windows. Soon, Nurse Bracken would come to check on them.

Emilia ran silently down the hall. She reached the infirmary door and pushed it open an inch, listening for Nurse Bracken. Everything was still. Slipping through the door, Emilia shut it quickly behind her.

"Don't move!" a voice said. "Whoever you are, you had better tell me where I am and then let me the hell out of here!"

"Claire?" Emilia's heart leaped straight out of her chest.

"Emilia?" Claire pushed herself wobblingly to her feet from behind a bed, clutching a lamp in one hand and a food tray in the other. "Emilia!" Claire stumbled toward her.

Emilia ran forward and grabbed Claire around the waist as she toppled toward the stone floor.

"You came to rescue me?" Claire asked. "We've got to work fast. I feel like centaur poop, and my magic is all fuzzy. I don't know how much help I'll be fighting, but—"

"We aren't going anywhere, Claire." Emilia hugged her tightly, tears burning in the corners of her eyes. "We brought you here on purpose, so they could help you."

"Help me?"

"The Pendragon," Emilia said, half-carrying Claire back to her bed and prying the lamp and tray from her hands. "He hit you with a spell, and we couldn't wake you up. Aunt Iz is still missing, and we couldn't put Proteus and the Tribe in more danger. The Academy was the only place we could think of. You've been asleep for two days."

"We're in the Academy?" Claire looked around the room. "Guess it makes sense why I thought I was stuck in a prison. Why weren't you waiting by my bedside? Where are Jacob, Connor, and Rosalie? Shouldn't they have been dabbing my forehead?"

"Rosalie didn't make it." Emilia's voice cracked, and Claire took her hand. "She sacrificed herself to get us out. Connor and Jacob are in the Academy, but they won't let them see us. Boys and girls are kept separate here. That's where I was—sneaking out to see Jacob, find out what he knows."

"Trapped in the Academy, Aunt Iz missing, still being hunted." Claire raised one very blond eyebrow. "Glad I woke up. Imagine if I had missed all the fun."

They sat in silence for a minute.

"What do we do now?" Claire asked.

"I go get Nurse Bracken, get her to check you over." Emilia stood and ran her fingers through her hair, making sure there were no signs she had been outdoors. "Then I storm into the headmistress's office, raise Hell, and see what happens."

"After Hell comes breakfast?"

"After Hell comes breakfast." Emilia walked over to knock on Nurse Bracken's door.

"You say I was out for two days?" Claire crawled back into bed.

"Yes." Emilia banged hard on Nurse Bracken's door.

"Then can you make Hell go quickly? I'm really hungry."

Nurse Bracken was furious at being woken up so early and shocked to find Claire conscious.

"Haven't you been trying to heal me?" Claire asked as Bracken muttered a spell over her. "Because if you were that doubtful of your own abilities, maybe we should reconsider coming to the Academy for emergency medical assistance in the future."

"I'll keep that in mind." Emilia smiled.

Even though Claire was shaky and pale, she was still Claire. Snarky and wonderful.

Tears slipped down Emilia's face.

"Oh, don't start crying," Claire said as Nurse Bracken did a spell that surrounded Claire's head in a pale green light and made her sound as though she were speaking from the end of a long hall. "If you start crying, Jacob will know you're upset and think I'm dead."

"No, he won't." Emilia squeezed Claire's hand. "He'll know."

Emilia stood and turned to Nurse Bracken. "How is she?"

"Healing remarkably well," Nurse Bracken said. "She should be able to move into the dorms in a few days."

"That won't be necessary," Emilia said, her tone shocking her. There was something in the way she had spoken. Not mean or rude. But in control. The way Aunt Iz had trained her. "I'm going to see the headmistress, and we'll discuss arrangements for the four of us."

"Mrs. Dellard isn't seeing anyone." Nurse Bracken narrowed her eyes at Emilia.

"She'll see me. I'm afraid she doesn't have a choice. The safety of my friends and the safety of this school need to be discussed." Emilia turned and walked toward the door. "The Pendragon will come whether we're ready or not."

Emilia stepped into the hall and closed the door behind her. It wasn't until she heard Claire clapping for her from inside the infirmary that Emilia began to crumple.

Claire was going to be all right. Emilia could go tell Mrs. Dellard everything. Tell her lying to her students and pretending the Pendragon didn't exist wasn't going to keep anyone safe. And if Mrs. Dellard threw them out, they could take Claire with them. Find a safe place. Or as safe as was possible with a horde of killers bent on murdering them.

The hallway was silent and still. The sun peered through the windows, but it didn't make the grey corridors seem any more cheerful. Emilia had always heard about the Academy being a terrible place. A last resort for young wizards born to magical families who didn't have the desire to teach them or the money to send them to be taught somewhere better. Or witches who were born to human families but couldn't find a Clan to take them in.

And the dangerous ones. The ones who couldn't control their magic well enough to be trusted in the outside world.

Dexter had wanted Jacob sent here. Emilia traced the thin golden line on her hand. Despite everything they had been through, Emilia knew Jacob wouldn't have been better off being locked in here.

Emilia wandered down the corridor. None of the doors were marked. And though some were larger than others, none of them seemed to indicate a headmistress's office.

"Well damn," Emilia muttered.

She was about to retrace her steps back to the infirmary when a man about the same age as Larkin came walking down the hall. He was dressed in a black uniform, had a shaved head, and the distinct look of someone who had just woken up.

"Excuse me," Emilia said, stepping in front of the man, "I need to find Mrs. Dellard's office."

"Mrs. Dellard isn't seeing anyone," the man said. "I suggest you return to the infirmary."

"I can't go back to the infirmary." Emilia stood as tall as she could. "I have vital information about the protection of this school that will affect the safety of the students, and Mrs. Dellard needs to hear it. Now."

"She isn't seeing anyone," the man said again.

"Look," Emilia said, trying to keep the pleading out of her voice, "you teach here, right?"

The man nodded.

"And I can't imagine you would choose to stay here if you didn't care about the students."

Emilia held her breath as the man stared at her for a long moment before nodding.

"I know more about the Dragons than she does, maybe more than anyone," Emilia said. "You've been kind enough to heal my friend and give us all shelter. The least I can do is make sure Mrs. Dellard knows what's really going on out there. Even if my friends and I leave today, it won't be long before the Pendragon comes for the Academy. You won't stay safe forever."

The man regarded Emilia for another long moment. "She won't listen. She thinks the school is impenetrable and too important to be attacked besides. Even after the Council crumbled and MAGI fell, she still thinks the Academy is invincible. We've heard about what the Dragons have done to humans, and Mrs. Dellard doesn't seem to care. If an army of humans shows up outside the gates looking for revenge on Magickind, we could beat them, but it would start the sort of war wizards might not come back from. And I haven't devoted my life to training the next generation of wizards just to see it all go to shit."

"None of us wants that," Emilia said.

"Turn left at the corridor, fourth door on the right." He began walking away before adding, "If she asks how you found her, say a student told you, and you don't know which one."

"Got it." Emilia walked down the hall as quickly as she dared, and in less than a minute, she was outside the door to Mrs. Dellard's office.

It wasn't marked in any way. The only thing that made it appear to be even the slightest bit special was the lack of doors on either side. Whatever room this door led to was larger than the others nearby.

Not giving herself time to wonder if she should come up with a better plan, Emilia raised her fist and banged on the door.

It was only a few seconds before an angry voice answered, "I have warned you, I am not seeing anyone."

"I am Emilia Gray, heir to Isadora Gray, and I command you to open this door and speak to me at once." Emilia's words rang down the hall. She held her breath, waiting for Dellard to scream at her, or worse, to laugh. Before Emilia had run out of air, the door swung open.

"You are an insolent little girl," Mrs. Dellard snapped, leaving Emilia to stand in the open doorway as she strode to her desk.

It took Emilia a moment to remember why she had come to the office at all. Not because Mrs. Dellard had yelled at her— Emilia had expected that—it was the office itself which caught her off guard.

The room was as large as Emilia had expected, stretched out to be as big as the whole infirmary. But, rather than the drab grey of the rest of the building, the walls had been painted a cheerful blue and decorated with paintings. A thick, colorful rug lay on the floor underneath the large and beautifully carved wooden desk that Mrs. Dellard sat behind as she glared at Emilia.

"Nice office," Emilia muttered as she closed the door behind her.

"An insolent child who mumbles," Mrs. Dellard said. "Isadora chose quite an heir."

"I'm not a child." Emilia forced her voice to stay calm. "And I am not insolent. I am coming to you as a courtesy." She took a deep breath. "I know you've kept everything that's going on outside hidden from your students. I know you've cut off contact with their parents. With everything that's been happening, some of their families could be dead."

"We do have a few new orphans," Mrs. Dellard said without a hint of sadness in her voice.

"Do they know?" Emilia balled her hands into tight fists.

"I see no point in disturbing them. It would make the other students panic. And I will not allow panic to creep into my school. Once this whole mess has blown over, I will inform all the students who have lost parents during the course of the Dragons' disruption at once. There is no point in breaking up the process into informing individual students. I would have to tell one a week about some family death or tragedy. I will not have disorder in my school."

"Disorder? No point in telling them their families are dead?"

"Well, would it make a difference to you? You stand in front of me, a courtesy I am only granting you because you are the acting Elder of the Gray Clan, whether Isadora Gray is dead or only being tortured has little—"

"Aunt Iz will be fine," Emilia growled, and for the first time the words seemed to ring true. "Aunt Iz will come back, and when she does I will tell her exactly what you've been doing here. Locking your students up, hiding the Dragons' existence from them when they could come for the school at any time. The school could be attacked, and your students won't even know who is trying to kill them!"

"The Academy will never be attacked." Mrs. Dellard stood, leaning over her desk as though she would like nothing more than to attack Emilia. "We have children here from every Clan. It is neutral territory. For a Clan to attack here would be to slaughter its own children."

"The Dragons are not a Clan." Emilia stepped closer to Mrs. Dellard's desk. "They are loyal to no one but the Pendragon. And when he decides he wants to attack the Academy—and believe me, he will attack—he will slaughter anyone who stands against him. Or maybe he'll just kill you all to get you out of his way."

"The Academy will not be attacked." Mrs. Dellard smacked her palms on her desk.

"The Pendragon will come," Emilia said, her voice frighteningly low. "Maybe tonight, maybe next week. But he will come, sooner than you can imagine. And if you aren't ready when he gets here, your students will die."

"You foolish—"

"He has *somnerri*. He used them to slaughter Edna Sable and her guards." Mrs. Dellard made a noise to interrupt, but Emilia kept talking. "They dug under her shield spells and came at us with no warning. He has more of them in his caves. You say the Academy is safe, but will it be safe from *somnerri?*"

Emilia waited while Mrs. Dellard sat, silently staring at her, finally looking the tiniest bit afraid. "The Pendragon is powerful. And he's crazy. He'd kill his own daughter if he got the chance. Hell"—Emilia squeezed her hands together to keep them from shaking—"he's tried. The Pendragon is coming for you. The only thing you can do is try to be ready so he doesn't murder all your students when he gets here."

Emilia turned and walked toward the door.

"What do you want me to do?" Hate filled Mrs. Dellard's voice as though Emilia herself were the threat to the Academy. "I can't contact MAGI or the Council. No one Clan would volunteer to protect the Academy."

"You're on your own, Mrs. Dellard. All of us are." Without looking back, Emilia walked out into the hall, shutting the door behind her.

Part of her wanted to curl up on the cold concrete floor and cry. She knew she was right. The Pendragon would come. If he knew she was at the Academy, he would have come already. Everyone in the Academy would be dead, all because of her.

Emilia shut her eyes so tight spots danced in front of them, blocking out the picture of Rosalie. Bleeding, still.

But crying wouldn't protect anyone. Emilia took a deep breath, letting go of the tears, and letting anger take over.

Mrs. Dellard may not be able to protect the school, but Emilia would be damned if the Pendragon walked up to the gates and met no resistance.

8

REUNITED

Emilia says take Connor to the infirmary.

Jacob stared down at the words that were already fading from his stinging arm.

He looked at the front row where the girl with the brown hair was glancing back at him while pretending to take notes.

C woke up. E says don't worry about Dellard, just go.

"Now?" Jacob silently mouthed.

No, wait until next week. You might actually learn something in this class.

Before those words had faded, new ones were being scrawled over them.

Yes, now!

Before he could worry about if the girl was actually telling him what Emilia wanted him to do or just trying to make class more interesting, Jacob stood. His chair made a horrible scraping noise on the concrete floor. Every student in the class turned to face him.

"What do you think you're doing?" Ms. Tellner said. "I don't know how they did things at the Gray house, but here, we do not interrupt class."

"I'm not interrupting," Jacob said. "I'm leaving."

"Students are not permitted to leave during class." Ms. Tellner looked as though Jacob had just threatened to burn down the Academy.

"I'm not asking permission." Jacob took Connor's arm and pulled him to his feet. "We're leaving."

"Finally," Connor said. "I don't think I could have stood another minute in here. Seriously, you think staring at a black-board is a good way to learn magic?"

"Overkill," Jacob whispered as he dragged Connor out into the hall.

"Whatever," Connor said, closing the door on the silent class. "Where are we going?"

"To the infirmary. Claire's awake."

"Are you sure?" Connor asked, pushing Jacob to walk faster while Jacob tried to figure out where exactly the infirmary was. Lee had pointed it out, but all the doors looked the same. "Is she okay? How long has she been awake?"

"I don't know. I got a message on my arm from that girl." Jacob peered down the hall. "She said Claire was awake and Emilia wanted us to come to the infirmary."

Finally, Jacob found the right door and flung it open. A flailing shock of blond hair launched at him.

"You really are alive!" Claire squealed, adding, "And you really did abandon my sick bed," as she punched Jacob on the arm.

"They were sent away, Claire," Emilia said, slipping her hand into Jacob's as soon as Claire let go of his neck.

"Claire." Connor stepped forward, his pale face blushing nearly as red as his hair. "You're, I mean, I…"

"I'm glad you're not dead, too," Claire said, hugging Connor. He wrapped his arms around her and pressed his cheek to her hair.

"Don't do that to me again," Connor whispered.

"I'll do my best."

Emilia slid into Jacob's arms, resting her head on his shoulder.

"I went to Dellard," Emilia said, not lifting her face. "I tried to warn her, but she wouldn't listen. I think she's too scared."

"So what do we do?" Jacob asked.

"We warn the students." Emilia pulled away from Jacob and ran her fingers through her hair. "We make sure they're ready to fight. And then we leave."

"Leave?" Claire asked at the same time Connor said, "Finally."

"Where do we go?" Jacob asked.

"No idea," Emilia said, "but we can't stay here. Now that Claire's better, we can't risk it."

"Or," Jacob said slowly, bracing himself for the anger he knew was about to come, "*we* leave, and Connor and Claire stay here."

"No!" Connor shouted. "No way in Hell! I am not staying in prison while you two go after the bad guys."

"But Claire could rest—" Jacob began.

"I just slept for two days! I may never need rest again!"

"We aren't staying here," Connor said with a fierce blaze in his eyes.

"Okay." Jacob raised a hand in surrender. "Then how about you go to High Peaks? You can be with your parents."

Connor glared. "And where do you two go?"

"With us," Claire said. "They can come with us. The four of us stay together."

"We can't," Emilia said.

"We're staying together," Claire said, her stern expression looking eerily like Emilia's.

"I mean, I don't know if we can go to High Peaks," Emilia said, explaining quickly as Connor's face paled. "I told Proteus about Stone and asked him to tell your dad. They might have moved somewhere safer."

"Okay, so we contact my dad and find out where they are," Connor said. "We go to them. They're Gray Clan. We should be with our own people anyway."

"I like it." Claire nodded. "The preserve folk have probably joined up with Proteus by now. We can be with them, and then Aunt Iz can come to us."

"It's the best we've got," Jacob said. "Unless you think it's better if we hide somewhere else."

Jacob could feel her heart aching, searching for some plan that wouldn't let anyone get hurt.

"Emi, there is no safe place," Jacob said softly. "We could go halfway around the world and hide, but running wouldn't help the people we left behind. We can't help anyone without being near them."

"But what if staying away from them is the best thing we can do?" Emilia said. "What if getting as far from Claire and Connor and Proteus and the Preserve is how we keep the most people alive?"

"She does know we can hear her, right?" Claire said.

"It's not." Connor stepped forward. "The Pendragon isn't just attacking you. He's trying to destroy the whole damn Magical Community. He's already murdered two Clan heads in their own homes. He won't stop until he's in charge of all things magical.

"And none of the Centaurs, none of the people from my parents' preserve, none of the Gray Clan will let that happen. They'll all fight until they die if that's what it takes to stop him. And if we're willing to fight and die, then sending away the only person we have who's had an actual conversation with the psycho murderer seems a little counterproductive."

"You're not just a target, Emi." Jacob pressed his lips to Emilia's forehead. "You're a weapon."

"What time is lunch?" Emilia asked.

"Yeah, that whole coma thing made me really hungry," Claire said.

"You don't want the food. It's rancid." Connor shuddered.

"We aren't going for the food," Emilia said.

"Shame." Claire raised both hands in surrender when Emilia glared at her.

"Meals are the only time the whole school is together, right?" Emilia asked Jacob and Connor.

"As far as we've seen." Jacob nodded.

"If we really want to spread the word and make sure everyone knows what's going on out there, we need to tell them all at once," Emilia said.

"They won't like it." Jacob paced between the beds of the infirmary, rubbing his palm over his mouth. "We'll have to get in and make sure we do enough damage Dellard won't be able to deny what we've told them. The boys already know most of it."

"And I told Maggie to tell the girls," Emilia said. "But if we're all whispering about it, Dellard can pretend it's not happening. If we get everyone together, we can make sure they know what's coming."

"The guys will want to leave with us when we go," Connor said, "and I think we should let them. They shouldn't stay locked in here while their families are in danger."

"First things first." A pain pinched between Jacob's lungs. "We have to figure out who still has families to go to."

"The teachers will try to stop us." Connor gripped his wand.

"I'm fine with fighting teachers as long as we get food afterwards." Claire stood up, twisting the ring on her finger.

"Let's go start a school rebellion," Emilia sighed, slipping her hand into Jacob's and letting him lead her out into the hall.

9

REBELLION

They were nearly to the cafeteria doors when the faint sound of footfalls began to echo behind them.

"This place is ridiculously creepy," Claire whispered. Even the soft sound of her voice seemed out of place in the hallway. "I mean, thank God I'm adorable and Aunt Iz agreed to take me to the Mansion House. I don't think I could have survived this concrete, pink-less pit."

"Do you have permission to be here?" a voice barked from the end of the hall. An angry looking teacher strode toward them, leading a group of terrified young boys behind him.

"I'm not asking for permission." Emilia's voice rang loudly through the hall. She took a breath, glad her nerves didn't sound in her voice. "I'm going into the cafeteria."

"This is the boys' side," the teacher said. "You girls will have to go to Mrs. Dellard and ask her permission to be—"

"I've seen Mrs. Dellard. She said nothing about my joining the girls." The hall was filled with boys now, all creeping in to get a closer look at Emilia and the others blocking the door.

Emilia wanted to turn and pull the door open. But what if

there was a spell she didn't know keeping it closed. Her palms began to sweat. "Let us in."

"The four of you aren't going anywhere but Mrs. Dellard's office," the man said.

"If he won't open the door when a lady asks him to"—a tall boy stepped forward—"I will."

"Thanks, Lee," Jacob said as the tall boy tapped the door with his wand before swinging it open.

"How dare—" the teacher began.

"Oh, come on," Lee said, bowing the others in, "I've got fifty days left here, and if I have to spend fifty days in the pit, at least I'll get to remember how pissed you look right now because a student opened a door at the Academy."

"Let's go." Jacob led Emilia into the cafeteria.

"I like your new friends," Claire whispered to Connor.

He looked at her, his brow knit together.

"Don't worry, you're still way better." Claire rolled her eyes.

The door on the other side of the room had swung open, and girls were filing in.

"So how do you want to do this?" Jacob asked.

Emilia's heart pounded against her ribs. She needed to speak to them. All of them.

"Just tell them the world is ending and their parents might be dead?" Emilia said. "I mean, how many of them could be orphans?" Panic and sympathy twisted into a knot in her stomach.

"It's okay." Jacob kissed Emilia's palm. "I'll do it. Can I have the skry mirror?"

Emilia pulled the enameled mirror from her pocket and pressed it into Jacob's hand.

"Break a leg." Claire punched Jacob on the arm before he walked to the center of the room and jumped up onto the rib-high wall that divided the boys and girls.

"My name is Jacob Evans, and I am a member of the Gray

Clan." He glanced down at Emilia, who nodded. "I've already met some of you, but this is something you all need to hear. And you need to listen together so no one can pretend you don't know.

"The Magical Community is crumbling. MAGI has fallen. The Council of Elders is gone. The heads of the Bonforte and Virginia Clans have been murdered in their own homes. All because of a group calling themselves the Dragons. They are rebels, terrorists who want to destroy the rules that have kept us all safe. They want the humans to find out about us. They want to control the humans, and wizards, and all magic, and they don't care how many people have to die to make it happen."

Jacob took a breath, and the silent room waited for him to speak again.

"The Dragons have already murdered a lot of people. They are dangerous and brutal. They won't care if you're a student of the Academy. They *will* kill you. I know, because the four of us"— Jacob looked to Emilia, Connor, and Claire—"we've fought them. Our family has fought them. And we've lost people."

The knot in Emilia's throat hardened.

"We've lost family, and you might have, too." Jacob looked out over the crowd of students. "You have a right to know if your family is dead or alive, you have a right to know what's going on out there, and you have a right to defend yourselves when the Dragons come. And they are coming."

"We'll fight," Lee said from his place at the head of the pack of boys. "All of us will fight."

"But what if," a weedy-looking boy toward the back said, his tone somewhere between fearful and defiant, "what if our families are with the Dragons?"

"Then we lock you in the pit with food, water, and a good book till we figure out how to keep your family from murdering us," Maggie said from the girls' side of the wall.

"Sounds fair." Connor glared at the weedy boy.

"But we don't know if our families are okay," a young boy next to Lee said, his brow knit together in a worried way.

"Your parents are human, Mikey," Lee said gently. "I'm sure they're fine."

"But mine aren't," a girl said. Frightened lines etched her face. "I'm Bonforte Clan. If they killed Olivia Bonforte, my family might not be safe."

"I haven't spoken to my family since this summer," another girl said. "I don't know what's happening."

Shouts of other students swallowed the girl's words.

"I need to find my uncle!"

"My sister wasn't old enough for the Academy!"

"This is quite enough!" Mrs. Dellard shouted as she stormed into the cafeteria followed by a line of teachers. "How dare you destroy the order of my school. I told you there would be panic, and now look what you've done."

"No one is panicking." Claire tossed her long, blond hair behind her shoulders as though preparing for a fight. "We're working out a plan to deal with the reality created by a bunch of murderers in black leather. If you had bothered to deal with this yourself, then a group of kids wouldn't have to."

"I will not allow you to say such things in front of my students," Mrs. Dellard said. "Take the four of them to the pit."

The teachers moved forward, coming toward Emilia, Claire, and Connor, while on the far side of the low wall other teachers pushed through the students to get to Jacob.

"Not going to happen." Lee stepped in front of Claire with two big, beefy boys. "We're done living under your thumb. You lied to us. We're not listening to you anymore."

"Do not make me use magic on you," a big, angry-looking woman growled.

"Bildge," one of the beefy boys said, "do you really want to fight all the students you've trained? You've been teaching us to fight, but Dellard's been hiding the battle from us. If the Dragons are coming, don't you want us to defend ourselves?"

Bildge pursed her lips. "We cannot have anarchy in the Academy."

"We don't want anarchy," Jacob said, still standing on the wall, protected from the teachers by the pack of girls that had closed ranks in front of him. "Let them contact their families. Find out what's going on out there. Help us figure out how to defend this place."

"I will not be told how to run my school!" Dellard shrieked. "*Viscerio!*" A streak of sharp blue light shot toward Jacob.

"Jacob!" Emilia screamed as the spell hit him square in the chest. Emilia dove through the crowd, but before she could reach the wall, Jacob had fallen out of sight.

Shouts erupted all over the room. A group of boys, led by Lee, charged Mrs. Dellard.

"Jacob!" Emilia screamed as students began pushing around in panic.

Emilia leaped over the wall with Connor and Claire right behind. "Jacob!"

She couldn't find him in the sea of people.

"Emilia!"

Emilia turned toward the muffled voice.

Maggie crouched next to the wall, a shimmering shield covering her, Jacob lying unconscious behind her.

"He's okay!" Maggie shouted. "Just get everyone calmed down before someone breaks my shield."

As if on cue, a spell shot overhead, cracking the ceiling.

Emilia leaped back up on the wall. "*Rovox!* Stop, all of you!" Her voice echoed over the chaos, but the students were still fighting, pinning down the teachers. "*Perluxeo!*" Instantly, all light was pulled from the room, throwing the chaos into blackness. "I said stop fighting!" Emilia held them in darkness for another moment before releasing the light back into the room.

"They attacked first!" a girl shouted.

"*Dellard* attacked first," Emilia said.

"We should throw her into the pit!" the beefy boy with Lee shouted.

"Lee," Emilia said, her calm tone shocking even herself, "take Dellard's talisman. Then escort her to the pit. Do not hurt her unless she tries to fight back."

"Got it!" Lee said, waving Dellard's wand triumphantly over his head before a group of older boys lifted the unconscious Dellard and carried her into the hall.

"The rest of you," Emilia said, taking a deep breath, "our fight is not with the teachers. It's with the Dragons. Any teacher who is willing to help us contact your families and plan for the protection of the school is an ally."

"I don't agree with students trying to pretend they know better than teachers," Ms. Bildge growled, straightening her rumpled blouse, and pressing back her flyaway hairs, "and I will not be locked up while this school is in danger. Do you really think the Academy isn't protected?"

"I'm sure it is," Emilia said, "but it's not enough, believe me… it's not enough."

"I'll help protect the school—that's my job, but I want nothing to do with a bunch of whiny brats calling home to mommy." Ms. Bildge spat on the floor.

"Fair enough," Connor said. "I can take a group and go through the defenses already in place with Bildge."

"Thank you, Connor," Emilia said.

Connor jumped off the wall, pulling some students from the crowd to follow him and Bildge from the cafeteria.

"I need to get him to the infirmary," Maggie said, her shield disappearing as she stood.

"I'm familiar with the infirmary," Claire chimed in. "I'll help."

"I want to talk to my family," a little girl said.

"We need to defend ourselves first," an older girl shouted.

"Claire, I need you to go with the girls, start organizing them into groups," Emilia said.

"I'll help Jacob," Mikey said. "I like him."

"Come on, squirt," Maggie said, levitating Jacob over the wall. The boy grabbed his feet, and together they steered Jacob through the air.

Emilia could feel Jacob's heart beating in her chest. Slow and calm as though he were sleeping.

He'll be okay.

"I'll help them organize," a teacher in a black uniform said from the back of the group.

"I always knew you had a heart somewhere deep down, Essec," Maggie called over her shoulder.

"Thank you," Emilia said.

"I'll keep an eye on him," Claire said, trotting toward the teacher.

"We need to find the skry mirrors," Emilia said.

"They're in the Hall of Mirrors, but Dellard locked the room and blocked skry spells on the bathroom mirrors," a girl called from the back.

"Well, let's unlock the hall." Emilia jumped down off the wall.

Most of the room had cleared out, either organizing a defense or following Bildge to see what the school already had in place, but about forty students had stayed watching Emilia, caring more about finding out what was happening at home than defending themselves.

The ones with real families. It was the Bonforte girl who had shouted about the Hall of Mirrors being locked. The girl looked pale. Fear darkened her eyes. Emilia gave the Bonforte girl a sympathetic smile.

"Lead the way," Emilia said, following the students desperate to find their families.

10

FACE IN THE MIRROR

"*Y*ou know," a voice pulled Jacob from the depths of sleep, "I sincerely hope when I was on the brink of death I looked cuter than you."

Jacob's eyes fluttered open. His head felt like a centaur had tried to cleave it in two. His stomach was sore like he had been violently ill for a week. And Claire was staring judgmentally down at him.

"What are you doing here?" Jacob pushed himself up onto his elbows, making the room wobble dangerously. "Where's Emilia?"

"Emilia finished rallying the troops." Claire sat by Jacob's feet. "Last I heard she was helping the students contact their families. I was assigned to help organize everyone into defensive groups. Finished with that and decided to come and get you out of bed. You've had your nap, now let's build a barricade and defend this place."

"How long was I out?" Jacob asked.

"A few hours," the brown-haired girl who had been sending messages to Jacob's arm said from the doorway. "I told her to let you rest."

"You also told me he wasn't dying," Claire said. "And he

should be with Emilia right now. So get up, Jacob, it's time to do things way above and beyond what should ever be asked of teenagers. Again."

"Right," Jacob grunted as he stood. Everything ached horribly. "Let's go find Emilia."

Claire took Jacob by the arm and led him to the infirmary door.

"Maggie, aren't you coming to the Hall of Mirrors?" Claire asked.

"I think I'll head to the cafeteria and see if there's anything I can do to help with the defenses," Maggie said. "Last I heard Mr. Essec was taking control of the students. I've always liked him, so I'll see what I can do to be useful."

"Don't you want to contact your family?" Claire asked.

"I don't have anyone on the outside," Maggie said. "Good luck."

"Wow." Claire dragged Jacob down the hall. "I can't imagine not having anyone I'd want to talk to."

"I don't," Jacob said. "Aside from everyone from the Mansion House, I don't have anyone."

"Well aren't you lucky our whole family is in this magical bloodbath together?" Claire said brightly.

She turned to an open doorway. The wood around the handle was cracked and splintered where someone had broken the door. Claire whistled. "Emilia's never been one to do things halfway."

A line of students waited in the center of the room. On either side were three full-length mirrors. A student stood in front of each of them, talking to the person in the reflection.

One boy was in tears, speaking to an older woman who was shaking and crying herself.

Jacob couldn't hear the woman's words, but he understood the grief etched on her face. She had lost someone to the Dragons. Maybe everyone. Emilia stood at the end of the room, directing students to mirrors as they became available. One small boy was crouched in the corner, speaking into Emilia's hand mirror. He looked overjoyed. At least someone's family was safe.

As soon as she spotted him, Emilia ran to Jacob, throwing her arms around his neck and holding him close. "Are you okay?"

"I'm fine." Jacob took a deep breath, letting her scent fill him. The pain ebbed from his body, and he held her closer.

"I wanted to go with you—"

"You needed to be here," Jacob whispered. "How's it going?"

"Well," Emilia said, pulling away from Jacob just enough to be able to look around the room, "this is the last group. Connor is still helping them figure out how to defend this place. But everyone's been put into groups and given assignments in case we're attacked. Essec has the older students patrolling the walls. He wants to have classes again tomorrow."

"Probably best if he doesn't want chaos." Claire nodded. "Not that I'm not a fan of chaos."

"What about the skrying?" Jacob asked, feeling the weight of his question settle into his chest.

"A lot of the students have lost someone," Emilia said. "We have two who lost everyone."

"The Bonforte girl?" Jacob asked.

"She managed to contact a cousin. That's the only relative she has left."

"Anyone have family in the Dragons?" Jacob asked.

"Only one that admitted to it," Emilia said. "He bragged about it like an idiot. We took him to the pit with Dellard."

"If any of them tell the Dragons we're here—" Claire began.

"Which is why we're leaving first thing in the morning," Emilia cut across. "I spoke to Proteus. We're joining the Elis Tribe. It's where most of the Gray Clan's strength is now."

"Great," Claire grumbled. "We get away from the centaurs, make it less than two weeks, and right back to them."

"It's the best plan we've got," Jacob said, threading his fingers through Emilia's.

Claire opened her mouth to protest, but before she could say anything, the small boy from the end of the hall tugged on Emilia's sleeve. He was young, the youngest student Jacob had seen at the Academy. And he looked terrified at his own boldness in touching Emilia.

"Umm, I, I mean," the young boy muttered, "Miss Gray, I was talking to my mom, but the mirror shimmered. And the lady, she wasn't very happy I had your mirror, and I think she wants to talk to you." The boy held up the mirror in his trembling hand.

Staring out of its surface was Isadora Gray.

11

FROM THE GRAVE

*E*milia looked into Aunt Iz's face.

"Emilia." It was Aunt Iz's voice coming from the mirror. The look of concern on the wrinkled face and tilt of her head as she examined Emilia were wonderfully familiar. It truly was Isadora Gray.

Emilia's knees buckled, dropping her toward the floor. Jacob caught her, wrapping his arms around her waist, steadying her by his side.

"Aunt Iz," Emilia whispered. "You're alive. Oh, thank God you're alive."

"Emilia, where are the others?" Aunt Iz asked.

"They're here," Emilia said. "We're all here at the Academy. MAGI Stone is a traitor, Aunt Iz. He told the Pendragon where we were hiding and where Rosalie was. The Pendragon kidnapped her, and we tried to save her, but she's dead and Claire was hurt and we had nowhere else to go. And…" Emilia's words were lost as tears clogged her throat.

"What about you?" Jacob asked. "Where are you? Are the others…did you all make it out?"

"We're fine," Aunt Iz said, her tone not matching the relief

Emilia felt. "Samuel and Dexter were not well enough to travel. We had to hide while we healed them."

"Where are you?" Claire asked, snaking under Emilia's arm so she could look into the mirror. "Tell us where you are, and we'll come to you. Or Emilia talked to Proteus, so we could all go to him."

"We can't stay where we are," Aunt Iz said, "and if Elder's Keep was compromised by Stone, we can't go there either. I don't want you traveling on your own. You've done well, Emilia. You've kept yourself, Jacob, Connor, and Claire alive. You have done beautifully. Stay where you are, and we'll come to you."

"Thank you," Emilia said. "I love you, Aunt Iz."

"I love you, too."

"Aunt Iz," Jacob said as it looked like Aunt Iz was about to disappear from the image, "you didn't look surprised when we told you about Stone."

"Someone betrayed us," Aunt Iz said, her tone deathly calm. "It was clear as soon as we were attacked in the tunnels. There are very few people who could have betrayed us to the Dragons. Stone was among them. And the others on the list, I don't think they would have betrayed us even to save their own lives."

"What do we do?" Jacob asked. "He knows so much about all of us."

"What to do about Stone will be Larkin's decision," Aunt Iz said, "and mercy is not a quality Stone ever sought to instill in her."

∼

*E*milia refused to be moved into the girl's dormitory, insisting the four of them stay together. With students and teachers patrolling the corridors, an attack on the outer wall seemed not only inevitable, but imminent. And if the time to fight came again, the four of them needed to fight together.

Nurse Bracken had allowed them to sleep in the infirmary for the night on the condition that the boys stay on one side and Emilia and Claire on the other.

Emilia wanted to be closer to Jacob. To be able to hear him breathe. But arguing with Nurse Bracken would only have made things worse. So Emilia lay in the dark, trying not to think of things to come.

Aunt Iz, Molly, Larkin, Samuel, and Dexter had all made it out of the Graylock caves alive. That was enough to be grateful for tonight, and tomorrow would come whether they wanted it to or not.

"Emilia," Claire whispered from her bed. "You're still awake, right?"

"Yep," Emilia whispered. "You need to sleep, Claire."

"I slept for days. I may never sleep again." Springs creaked in the dark as Claire climbed out of her bed and perched next to Emilia. "Besides, I have something for you."

"What is it?"

"So here's the thing," Claire said. "We all know interfering is something I'm really good at. Remember when we were in the car with Rosalie and we were all going *someplace safe?*"

Emilia didn't say anything. She didn't want to talk about Rosalie.

"You fell asleep, and I might have told Rosalie that, seeing as she's your mother, she should say really nice things to you before going into human hiding. She didn't take too kindly to that, but I nagged her until she agreed to write a note." Claire pulled a piece of paper and a shining pink stone from her jeans pocket. "I was supposed to save it until things had calmed down, but that doesn't seem like a great idea with all the impending doom."

Claire pushed the paper into Emilia's hand and fidgeted with the stone as she moved back to her own mattress as though to give Emilia privacy. "It's a little wrinkled and gross from being in

my pocket while we were fighting our way through the tunnels…
and stuff. But I think you should read it."

There was a long pause before Emilia managed to say
anything. "Did you read it?"

"No. But she did cry a bit toward the end of writing it, so that
must mean something."

"Thanks, Claire." Emilia held the paper tight in her hand. She
wanted to read it. To open it and find her mother's last words to
her. But the letter was from Rosalie. A woman she had spent
barely a week in the company of. The same woman who had left
Emilia on Aunt Iz's doorstep when she was only a baby.

Aunt Iz was Emilia's real mother. The one who had loved her
and raised her. Aunt Iz was the one who Emilia could always rely
on, who had given Emilia a home, a Clan, and a family.

Emilia tightened her fingers to tear the paper in half, then
stopped.

Rosalie had been tethered to the Pendragon. She had lived
with him at Graylock. If there was even a tiny piece of information that could help them destroy the Dragons, she had to know.

Emilia slipped out of bed and lowered herself to the cold
stone floor, before saying in a shivering whisper, *"Inluesco."* A tiny
blue light appeared in her palm. *"Elevare."* The light floated in the
air as Emilia unfolded the paper with trembling hands.

My Daughter Emilia,

*Your little blond friend just shoved a piece of paper under my nose
and insisted I write you a note. She says these are uncertain times and I
shouldn't count on being able to see you again. I'm sure she'll read this
letter before it gets to you. So, little blond girl, you are right. People die.
People change. They betray and lie, and nothing in the world will ever
change that. It doesn't matter if the people you love and trust are
wizards or humans, they can hurt you just the same. And the worst of it
is knowing you've hurt them back.*

But there's nothing to be done. The world is cruel, magic is cruel, and survival is the most painful part of it all.

I wish I could say I regret loving Emile. I wish I could say I regret leaving you, Emilia. But I don't. I made my choices. I chose who to love, and I chose when to run. I don't regret leaving you with the Grays. They made you who you are. I said my goodbye to you a long time ago. I cried and left a note. I don't want to do it again.

You are stronger than I ever was. You don't need me to hold your hand or protect you. You are everything without me.

If there had been a spell to let me see you grow up without you ever knowing I was watching, I might have used it. But I never would have had the strength to stay away. So, I won't apologize for missing seventeen birthdays. There was always bound to be pain. I've done my best not to make it worse.

Fight, my little Emilia. Fight for what the Grays have taught you. Fight for the one who loves you with or without magic. And when the fight ends, survive. Live. That is all I could ever hope for.

Rosalie

*E*milia touched her face with her frozen fingers. There were no tears on her cheeks. Rosalie wouldn't have wanted there to be. Rosalie was free. The Siren couldn't hold her, Emilia couldn't drag her into a world she hated, even the Pendragon couldn't hurt her. Rosalie's pain had ended.

Emilia folded the letter and slipped it into the pocket of the coat on her bedside table.

Rosalie was free. But the rest of them would have to fight. Emilia wanted to scream, to shriek loud enough to wake the whole Academy. Rosalie was gone, but the rest of them would have to fight, and bleed, and hurt, and kill.

Warm arms wrapped around Emilia, the scent of fresh grass

and the woods in the fall covered her. She didn't need to look to know it was Jacob who lifted her into her bed. Jacob who draped the warm covers over her.

"Sleep, Emi." Jacob kissed her forehead. "Aunt Iz will be here tomorrow. Things will get better."

Emilia took Jacob's hand and pressed it to her lips.

"Thank you," Emilia whispered.

"For what?"

"Never leaving me."

IN THE CORNERS OF EVERYTHING

*T*he cool wind of the ocean tickled Emilia's cheeks. The tang of the salty air filled her lungs. Waves lapped at the sand, but even without knowing why, she knew it was wrong. Black sand covered her toes and marked her hands like a stain that would never come clean.

The grey sky hovered over the horizon, and the green flash of dawn had frozen as a bright blast of light, a permanent scar above the waves.

"It's always like that," the Pendragon said from behind Emilia's shoulder.

She recognized his voice, but when she spun to face him, it took a moment to understand his face. It was Emile LeFay, but unlike Emilia had ever seen him. He was younger, his face missing the lines of anger that now marred his brow. His eyes were bright without the hatred that now filled them. Even the black uniform with the golden dragon was missing. This was Emile as Rosalie had known him.

"What are you doing here?" Emilia took a step backward, but Emile caught her by the arms and pulled her away before the waves could touch her feet.

"Don't touch the water." Emile swept Emilia into his arms and carried her to a table with two chairs, which sat in the middle of the black sand. "It will pull you under and far away."

"This is a dream." Emilia shoved Emile away as he knelt to speak to her like she was a small child. But he didn't waver or fall into the sand. He was frozen, steady like a wall.

"It doesn't matter if it's a dream," Emile said. "The light is there in the corners of everything."

"What light?" Emilia asked, but she didn't need Emile's reply.

As soon as she thought to look for it, she could see the light every-where. A pale green mist to match the green that scarred the sky and hovered over the waves as they lapped against the shore. The light clung to the corners of every shadow, as though waiting for a chance to break free.

"It is always there waiting." Emile stared at the mist with a furrowed brow.

"It's the Siren." Emilia's heart quickened as if saying the name would make the Siren herself appear.

"I'm afraid you're right. Though, I do not know why it's here."

"You were feeding her power for seventeen years," Emilia laughed cruelly. "Maybe she just wants to pull you under the waves and keep you forever."

"Perhaps." Emile sat in the chair opposite Emilia and stared out at the waves.

"Why are you in my dream?" Emilia asked after what seemed like hours.

"If this is your dream, then that would be a question to ask yourself." Emile turned to Emilia with a smile. "Perhaps you are longing for a father to show you the way?"

"I don't need you." Emilia dug her fingers into the table, turning her knuckles white under the smeared stains from the black sand.

"Then perhaps you're here to save me from the mist?"

"The Siren can have you," Emilia growled. "In fact, it's a better fate than you deserve."

"And yet you dragged Rosalie from the Siren's Realm." Emile laced *his fingers together, resting his chin on his knuckles. "If she needed saving, wouldn't the Siren's Realm be a good enough condemnation for me?"*

"Rosalie was there because she was afraid of you!" Emilia shouted, her voice echoing out over the ocean, making the mist vibrate where it lay. "I brought her back so she could help me kill you. So she could have a life of her own!"

"She did help you kill me." Emile pulled down the neck of his shirt, showing a horrible red scar that cut right over his heart. Right where Emilia could always feel the tug in her own chest that led her to Jacob.

"I'm wounded. Broken," Emile whispered.

"I don't think you have enough of a soul for Rosalie's death to hurt you, and it's your fault she's dead."

"It's no more my fault than yours." Emile's eyes had begun to harden, their steely grey filling with the malice Emilia knew too well.

"She killed herself to stop you from murdering your own daughter."

"She killed herself because you dragged her back into a world she couldn't stand!" Emile raged.

"You could have left her alone. We left her someplace safe. She would still be alive—"

"I would never abandon the other half of my soul."

"But you would try to kill your own daughter?" The waves crashed violently against the shore, tearing the black sand away in great strips.

"You betrayed me!" the Pendragon shouted, and he did look like the Pendragon now. Gold shimmered on his chest, taking the form of a dragon. "I tried to give you the world! A world where magic will never have to hide in the darkness again."

"You're a murderer who kidnapped me and tethered me against my will."

"Doing the right thing is not always pleasant. I was protecting my only child."

"You tried to kill me." Emilia balled her hands into tight fists.

There was something in that simple movement that made her

remember the tingle in her fingers, remember what that feeling meant. "Manuvis." A sparking orb of light appeared in Emilia's hand.

The Pendragon looked surprised only for a moment before she threw the crackling ball at him, hitting him right in the chest, sending him sprawling onto the sand.

He stood, laughing, not bothering to wipe the blackness from his face. "You ran from my home, destroying it. Bonding yourself to the boy who had already murdered in my home. What did you want me to do, Emilia? I offered you a chance to come home, and you ran away with a killer."

"Jacob is not a killer."

"He has blood on his hands," the Pendragon growled.

"He has only ever fought to defend himself. You've murdered hundreds for no reason at all."

"I have the best reason!" the Pendragon roared. "I am fighting for freedom for Magickind. For me, for the men who serve me. For the ones hiding from the humans so deep in the wild they have yet to realize a new day is upon us all."

"Murder is not the way to make things better. Sustaura!"

The Pendragon doubled over as though an invisible fist had punched him in the stomach. He took a gasping breath before speaking. "I would have protected you. I would have made sure your children could walk in the sun, letting their magic shine for all the world to see."

"And now you just want me dead?" Emilia laughed. "How fitting. Destroying the future before you can create it."

"You could still come home," the Pendragon's voice dropped, but its low kindness was more frightening than his shouting had been. "You will be forgiven. You will be honored and protected. You will be there to see the rise of a new and glorious world."

"I would rather die than be locked up while you slaughter innocent people," Emilia whispered. Her words rushed through the air, stirring the storm that had been gathering in the grey sky, pushing the green mist closer so soon there would be no hope of escape.

"Then my sweet Emilia, you will die," the Pendragon said without a hint of sadness in his voice.

"Not if I kill you first." Emilia stepped in so close to the table she could have smacked the Pendragon.

"My child"—the Pendragon smiled pityingly—"you will never kill me. You don't have the strength for such blood."

"Yes, I do," Emilia whispered, staring straight into the steel grey eyes that perfectly matched her own.

The storm raged, drawing up the black sand and green mist, mixing them with clouds.

"I know you, Emilia. You will never kill me."

The storm became streaks of color, blurring everything, whisking the Pendragon away.

"If you really believe that," Emilia spoke softly into the storm, "then you don't know me at all."

13

OUT OF THE CAVES

*I*t was the banging on the door that dragged Jacob from his bed, though he wasn't sure he had ever slept. Whoever was on the other side of the infirmary door didn't seem to care that it wasn't locked or that the sun had barely come up. They just kept banging.

"Are you kidding?" Connor mumbled, grabbing his wand at the same time Claire and Emilia came running from their beds on the other side of the room.

"Do we open it?" Jacob pointed his wand at the door.

"I think we have to." Emilia stepped toward the handle. The whole door bounced, shaking from the banging.

"Aw come on," Claire said before calling, "Who's there?"

"It's Mikey!" a voice on the other side of the door shouted. "Lee sent me from the gate, he said to wake you up and make you come now!"

Jacob pulled open the door to find Mikey's excited face on the other side. "Why does he want us at the gate?"

"There are people there." Mikey seized Jacob's hand and dragged him down the hall. "But I don't think they're here to kill us. I think they know you."

"Aunt Iz!" Emilia ran so fast Mikey had to let go of Jacob and sprint as fast as he could just to try and keep up.

"You know, you could have shouted that our family was here," Claire said between gulps of air as they tore through the corridors, "or just come in and told us."

"No, miss," Mikey said, his face momentarily losing the redness running had given it. "I knew there were girls in there, and it's not right for a boy to go barging in where girls are. I had to do the right thing and knock."

"And who said chivalry was dead?" Claire snarked as they tore out the front doors and onto the snowy lawn.

The freezing air bit through Jacob's clothes, but he didn't care. Down at the end of the driveway he could see the gate. A row of students stood behind two black-clad teachers, and on the other side of the gate, five people stood facing them. Waiting to come in.

"Aunt Iz!" Emilia shouted, running full tilt toward the gate. "Let them in!"

The two men in black obeyed, pushing the gate out toward the street.

The gate swinging toward them made Aunt Iz and the others step back. Samuel leaned heavily on Molly's arm, and Dexter stumbled so badly Larkin had to catch him around the waist to keep him from falling.

"Emilia," Aunt Iz breathed, pulling her into a tight hug. "You're all right. You're all right."

"Aunt Molly!" Connor bolted to her, throwing his arms around his aunt before taking Molly's place at Samuel's side. "You okay, Samuel?"

"Fit as a fairy," Samuel half-grunted as Claire stepped up to his other side, giving him a quick hug before helping him through the gate.

Jacob stood back watching it all. Emilia left Iz and hugged Larkin.

"Look at you, keeping the others alive. I'm impressed." Larkin smiled.

Dexter nodded to Emilia but said nothing as Larkin half-dragged him through the gate.

Jacob wanted to step forward. To say how glad he was they had come back from Graylock and now they could all be together again. But there was a lump in his throat that seemed to make speaking impossible. And his arms and legs had gone so numb he couldn't quite remember how to move them.

"Jacob," Aunt Iz said gently as she reached him.

He nodded, feeling stupid for not being able to find the words to say how glad he was they were there.

But Aunt Iz apparently did not think him stupid at all. She pulled him into a tight hug.

Tears burned in the corners of his eyes.

"Thank you for taking care of Emilia," Aunt Iz whispered.

"She didn't—" Jacob began, his voice coming out all creaky. "She took care of me, too."

"That's the way it's supposed to work." Aunt Iz looked deep into Jacob's eyes, and he knew she understood. They had survived together, and she was grateful.

Claire bounded over and threw herself at Aunt Iz. "I'm so glad you're back! It's been terrible. I was in a coma, and the head-mistress here is psychotic, and that was after the underground labyrinth the Hag set up—"

"The Hag?" Molly cut across.

"Yep," Connor said, still supporting Samuel. "She took our magic, made us suffer, and then dumped us at the Pendragon's feet."

"Well, if you want to tell the boring version." Claire shrugged.

"We should talk about this inside," Larkin said with a glance to the pack of students and two teachers who were close enough to hear.

"I'll lead you to the infirmary," Claire said. "I'm very familiar with it."

Jacob stepped in to help Samuel up the stairs.

"I'm glad you made it," Jacob said, knowing his words were insufficient when what he really should have been saying was *I'm glad you didn't die while being tortured for months after rescuing me and Emilia.*

But Samuel just nodded. "Me too, Jacob. Me too."

The students hadn't been called to morning classes yet, so the cafeteria was rumbling with noise as they passed. There was no laughter, only talking, and the voices sounded afraid.

"I should speak to the headmistress as soon as possible," Aunt Iz said as they neared the infirmary.

"I mean, you can if you want," Claire said, her tone a little too cheerful as she led the limping group, "but we threw her in the pit for cursing Jacob."

"Mr. Essec is in charge now," Emilia said. "I can take you to see him if you want."

"Yes, thank you." Aunt Iz stopped at the door while the others filed into the infirmary. "We need to discuss our immediate plans. And I need to be sure the students at this school are actually safe."

"I'll be right back," Emilia whispered to Jacob before leading Iz down the hall.

Jacob followed the others in, closing the door to the infirmary behind him.

Nurse Bracken stood in the center of the room, looking for all the fairies in the world like her head was going to explode.

"Who—What—" she stammered. "Why are there—not even students! Why are you here?"

"They're our family," Connor said, helping Samuel sit down on a bed. "They've been fighting the Pendragon, and now they need you to heal them."

"I am the Academy nurse, not a field medic!" Nurse Bracken squawked, finally finding her words in a surge of indignation.

"And I'm a thirteen-year-old kid, not a fighter, but you do what you have to do." Claire planted her hands on her hips, raising one blond eyebrow.

"She's right," Jacob said. "They're patients just like any other. They need your help."

"Fine," Nurse Bracken said, "but this is an exception, not a practice that will become standard in *my* infirmary." She rounded on Dexter. "What have you done to yourself anyway?"

"A bunch of rocks fell on me." Dexter groaned as she pushed him down on a bed.

"We did all the healing spells we could," Larkin said before Dexter could speak again, "but the best we could do was get him well enough to travel."

"And that one?" Nurse Bracken asked, jerking her head toward Samuel.

"Captured and tortured for half-a-year by the Pendragon himself," Samuel said, his voice so low and dark it made Jacob's spine tense.

"Well," Nurse Bracken said after a brief and painful pause, "if I'm going to be working on this much damage, I'd prefer to work with Maggie's assistance."

"I'll get her," Jacob said.

"You can all get her." Nurse Bracken waved them toward the door. "Unless you have an injury that needs healed, get out of my infirmary."

Jacob bowed the others toward the door. Larkin, Claire, and Connor all went into the hall, but Molly stayed, eyeing Nurse Bracken.

"Are you in need of medical assistance?" Nurse Bracken asked Molly.

"No, I am perfectly willing to leave your infirmary," Molly said using her calm and dangerous tone that made anyone with a self-preservation instinct want to run away. "But I need you to understand that both of these men are members of the Gray Clan. The head of the Gray Clan is here, and she would take it as a personal affront if both of these men did not receive the best medical care you have to offer."

Jacob held his breath for a moment as both women glared silently at each other.

"I will be back in one hour to check on them." Molly spun on her heel and strode out into the hall.

Nurse Bracken turned her angry gaze to Jacob as though looking to him to apologize.

He followed the others without a word.

"Wow, Aunt Molly." Connor nodded appreciatively. "Nice one."

"Where is this girl the Nurse wants?" Larkin asked.

"In the cafeteria." Jacob led the way. "If we hurry, we should be able to grab some food."

It took Jacob only a minute to find Maggie, and she ran out of the cafeteria as soon as he delivered word Nurse Bracken wanted her.

A group of young students both boys and girls cleared away from their table, offering it to Jacob and the others. The children stood nearby, watching them eat until the bell rang for them to go to class.

"Well?" Connor asked as soon as the cafeteria door closed behind the last student.

"Well what?" Larkin asked.

"Come on, you escaped the caves." Connor leaned forward, speaking quickly. "Emilia said there was a cave-in. She didn't know if you had made it out. We couldn't get ahold of you for three days. You finally get in touch with Emilia who tells you we almost died, and then you show up limping at the Academy gate."

"How did Emilia know about the cave-in?" Larkin asked.

"The Hag." Jacob rubbed his hands over his face, feeling like the mere mention of her would bring her close. "She made Emilia watch what was happening. You rescuing Samuel, the *somnerri* attacking, Dexter causing the cave-in."

"We know you were trapped," Claire said. "What we don't know is how you got out."

"There's no point in sheltering us," Jacob said. "We're not kids who need protecting. We're targets. All of us are."

"We're in this together," Claire added.

Larkin and Molly exchanged looks before Larkin sighed. "We are all targets, and I don't think it's anywhere near over."

"We were penned in," Molly said, her face turning grey just mentioning the caves. "We had gotten to Samuel, but they knew we were coming."

"It was Stone," Larkin said. "He must have told them. As soon as we had Samuel, they came for us."

"They had *somnerri*." Molly sounded far away. "They were coming out of the walls, and it was all I could do to keep Samuel standing."

"I didn't think we'd make it." Larkin reached over and squeezed Molly's hand. "But Dexter, he collapsed the ceiling, made us a way out. But he used his shield to protect us instead of himself."

"At least he did something right," Claire growled.

"I managed to get him out of the rocks," Larkin said, not seeming to have heard Claire. "Iz was fighting the Dragons on the outside, and Molly was trying to move Samuel."

"Then Isadora was hit," Molly said. "I thought we'd lost."

"How did you get out of that?" Connor whispered.

"She fought her way to her feet," Larkin said. "She stood and everything sort of went still. Molly cast a shield, and we all made it to the surface. They were charging us. But Samuel, he started to fight. It wasn't much, but seeing him standing seemed to scare the Dragons."

"Larkin used a hover spell on Dexter," Molly said. "I don't

know how Isadora managed it, but she was running, leading us all away."

"The ground was cracking, water flooding up to the surface."

"And then we were at a rock face. Isadora made a shield large enough for all of us. We hid in the spell."

"Iz collapsed as soon as we were all in." Larkin's hands shook. "We did the healing we could on the three of them. But none of them were strong enough to move on their own. And with two of us and three of them, we had to stay put."

"We stayed for two days," Molly said. "We couldn't contact anyone through the shield, and we didn't dare leave it. Iz woke up first, Samuel..."

"He was awake." Larkin's voice was low. "But he couldn't fight. And Dexter..."

"We thought we'd lost him," Molly said. "We couldn't wake him. He was in very, very bad shape."

"When he finally woke up, Iz decided we should make a run for it," Larkin said. "We met a few Dragon guards patrolling, but we fought our way through. As soon as we got far enough away, Iz contacted Emilia. We knew someone had betrayed us. We didn't know it was Stone. I didn't know. I never even suspected. He trained me—"

"He fooled all of us," Jacob said.

"Yeah, that—" Connor let loose a long stream of curses describing Stone. It was a mark of how angry Molly was with Stone that she didn't even try to object.

"Once we found out where you were," Larkin said, "we found a road and a car. Flying wasn't an option with Dexter and Samuel being so weak."

"But Dexter flew you back to the Mansion House on a broom when you were hurt," Claire said, turning to Larkin.

"Dexter got lucky," Larkin said. "We needed to travel below the Dragons' radar. And considering we made it here alive, I think it worked."

They all sat in silence for a moment.

"So what do we do now?" Jacob asked. "I mean, we're all together, so there's got to be something we can do."

"We wait for Isadora to get back from talking to Mr. Essec. We check on Samuel and Dexter and see how soon they'll be fit to fight." Molly stood as though ready to begin everything right away.

"And after we're all in fighting shape?" Claire asked, not hiding the hint of excitement in her voice.

"We make sure the Dragons can never hurt our family again," Larkin said.

"Good plan." Connor smiled, standing next to his aunt.

"Fighting is never a good plan," Molly said, "but sometimes there is no other choice."

14

CAKE

*E*milia sat outside Mrs. Dellard's former office. She had been in on the first part of the meeting between Essec and Aunt Iz, but when they stopped discussing the Gray family taking up residence in the infirmary and moved on to protecting the school, Essec had insisted Emilia leave.

She had wanted to argue, to stay close to Aunt Iz. It had been less than two weeks since she had last seen Iz and the rest of the rescue party at the Green Mountain Preserve with the Elis Tribe, but it felt like forever. Too much had happened. Having Aunt Iz out of sight, even if it was only behind a door, was too terribly painful.

"Pull yourself together, Emilia Gray," Emilia whispered.

"You okay?" Jacob asked from the end of the corridor as though answering Emilia's call.

"Fine." Emilia nodded, knowing full well he could feel she was lying.

"I've been to the infirmary." Jacob slid down the wall and sat next to Emilia. She took his hand in hers without thought. "They're both okay. Samuel is…"

"As bad as Larkin?" Emilia asked. Larkin, too, had been locked up and tortured in the tunnels under Graylock.

"Worse maybe." Lines pinched between Jacob's eyebrows. "She was scared and angry. Samuel's hollow."

"He's in shock," Emilia said. "What both of them went through, to have survived months of torture…"

"But they made it out alive." Jacob squeezed Emilia's hand. "Alive is good. We can work on getting better later."

They sat in silence for a moment, listening to the low rumble of voices filtering through the office door.

"Did Aunt Iz tell you what happened?" Jacob asked.

"I heard the parts she told Essec." Emilia laid her head on Jacob's shoulder. "I'm sure there's more."

"I'm just glad they made it out okay."

Emilia's eyes began to slide shut. There, in that moment, she was safe and warm. Aunt Iz's voice carried through the door, as though she wanted to be sure Emilia knew she was still in the office.

But before Emilia could fall properly asleep, the door to Mrs. Dellard's former office swung open and Mr. Essec bowed Aunt Iz out.

"I appreciate any help you can give," Essec said, the tone of his voice making it clear his gratitude was grudging. "The most important thing we can do right now is protect our students."

"As it always is," Aunt Iz said. "I will contact my Clan and look forward to meeting with you again as soon as there is news."

Jacob and Emilia scrambled off the floor, and Essec glared at them.

Aunt Iz didn't seem to notice or care as she led Jacob and Emilia away.

"How did it go?" Emilia asked quietly as they moved into the next hallway.

"As well as can be expected when dealing with a man in denial who is still enamored of his newfound authority."

"So, great then?" Emilia heard the smile in Jacob's voice.

"The best plan would be to send all the students home," Aunt Iz said. "Without MAGI or the Council there is no one left to properly defend the Academy. No Clan would want to take charge of it with so many children that don't belong to them attending."

"Can't *we* protect the Academy?" Emilia asked, her heart sinking as she thought of Maggie. She had no family to return to.

"I wish we could," Aunt Iz said, her face looking older and sterner than Emilia had ever seen it, "but we are fighting the Dragons. No other Clan has come forward to fight with us. We have to protect our people and concentrate what resources we have on stopping the Pendragon. We don't have the numbers to protect the school."

"So then what are they going to do?" Jacob asked as Iz stopped right outside the infirmary door.

"Essec is going to begin contacting the families of the human-born students. They will be sent home as soon as safe transport can be arranged."

"But—" Emilia began, not quite able to wrap her mind around what Iz was saying. "You're going to bind all of their powers and send them home without magic?"

"It's the best option they have," Aunt Iz said. "The students with magical families will be sent home next."

"And what about the kids who have nowhere to go?" Jacob asked, his hands balled into such tight fists that white shone on his knuckles.

"They will have to stay here," Aunt Iz said. "If no one in the magical or human world is willing to claim them, they have to stay. And we are going to help Essec arrange the best defense possible for the school. We'll set up as many shield and protective spells as we can."

"What are you contacting the Clan for?" Emilia asked.

"To assist in arranging transport," Aunt Iz said.

"You want to borrow a car?" Emilia asked.

"In essence." Aunt Iz nodded, turning to go into the infirmary.

"There is something else we could do," Jacob said, stopping Iz mid-step. "We could ask the Hag to protect the Academy. Her spell at Elder's Keep held even when the Pendragon knew we were there. She could cast the same sort of spell here."

"That kind of spell requires secrecy," Emilia said, feeling Jacob's hope ebb away. "There's too many people here, and I don't think they'd all agree to being trapped."

"And even if it would work," Aunt Iz said, "the Hag doesn't simply come when you call her. And even if she did, would you really trust her when she arrived?"

"No," Jacob said after a long moment. "No we couldn't trust her."

Iz pushed open the door and led Jacob and Emilia into the infirmary.

It was the same as always—at least the furniture was in the right places—but now it was full. Not stuffed with people. The room wasn't even noisy. But there was something about having everyone in there that made the room stop feeling like a tomb. If only the professor had been there her family would be complete. As soon as she had the thought, the letter in Emilia's pocket seemed to grow heavy.

"Emi?" Jacob turned to her with concern in his eyes.

"Nothing," Emilia murmured. "It's nothing." She tried to force the knot in her chest to relax. There was nothing Jacob could do to help her. He didn't need to feel her pain.

"How are the patients?" Aunt Iz asked a harassed-looking Nurse Bracken.

"Well," Nurse Bracken said, "they aren't in as bad a shape as they could have been. The healing you did might well have saved that one's life." She pointed to Dexter who lay on a bed away from the others, who all surrounded Samuel.

"His name is Dexter," Emilia said softly.

"I would think you'd care more about whether or not I've healed him than learned his name," Nurse Bracken said. "The other one—"

"Samuel," Emilia said firmly.

"—is in decent condition," Nurse Bracken said loudly enough that Samuel would easily be able to hear from his bed fifteen feet away. "He's clearly been abused, but they seemed intent on keeping him alive. I've done the healing spells I can to relieve him of immediate pain, but some of the damage and scarring are likely to be permanent."

The others by the bed had gone silent.

"I'll work on some potions for both of them, and we can see what relief they bring," Nurse Bracken continued, seemingly oblivious to the angry glares of the people around the room. "I just hope you understand how lucky you are to have found someone with competent healing skills."

"It wasn't luck," Jacob said, the levelness of his voice making his anger clear, though his words were kind. "We came here to get your help, and we're grateful for it. Everyone we've brought in here for your help has been hurt fighting the Dragons. Because that's what happens when you try and stop the bad guys from destroying everything you love. People get hurt, and you need a healer. Who hopefully appreciates the fact that what you're fighting for benefits them, too."

The room was brutally silent. Nurse Bracken stood frozen, glaring at Jacob as though unsure whether to yell at him or thank him.

"I got the best soup I could get the cook to make," Maggie said, coming through the door with a tray hovering in front of her. She looked at the silent group. "Don't count on it being too good. By *best* I mean tastes like cardboard not sewage. So…eat up."

Maggie steered the tray over to Samuel's bed where Molly took a bowl.

Molly sat down next to Samuel, sniffing the soup, and cringing before holding the spoon out to him.

"I can feed myself, Molly." Samuel's voice was gravelly and low.

"It's not for you that I want to do it," Molly said, firmly holding the spoon an inch from Samuel's lips. Their eyes locked for a moment before he opened his mouth and allowed her to deposit the brownish-orange goo.

"How is it?" Claire asked.

"Awful." Samuel barely had time to say the word before Molly shoved another spoonful of soup into his mouth.

"Maybe you could go into the kitchen, Aunt Molly," Connor said casually. "You know, really show them how it's done. Make up a dinner to give them an example of what food fit for wizards tastes like."

"Thinking of your stomach at a time like this." A hint of a smile crept into the corners of Molly's eyes.

"Well, I am still growing." Connor sounded a little guilty. "And we do all need our strength."

"And cake!" Claire said cheerfully, giving an exasperated sigh when no one cheered her suggestion. "Death's claws missed our sorry hides this time. We should eat cake!"

"Cake might be nice," Larkin said. "I mean, after all we've been through."

Molly sighed and passed Samuel's bowl of soup to Larkin before walking toward the door. "Train the children to fight Molly, go on a rescue mission Molly, heal us Molly, don't take care of us Molly, make us cake Molly."

"You know you love us." Connor beamed at his Aunt.

"More than anything in this world or any other. So now, I'll go make cake." Molly walked out of the infirmary as Connor and Claire high-fived.

"Samuel, we got her to make you a cake." Claire sat down on

the edge of Samuel's bed and gave him a careful hug. "Cake makes everything better."

Samuel took a slow bite of the goo. "As long as the cake doesn't taste like this soup."

15

BROKEN AND BOUND

*T*he rest of the family had filtered out of the infirmary. Jacob to help Lee with patrol, Claire and Connor to help Molly train the students, while Larkin and Aunt Iz had followed Essec away. Emilia was left alone sitting next to Samuel's bed. He had drifted off after his second piece of cake. He wouldn't even know if she left the room, but she wanted to sit with him. To watch his chest rise and fall and know he was alive.

Maggie had come in earlier and gone straight to Dexter's bed with a tray of food. He had refused Molly's cake, and none of the Grays tried to argue with him.

Maggie sat perched on the edge of Dexter's bed speaking softly to him. Dexter was sitting up now. His face had more color, but the heavy lines that creased his brow hadn't disappeared.

"The rest of your family are working on helping protect the Academy." Maggie's voice was barely loud enough for Emilia to hear.

"They aren't my family." The strained sound of pain in Dexter's voice made Emilia's heart drop. "I don't have any family."

"Neither do I," Maggie said, "but what you do have is a bunch of people willing to haul your half-dead body through the woods instead of leaving you behind. They may not be your family, but it's a hell of a lot better than nothing."

"It's a lot better than I deserve."

Emilia stood and crept out into the hall, leaning against the cold wall as soon as she closed the door.

Dexter had betrayed her, betrayed her whole family. But he had saved them, too. The split instincts to slap him and hug him were driving her crazy.

Aunt Iz was right to have pulled him out of the rubble at Graylock. They couldn't abandon him. He was a part of their battle, and he was fighting on their side. He had protected them, and now they would have to protect him.

Jacob would understand. Claire and Connor wouldn't.

"You okay?" Maggie asked as she joined Emilia in the hallway.

"I'm fine." Emilia exhaled. "It's just a lot. There's just…a lot."

"Yep." Maggie nodded. "Immanent doom. Your ex fighting for your clan."

"What?" Emilia stood up straight, turning to Maggie. "What did he tell—"

"Dexter didn't say anything. But the way he looks at you and the way Jacob refuses to look at him, it's pretty obvious."

"It was before Jacob." Emilia rubbed her face. "It was before all of this."

"So, I take it Dexter isn't seeing anyone?" Maggie asked, her tone a little too casual.

"What?" Emilia's left eyebrow shot up her forehead.

"I just mean there is no girl out there in the world that's waiting with bated breath to find out if he survived the Dragons?"

"No." Emilia shook her head, not quite able to keep the confusion from her face. "I don't think there is."

"Good to know." Maggie grinned. "I think I like him. Handsome, mournful, even more damaged than I am. He's just my type."

"O-okay."

"Look, I get it. The world is ending and we could all be slaughtered tomorrow. But if I'm going to be brutally murdered tomorrow, what's the harm in flirting with a really hot guy today? I've been locked in the Academy long enough to know that tall, dark, and emotionally impaired is my type."

"Good." Emilia's voice sounded pitchy in her ears. "That's good. But be careful, okay? Dexter is, I've known him for a long time, and he's, he can be a good guy. But…" Emilia searched for the words.

"Don't worry about me getting hurt," Maggie laughed. "I'm not counting on having a long, full life, let alone finding true love on the eve of destruction. But as long as it won't hurt you, I might as well have some fun while I've still got the chance."

"I'm fine." Emilia smiled, feeling a weight lifting from her chest as she knew the words were true. "I want Dexter to be happy and safe. As long as you want that too, that's great."

"Good." Maggie loosened the pins that held her bun and let her hair fall around her shoulders. "Then I'm going to go grab some of this famously great cake from Molly and sit consolingly by Mr. Brooding's bedside until I can convince him to eat it." Maggie started down the hall before turning back with a whip of her hair. "Because sadly enough, that'll be the most fun I've had in months locked in this grey Hell hole."

Emilia watched Maggie disappear down the hall, unable to wipe the smile from her face. The world was falling apart and flirting was still happening. Something that simple still existed. And it was exciting and amazing.

"You all right?"

Emilia jumped at the sound of Larkin's voice.

"I've been hearing that question a lot lately," Emilia said.

"That's what happens when you're surviving in panic mode."

Larkin shrugged. "Don't worry, I get it all the time, too. Just got it in Essec's office. They want you there, and apparently I'm better at fetching you than defending the Academy."

Emilia laughed and hugged Larkin tightly. "At least we're a mess together."

"But seriously, Emilia, are you okay?" Larkin pulled away and stared into Emilia's eyes in a very Aunt Iz-like way.

"I'm great." Emilia nodded. "Maggie has a thing for Dexter. She wanted to make sure I was fine with it, and I am. And you're here. Aunt Iz is taking care of the Academy. It'll only be a couple of days before we get out of here and join the Elis and Wright family. And then we can fight. We can end this thing."

"It won't be easy," Larkin said. "We could lose more people."

"I know." Emilia pushed the words past the knot that had leaped right back up into her throat. "But we can plan an attack. It'll be better than being chased and trapped and picked off one at a time."

"You would have made a great MAGI," Larkin said. "In a different lifetime."

"Well, when you re-form MAGI after we get to the end of this, maybe you can train me."

"Can't," Larkin said. "Clan heirs aren't allowed to join MAGI."

"They weren't," Emilia said. "But being an heir hasn't kept me from needing to fight. And since MAGI will have to be rebuilt from the ground up, you can change whatever rules you like."

"I guess we can figure out what the new rules should be together," Larkin laughed, and a hint of true joy shone in her eyes.

∼

"We have enough teachers willing to act as guards to get the human-born children to safe places," Aunt Iz said. "Claire has been kind enough to arrange bus and train transport for each of them."

"Do you really think they'll be safer on a bus alone than they would be here?" Essec asked. His voice wasn't combative, or hateful, just tired and a little sad.

Jacob had been watching the man deflate for the past few hours. First as Larkin showed him all the weak points where the school could be entered. Then again when Connor came in, an hour after Essec made the announcement in the cafeteria about the evacuation, with the list of students who wanted to be in the first group to leave.

Most were from magical families, but some were human-born who, even knowing their magic would have to be bound, wanted to leave immediately. The rest of the human-born students had looked like they would drag Essec off the low wall in the cafeteria as they shouted about the unfairness of having their magic taken away.

Claire slipped out of the cafeteria as soon as the shouting started. She had made the exact same argument when Aunt Iz had tried to send her home, and it had worked.

But Iz was having none of it. Essec tried to explain that there was really no other choice. Aunt Iz made promises to personally ensure each of the students would be collected and their powers unbound, but it was Lee who finally calmed everyone down.

"Look, none of us like this place," he said, ignoring Essec's huff behind him. "All of us would be happier somewhere else. And now we can't stay here. Those Dragons are coming. We know they are. Essec is finally going to let us out of here. And for the ones who have to go back to human homes, at least you have families to go back to. Some of us aren't as lucky. If the Dragons win this thing, then you'll survive longer out there. If the good guys win, they'll come and get you."

"Who says we'd all die if the Dragons win?" a girl in the back of the crowd asked. "You've never even met them."

"Well," Lee said with a grimace, "the only way you'd survive the Dragons would be to join them. And I know you're not a good fighter, Alice, so if you did join the Dragons, then we'd take you out ourselves."

"You have to go home," Jacob said. "The Academy can't stay open. You aren't old enough to live on your own. And you can't stay with humans and keep your magic. The best thing you can do is hide. Stay with your families, and we'll come get you when this is over."

"I don't want to not have magic," Mikey said, tears glistening in the corners of his eyes. "I don't want to go home."

"I know, Mikey." Lee patted him on the back. "But there's nothing else we can do. Sometimes war means you fight. Sometimes it means you get the hell out of the way so other people can do what they need to do. You love magic. You want our world to survive. The best thing you can do is keep your head down. But I will say "—Lee turned to Aunt Iz and Essec—"I have no family, I have nowhere to go. I'm forty-eight days away from getting out of here. I want to fight with you. I'll stand with the Gray Clan. And I think anyone else who wants to fight with you should be given the option, too."

"I'll fight!" Mikey raised his hand.

"Not young ones, Mikey," Lee said. "You're too little. They'd eat you alive. But the older ones should get the choice. Jacob and the others are going with you. We should be able to go, too."

The room went so quiet Jacob could have heard a fairy flying as everyone waited for Aunt Iz to speak.

"Anyone who is in their last year of school who wants to join the Gray Clan, come and speak to me. I will make the decision on an individual basis, and yes"—Aunt Iz's gaze flicked to the girl from the Bonforte Clan—"your family ties will be taken into consideration."

The Bonforte girl nodded.

"But you're letting the younger boy and girl from your Clan fight," a girl who looked to be the same age as Claire said with her arms folded over her chest.

"We're different," Connor said without missing a beat. "We've already been forced to fight the Pendragon. He knows who we are, he'll hunt us down whether we fight him or not. We're already screwed. Believe me, I wish I had never seen the Pendragon. It's too late for us. But some of you can still get out of this without watching anyone die."

"He's right," Essec said, "and I agree with Isadora. Human-borns who are too young will have their powers bound and be sent home. Those who are old enough should be allowed to fight if they wish."

"How soon can we go?" asked a girl who looked young enough to be in elementary school.

"We're working on that," Aunt Iz said. "I hope to send the first group tomorrow. Connor can take the names of those who wish to leave first." Connor nodded his silent assent. "Those who wish to fight, come to the headmaster's office."

It had taken nearly an hour for Aunt Iz to speak to all the students who wanted to join the Gray Clan. Some were too young, not even sixteen yet. Iz sent almost all of them away. The two who had lost their families were allowed to stay. Nearly twenty students were chosen in all. Molly marched them directly to the gym where Connor and Jacob had practiced sparring with the boys.

Jacob didn't envy them. Molly may have made a wonderful cake, but she was a terrifying fighter.

Connor and Claire returned not long after Aunt Iz was done, Claire pouting about the lack of sufficient wifi and the terrible processing speed of the laptop she had borrowed.

Three hours. It had only taken three hours to book tickets for the human-born, decide who wanted to go first, and set up transport to the train station. In three hours, they had dissolved the Academy. And now, Jacob was stuck in Essec's office, watching the teacher crumble as they pulled apart the school he had devoted his life to.

"We'll set up extra guards for tonight from the students who want to stay." Aunt Iz stood in front of Essec's desk.

Larkin and Emilia slipped silently into the room, supporting an exhausted-looking Samuel between them.

"I hate to be rude"—Aunt Iz gave Essec a nod—"but I would greatly appreciate the use of your office for a few minutes while I discuss plans with my family."

For a moment it looked as though Iz had finally crossed the line. Essec's face turned a bit purple before he stood and left the room, closing the door loudly behind him.

"Now that we know what we are going to do with the school," Aunt Iz said as Larkin and Emilia gently lowered Samuel into a seat, "we need to decide what we are going to do with ourselves."

"We're going to join the Elis and my family," Connor said, looking to Molly for support. "They've all banded together. We should go and be with them."

"If anyone even mentions trying to hide *the children* someplace safe, I swear I am going to scream and curse the lot of you," Claire said.

"We have nowhere left to hide anyone," Samuel said. His voice sounded more like Jacob remembered than when he had arrived that morning, but it was shallow, like a part of Samuel had been carved away. Jacob didn't know if it would ever be the same.

"We need to fight back," Larkin said. "We have the Elis and the preserve folk. We take them and come at the Dragons head on."

"It's the best chance we have," Molly said.

"We should wait," Samuel said. "Ask our allies for help."

"It would take too long," Larkin said. "We need to hit them

now before they can rebuild the tunnels."

"I agree," Aunt Iz sighed, "with Larkin. We need to attack. All waiting will do is allow more innocent people to be killed."

"So do we go to the Elis and my parents, or ask them to meet us here?" Connor asked.

"We go to the Elis," Aunt Iz said. "We leave you four and the other students at the preserve. We take the warriors and go to Graylock."

"You're leaving us!" Claire shouted. "We all almost died, and you're just going to dump us right back in the woods?"

"We need to come with you," Jacob said as Emilia walked over and took his hand. "Emilia knows more about the Pendragon than you do, and we can fight him. We've done it twice."

"And you've done very well," Samuel said. "You've survived. That's better than most adults could have done."

"Then let us help you," Emilia said. "The Grays got dragged into this because of me. I need to see it through to the end."

"That's the point," Larkin said. "You and the other students aren't going to be hiding from the fight. You'll be there if we fail. You'll be there to protect what's left of the Gray Clan. If attacking them head on doesn't work, there will still be someone left with a shot at finishing the Pendragon."

"So if you all die," Claire began slowly, "then you want us to go and try to kill the Pendragon ourselves?"

"You won't be alone," Samuel said. "The preserve folk and the rest of the Elis Tribe will stand with you."

"But we'll have a better chance if all of us fight together," Jacob said. "If we hit them with everything we've got—"

"It's a gamble we can't afford," Aunt Iz cut across him. "We aren't just talking about the lives of the people in this room, the lives of the people I care for most in this world. We are talking about preserving the Magical Community. And if there is nothing left of the Gray Clan, I don't know who will be there to make sure we don't lose everything we have fought for hundreds of years to achieve."

The room fell silent.

Jacob waited for Emilia to argue, but instead she said softly, "For the good of the Clan."

"For the good of us all," Aunt Iz said.

"So that's it?" Claire planted her hands on her hips and stepped in between Emilia and Aunt Iz. "You just dump us in the woods with twenty of our newest Academy-provided friends, and we hope we get to see you again?"

"That's exactly it," Samuel said. "We don't get to choose where we want to be or if we want to fight. But we can choose how. And we have to choose to preserve a legacy for the future. You and the other students, you're that legacy."

"You planned this before you ever got here." Connor glared at his aunt. "You knew you were going to leave us before you even knew if any other students would come with us."

"We knew." Molly nodded. "And it was decided because there is no other choice."

Connor let out a long string of curses, railing about his aunt's betrayal and all the other choices they could have made. No one tried to stop him or even bothered to look shocked.

"What about Dexter?" Emilia asked when Connor had finally run out of things to say.

"He'll be coming with us," Aunt Iz said.

"But if he's allowed to fight—"

"It is a point I will not be swayed on," Aunt Iz said, silencing Claire.

"You won't be swayed on anything," Connor growled.

"The choices we've made, we've made out of love," Molly said, reaching for Connor and looking desperately hurt when he shrugged her away.

"When are we leaving?" Emilia's voice was painfully calm, more detached than Jacob had ever heard it.

"The day after tomorrow," Aunt Iz said. "We have to be sure the human-born students have their magic properly bound and get them loaded onto the bus Claire so kindly found for us to borrow."

"Wish I hadn't," Claire muttered.

Aunt Iz continued as though she hadn't heard. "From there, Essec should be able to handle everything."

"So you spend tonight binding their magic, tomorrow a school bus comes and takes them away, then comes back for us the next day?" Claire asked.

"More or less," Larkin said.

"This is bullshit," Connor said.

"I'm going back to the infirmary," Claire said. "I helped you buy the train tickets, but I'm not going to escort a bunch of kids to the gym to get their magic bound." Without another word, Claire stormed out, slamming the door behind her.

"Do you need us to help?" Emilia asked, her face pale and her hands shaking. "Do you need us for the binding?"

"Go to the dormitories and let them know it's time," Aunt Iz said, adding as Emilia, Jacob, and Connor were most of the way out the door, "and thank you. I know how painful and difficult this must be for all of you—"

"No," Connor said. "You really don't."

16

HAPPINESS

*E*milia stood on a chair, watching the sunset. It would be time soon. All the human-born students had been rounded up, and in just a few minutes they would be without their magic. Emilia remembered what it felt like. Her skin dull and thick. As though her whole body had been wrapped in dense rubber.

Would the binding spell be painful? It had been for Rosalie, but then her tethering had been broken, too. Her soul had shattered.

Emilia's heart raced as panic surged through her at the mere thought of losing her tie to Jacob. But she could still feel him. Frustrated but calm. He had been trying to talk sense into Connor and Claire for an hour. The problem was, he didn't believe what he was saying.

He and Emilia both wanted to go to Graylock and fight. But Iz was right, too. If it all went wrong, if they were all lost...

Emilia swallowed the bile that crept up into her throat.

The only reason to leave them behind was in case everyone else died. If more than half of her family died.

Emilia dug her nails into her palms, willing herself not to cry.

"You're not going to the binding?" Dexter asked from behind Emilia. She spun around, and the chair she was standing on tipped.

Before Emilia realized she was falling, Dexter caught her in his arms. "Careful!"

"I'm fine," Emilia said, though her heart had leaped up into her throat. Her face was right next to Dexter's. They were closer than they had been in months. She could feel his heart pounding into her chest. "Thanks." Emilia jumped out of Dexter's arms. "I'm fine though. Really fine."

"So you're fine then?" Dexter grinned, and a shadow of his old self passed over his face.

Emilia laughed breathlessly, not sure whether to run away or smack him upside the head.

"No binding?" Dexter asked again.

"I couldn't watch it." The racing of Emilia's heart was replaced with dread. The sun was nearly down. "I watched Rosalie's. Never again."

"Are the others there?"

"Larkin, Molly, and Samuel are helping Aunt Iz. Jacob's trying to calm Claire and Connor down. I just couldn't face it." Emilia dragged her fingers through her hair. "I know I should be there. Helping to keep everything together, but Rosalie, it almost killed her."

"It was different for her," Dexter said. "It won't hurt for them. I've seen it happen. My father had to bind—"

"Your father's done a lot of things"

Dexter only nodded, his face set back in the lines Emilia had grown used to seeing.

"But you aren't him."

"Is Maggie helping with everything?" Dexter said as though Emilia hadn't mentioned his father. "She knows her way around this place and seems like she can be trusted."

"Maggie's nice." Emilia followed Dexter's gaze up to the darkening window.

Dexter nodded but didn't say anything.

Emilia bit her lip for a moment before continuing. "She likes you."

Dexter gave a laugh that caught between a sigh and a growl.

"You should eat lunch with her," Emilia said. "Tomorrow before we all leave."

"I don't think that's a good idea." Dexter turned to face Emilia.

"Why? Because you might like it? You can be happy, Dex."

"Some people don't deserve to be happy." Dexter turned back to the window, looking so much older than his eighteen years.

"You're right," Emilia said, "some people don't deserve happiness, but you do."

Dexter froze.

"I saw what you did in the caves," Emilia whispered, visions of blood and fighting flashing in her mind.

"What do you—"

"You almost died saving Samuel, and again saving all of them," Emilia said.

"How do you know?"

"The *how* doesn't matter. It's messy and more complicated than you'll understand." Emilia took Dexter's hand. His touch felt familiar, something from a past life. "What matters is that you saved my family. The only real parent I've ever had. I can't forget what happened before, but I forgive you. Whatever penance you think you have to do is done. The way you were fighting in those caves, it was like you wanted to die."

"I was helping." Dexter didn't shy away from Emilia's gaze.

"You can help without trying to get yourself killed. We've lost enough people, Dex. We don't need to lose any more. You can be happy. You deserve to be happy."

"Em."

"Why are you going with them? They won't let the rest of us

go. And I know why, they want to keep us from being killed. Because we're young. Because we're the next generation, the future this whole fight is supposed to be protecting. But you're one of us, Dexter. Why would they take you and not us?"

"I'm not worth anything," Dexter said without a trace of sadness in his voice. "I'm not fit to lead, can't be trusted to defend. There is no future for me. Not while the Dragons are around. My father is with them. My Clan is fighting with them. I'm worth more dead than alive."

"That's not true."

"Do you think Iz would leave me with you? With Jacob and the others?" Dexter's eyes gleamed in the fading light. "I've lost everything I've ever loved, and the only thing I can hope for is that something I care about can survive after I'm gone. You're what matters, Emilia." Dexter took her face in his hands. "All that matters is protecting you. I have to protect you. Even if I shouldn't."

"I have Jacob, Dex. He'll protect me. We'll protect each other. You don't have to make up for anything. You don't have to worry about me. You just have to survive. Get through this awful mess. Be happy. Someday when this is over. Be happy, Dex."

Emilia placed her hand over his heart, wishing she could make a happy ending for all of them.

But the sun had set. Night had come, and it would be hours before the dawn.

BREACHED

*J*acob lay in the dark, listening to Emilia breathe. He wished he could be closer to her, have her head on his chest, feel her warmth. Aunt Iz had let them sleep at the same end of the infirmary, but that was as far as she was willing to go.

He knew he should be asleep. Larkin had taken Connor, Claire, and Lee to help her lead the first watch of the night. Soon she would come for them, and Molly would take Jacob and Emilia to the girls' dorm where they would collect Maggie and the others who wanted to fight, and then it would be their turn to patrol the frozen grounds.

Dawn would come, and the human-born students would be sent away. Then whatever transportation had taken them would return for the Gray Clan, complete with their brand new members.

In a way, it all seemed incredibly fast.

They had only been at the Academy for a few days, and now they were going back out to the woods. Away from the medical help they had come running to the Academy for. But Claire was fine. Samuel had argued with Iz about not being allowed to take a watch. Just listening to him argue had proven how much Nurse Bracken had helped. They were all as healthy as could be expected. They needed to make a move.

And that's where it began to feel much too slow. The Dragons had had days to repair the tunnels. They had magic and more people than when Emilia had collapsed the tunnels last summer. Five days to rebuild and regroup. Five days for the Pendragon to plot revenge.

But he had lost Rosalie five days ago. His heart had been torn in two. He had lost the other half of his soul. How long would it take a person to recover from that? Jacob knew the answer without even thinking.

Forever.

The Pendragon would never recover.

But had it weakened him, or turned him into even more of a maniac?

Jacob buried his face in his pillow, willing sleep to come. Soon there would be no more chances for rest. Would they have enough beds for all of them on the Preserve? Would he and Emilia be allowed to share a tent?

Proteus wouldn't mind, but the Preserve folk might. Jacob could ask Connor. Maybe he could convince his parents Jacob and Emilia should be able to stay together. They could share with Connor and Claire like they had before with the Elis Tribe. Just as long as he could be near enough to protect her.

Jacob watched Emilia sleep. She was with him. She was safe. Everything was fine. He closed his eyes. They would be allowed to stay together. He would make sure of it. His heart slowed as he drifted to sleep. At least he would get a few minutes' rest before Larkin came to wake them.

Larkin would want him and Emilia to stay together. Larkin would fight for it. Larkin was good at fighting. She had been in battles. So many battles. With screaming and shouting. And someone crying desperately for help.

Jacob's eyes flew open. The sounds weren't in his mind. They were real. Shouts carried from the grounds.

"Wake up!" Jacob leaped out of bed and tore back Emilia's covers. "Everyone wake up. There's something wrong."

Molly and Iz were out of bed in an instant.

"What's going on?" Dexter raced toward them from his bed in the corner.

"They're here," Samuel said, his voice frighteningly calm. "They've found us."

"We need to get outside." Iz ran for the doors.

"You three stay here," Molly shouted at Emilia, Jacob, and Samuel as she followed Aunt Iz into the hall.

"Not a chance, Molly." Samuel ran after her as fast as his limp would allow.

Jacob took Emilia's hand and grabbed his wand before starting for the doors.

"You need to stay in here," Dexter said, trying to block them from the hallway.

The sounds of the fighting had come closer, right near the outside wall of the building. If whatever was out there got inside, there would be no more barriers protecting the students.

"We're going out there," Emilia said. "I'm not going to wait in here and see what happens."

"You need to stay safe." Dexter still didn't move.

Shouts came from the halls now. Terrified students screaming in confusion.

"There is no such thing as safe, Dex," Emilia whispered.

Sadness passed over Dexter's face before he nodded and stepped aside, letting Emilia lead the way down the hall toward the front entrance.

Students stood with their backs pressed to the doors, as though hoping to keep the attackers out with the weight of their bodies.

"We have to go back out there!" Claire screamed at the group blocking the entrance. "There are still people out there."

"No." It was Lee who stood at the center of the double door. "If we open the doors, those things will come in here. We can't let them in here."

"Larkin," Molly shouted when she spotted Larkin lying bloody on the floor.

"I'll be fine Molly," Larkin said, her voice weak but calm. "It's the *somnerri*. There are dozens of them."

Molly dropped to her knees and muttered a spell over Larkin's bleeding leg.

Larkin gasped as the healing spell made her torn flesh shine. "I don't know how they got in, but we were surrounded. I had to get the kids out."

An ear-splitting *screech* came from the other side of the doors, like metal grinding on concrete.

"They're trying to get in," Lee whispered.

"Get to the dorms," Iz ordered Lee, who nodded through his terror. "Make sure every bound student is with one that has a talisman. Have them all go to the cafeteria. We will meet you there."

Lee turned to an older girl. "You get the girls."

She nodded, and both of them sprinted down the hall.

"Lee's right, we can't let the *somnerri* in here," Claire said. A deep purple bruise blossomed across her right cheek, and she held her left arm awkwardly at her side.

"It'll be a massacre if they get to the students." Samuel stepped forward and laid his hands on the doors. The five remaining Academy students all backed away as though expecting him to fling the doors open.

"We can't fight them out there," Larkin said through gritted teeth as Molly helped her to her feet. "There's too many of them, and it's dark."

"We'll keep the doors closed for as long as possible," Aunt Iz said. "The walls are protected, and so are the windows. Even those monsters shouldn't be able to get in anywhere but through these doors."

"But they got onto the grounds," a scared-looking girl squeaked.

The scraping on the outside of the doors quickened as if in response.

"I know," Aunt Iz said, worry echoing in her voice.

"They can dig deep," Dexter said. "Deeper than the caves. Deeper than a shield spell. They must have come up from below, just like with the Virginia Clan."

"So it'll just be bug men then?" Claire asked. Molly had moved on to Claire's limp arm, and she hissed a curse as the healing began.

"I don't know." Dexter's words rang through the entryway.

"The doors seem to be where they're concentrating their efforts. We get the students someplace safe, guard the doors, and when they do manage to break through, we bottleneck them. Fight them as they come through to keep ourselves from being surrounded." Samuel leaned against the wall.

"Emilia and Jacob, take Connor and Claire to the cafeteria with the others—" Aunt Iz began.

"We have to stay with you, Aunt Iz." Emilia stepped forward. "You can't fight all of them with five of you, and Larkin's hurt. Samuel doesn't even have a talisman."

"There are more than a hundred innocent lives that need protecting, some of whom are utterly defenseless. I am not asking you to run away, Emilia Gray. I am asking you to fight to protect the students of this school." Fire burned behind Aunt Iz's eyes.

"We'll stay," a girl said to Aunt Iz. "We said we wanted to fight with you. Your lot can go protect the others, and we'll back you up here." The other four at the doors nodded.

"Thank you." Dexter raised his hands toward the doors. The wrist cuffs that were his talisman sparked in the dim light.

"There is no other way into this school, Emilia," Aunt Iz said. "If we stop them here, there won't need to be a battle."

"There is another way in." Jacob's heart disappeared as he remembered a freezing breeze drifting through a concrete wall. "There are two other ways."

Emilia turned to Jacob with terror in her eyes. "The way out."

18

MONSTERS

"What way out?" Larkin asked, leaning against the wall, testing her weight on her newly healed leg.

"It's how the students sneak out onto the grounds," Emilia said, the words tumbling from her mouth in her panic. "There are two we know of. Missing bits of wall. They're only covered by a mirage spell, so it looks like wall, but there's nothing really there."

"There's one near the girls' dorm and one near the boys'," Jacob said. "And it would be a way in. There's no one guarding those entrances."

The last of the color in Aunt Iz's face drained away a second before the first scream shook the hall. A blood-curdling cry of fear and pain. Chaos came a moment later.

Snarls and shouts echoed through the corridors.

"We have to help them." Molly started toward the dorms.

"No, Molly, stay here." Aunt Iz raised the tip of her wand. "Samuel, Jacob, and Emilia with me. Larkin, stay with Molly and the students and guard the doors."

Aunt Iz ran down the hall without waiting to see if her orders would be obeyed. There wasn't time to wait. The screams were getting louder. The sounds of breaking bones and tearing flesh joined the snarling and howling.

Blood pounded in Emilia's ears so loudly the noise of the hall disappeared. She reached up to her neck, feeling the sapphire pendant Rosalie had left her. But she didn't need the sapphire. She had her ring.

"Use this." Emilia slipped off the necklace and lifted the chain over Samuel's head. He let the talisman fall around his neck without question.

As they rounded the last corner to the girls' dormitory, the world morphed into an incomprehensible nightmare.

The vivid red blood that covered the grey floor. The students running past them. The ones who couldn't run. Torn and bloody on the floor. Not moving. Eyes dull.

And something beyond the bodies still moving, dark with blood covering its white fangs. Larger than a wolf and more frightening than the *somnerri*.

The beast turned its horribly bright green eyes toward Emilia, holding her gaze with its own.

Sound rushed back as the thing growled and launched itself at another student, tearing through her chest before Aunt Iz could scream *"Contosus!"* The beast bounced away a moment too late, fresh blood soaking its dark fur.

"Nandi," Emilia whispered as another great beast streaked down the hall toward them. "They've sent Nandi into a school."

"Stay behind me." Samuel stepped in front of Iz as both the Nandi turned to him, red dancing in their green eyes.

Students were trapped behind the Nandi. There was no other way out of the hall. Emilia wanted to shout at them to go back into the dormitory, but the door was shredded and hung uselessly from its hinges.

Claire. Connor. They were supposed to be coming to the dorms. Emilia searched the floor. There was no blond or red hair. But where were they?

Samuel walked toward the Nandi.

Emilia wanted to scream for him to step back, but Iz stood behind him, her wand raised, letting Samuel get closer to the monsters.

There were more screams coming from farther behind them, from the front entrance.

"You go, Isadora," Samuel said, not looking over his shoulder. "I'll take care of the beasts."

Aunt Iz ran down the hall toward the sounds of the fighting.

Emilia wanted to follow her to make sure the others were all right, but she couldn't leave Jacob and wouldn't leave Samuel to fight on his own.

Aunt Iz's sudden movement seemed to have roused something in the Nandi. Both beasts drew their lips back, baring their fangs at Samuel as they growled. One of the Nandi took a step forward. The movement made a clicking sound on the stone floor. Emilia glanced down at the Nandi's feet. Sharp claws, six inches long and already dripping with blood, scraped against the ground.

"Hey, hey." Samuel raised his hands in the air. "You've come for blood." His voice was calm and steady. "Take mine."

"Samuel." Jacob took a step forward, but Samuel didn't seem to hear.

"If it's a hunt you want, why choose children?"

The beasts growled and stepped forward in unison.

"Fight me."

Samuel pointed calmly at the closest of the beasts. For a moment the Nandi froze, before leaping onto Samuel.

"*Primurgo!*" Emilia shouted as the monsters leaped into the air, not knowing if a spell like that could even block an animal.

The Nandi didn't stop at the edge of her spell but slowed as though falling through thick mud.

Samuel brought his fist down hard on the head of one of the

monsters before lightning flashed in his palm, hitting the other in the ribs.

"*Inexuro!*" Jacob shouted. Flames shot from the tip of his wand, scorching the Nandi's fur. But if the beast's flesh was burned, it didn't seem to notice or care.

"*Terraminis!*" Emilia shouted, gagging on the putrid stink of burned hair and blood as the Nandi reared to pounce on Samuel.

The hall shook, and *snaps* rent the air as cracks climbed the concrete walls. A jagged piece of concrete fell from the ceiling, and Samuel caught it as though he had summoned the debris. In the split-second before the Nandi and Emilia recovered their footing, the shard of concrete had lengthened into a staff as tall as Samuel himself.

The Nandi faltered, staring at the staff, and Samuel attacked, plunging his weapon deep into the first Nandi's side. The Nandi howled in pain, but the other beast growled, baring its razor-sharp teeth.

The beast lunged for Samuel, but his stone staff was still buried deep in the dead Nandi's side. Jacob threw himself at the Nandi, knocking it away from Samuel before it could sink its claws into him. The two fell to the ground, the Nandi hissing and spitting.

"*Fulgurmortus!*" The shining red bolt formed in Emilia's hand, and she charged forward, plunging it into the Nandi's side.

The energy of the bolt radiated up Emilia's arm. Agony seared through her bones as she held on, driving the bolt deeper into the monster.

The Nandi howled a terrible, rage-filled cry before crumpling on top of Jacob.

"Jacob!" Emilia screamed, trying to push the Nandi off of him. His face was covered by the massive animal's body. She couldn't see if he was breathing. "Jacob!" Her arm was numb, and the monster was heavier than she could move.

"Perectus!" a voice shouted, and the monster was lifted off of Jacob, tumbling limply away.

Jacob coughed as soon as his face was free of the fur.

"Jacob." Tears coursed down Emilia's cheeks

"Are you hurt?" Maggie knelt next to Emilia.

"I'm fine," Jacob coughed as he struggled to his feet. "Are you okay, Samuel?"

"Fine," Samuel grunted, "but we need to get back to the others."

He was right. The sounds of fighting had disappeared from the dorm, leaving behind only frightened crying. But near the entrance, shouted spells could still be heard.

"Connor and Claire?" Emilia asked Maggie. "Have you seen them?"

"No." Maggie shook her head. "I was stuck in the girls' dorm."

"You have to get to the cafeteria," Jacob called to the girls at the end of the hall who cowered in the shadows of the shattered dorm door. "Follow us, and stick together. We have to go right now."

"Lead the way," Maggie said.

Emilia ran down the hall toward the sounds of the fight, a thunder of footsteps following behind her.

The *somnerri* had made it into the hall. The noise of their hard plated arms smashing into the walls pounded toward her before she could see the monsters.

The battle had swallowed the entryway. There were more people than should have been there. For a terrible moment, Emilia thought the Pendragon had sent his men into the Academy. But it was students. Boys from the dorm had joined the fight.

A few were already lying on the ground, unmoving, but a dozen more were fighting the black creatures the Pendragon's spell had disfigured.

What had once been normal wizards now had hard armor

covering their bodies. Soft flesh was gone, replaced with shining black. Claws had taken the place of hands, and even their voices had changed. A low hissing that never should have come from a wizard's mouth filled the hall as they taunted the students.

"Come and fight us, come and die," a *somnerri* hissed, twisting his talons through the air as he closed in on Lee and two other boys.

"Oh, we'll fight you," Lee growled. "*Ignerrum!*" A long sheath of fire appeared in his hands, and he lunged at the beast.

The *somnerri* stumbled back for a split second, but the spell wasn't enough.

"*Refecto!*" another boy yelled.

"*Scorepio,*" Emilia shouted.

The monster turned to look at her, and Emilia's heart stopped beating. The spell hadn't worked. It wasn't enough.

"*Manuvis!*" Jacob shouted. A red sphere of light formed in his hands, and he threw it at the *somnerri*.

A hole the size of a fist appeared in the monster's chest. The black shell began to crumble, turning to dust and falling to the floor. The beast let out a wail, but Emilia didn't watch him disintegrate. She had already turned to the rest of the battle.

There were seven more *somnerri* in the hall. Larkin had one backed against a wall, and Samuel rushed forward to join her, raising his staff to attack.

Dexter and Iz were by the front doors, both fighting two *somnerri* each.

"Get back!" Molly shouted. "Children, get away from them." She charged down the hall, her wand held high. Three students followed her. Connor and Claire, both very much alive and seemingly unhurt, and a little boy.

"Go back, Mikey!" Connor shouted before launching a spell at a *somnerri*.

The monster turned away from the two girls he had been fighting, two of the students who had agreed to stay at the doors.

They both looked exhausted. One swayed on her feet as blood dripped from her clenched hand.

"Time to fight the Gray," the monster hissed. "Time to take the Gray away."

"But that's the problem with Grays." Claire smiled and stepped up next to Connor. "You can't fight just one of us."

The *somnerri*'s face twisted into a horrifying grin. "We shall see."

Claire raised her hand to fight, but another beast had run toward Molly.

"Molly, watch out!" Emilia yelled, but Molly had already rounded on the monster.

Two more were running toward Jacob and Emilia.

Emilia tried to watch the others out of the corner of her eye. The students were helping each other. Nine students fighting two monsters. Molly had drawn her *somnerri* down the hall. Larkin and Samuel's opponent had been joined by another. There were too many *somnerri*, more than had been there before, but there was nothing to do but fight.

Searing heat cut across Emilia's shoulder as a stray spell grazed her.

Through her cry she heard a voice shout, "Mikey, get out of here! It's not safe!"

She blinked back the dizzying spots from the pain.

Jacob cracked the ground beneath the *somnerri*'s feet, and the monster stumbled just long enough. "*Lancanus!*" The beast fell face first into its own blood, a shard of silver light protruding from its back.

But something was wrong. Very wrong. More monsters were at the doors. And screams shook the end of the hall.

"No!" a voice wailed.

Emilia turned to see claws digging deep, eyes growing wide. And little Mikey crumpled to the ground.

19

THE FALLEN GRAY

"*M*ikey!" Lee caught the boy before he hit the floor.

"Mikey!" Jacob echoed Lee's scream, running forward to take on the beast.

"*Expulsio!*" Emilia shouted behind him, and the beast spun towards them.

"Help him!" Lee screamed. "Maggie, help him."

But the boy's eyes were open and vacant. Mikey was already gone.

Maggie ran forward, ducking through the fight to reach them.

"*Subnicio,*" Jacob yelled, his voice barely audible over the chaos of the fight.

"Samuel!" Larkin screamed.

Jacob couldn't stop himself from glancing just for a moment.

Three clawed beasts stood in front of the doors, blocking Larkin and Samuel who fought as furiously as they could.

Samuel blocked one of the monsters' talons an inch from his neck. Something black flashed in Larkin's hand as she used a claw of one of the fallen *somnerri* to cut deep into the neck of Samuel's attacker. Thick red blood spurted out, covering Samuel, but he didn't pause before moving on to the next monster, desperately trying to get to the doors.

"Aunt Iz!" Emilia shouted. "Where is Aunt Iz?"

Jacob spun, searching the fight for Iz, but she was nowhere to be seen.

"Aunt Iz!" Emilia screamed.

Connor and Claire had killed their *somnerri* and moved on to help the other students. Molly ran down the hall toward them, favoring her right leg but still moving quickly. The rest of the fighting was by the doors, where Iz and Dexter had been the last time Jacob had seen them.

Jacob ran forward to join Larkin and Samuel who were still trying to fight their way through the doors.

Another beast blocked his path before he had made it ten feet. The thing was limping and drawing in rattling breaths.

"It's too late, little Gray," the monster said to Emilia as she stepped up to Jacob's side. "The Pendragon shall be victorious."

"*Fulgurmortus!*" Emilia shouted and thrust the bolt into the wound, which had already cut through the armor on the *somnerri's* chest. The monster twitched as it fell to the ground.

Jacob swallowed the bile that rose in his throat as the beast bled on the floor. There was no time to worry about who that wizard had been before he became a monster.

Screams drifted in through the doors.

"Aunt Iz." Emilia leaped over the dead *somnerri*. "Dexter!"

Samuel and Larkin were still trapped by the doors, unable to move forward through the throng of monsters.

"Aunt Iz!" Emilia shrieked as she attacked the first beast. The thing seemed to laugh for a moment before crumpling to the floor, dead.

Jacob's heart raced as he fought, not fearing for his safety but for Emilia's, who had battled her way to the head of the group, and for Aunt Iz and Dexter, who were still out of sight.

They were alive. They had to be alive. There were spells flying beyond the doors. Someone was still fighting.

"Get behind me," Larkin shouted, shoving Emilia back and meeting her opponent head on.

They were almost to the doors. If they could push the beast another two feet back, they would be outside and able to see.

"*Sonivox!*" Larkin's spell pounded through the hall. Her voice seemed to have gained power and substance, for as it reached the walls, they began to shake. As its echo pounded through the air, the *somnerri* were pushed back, stumbling and flying over each other out the front doors.

"You are out of time!" Jacob could barely hear the monster's scream over the pounding in his ears. "We are all out of time!"

Samuel silenced the monster, bringing his staff down hard on the thing's head.

But the *somnerri* hadn't been talking to the Grays. He had been shouting to the *somnerri* behind him. The beasts that had been pushed from the Academy ran to join a group fighting in the middle of the lawn.

There were two battles happening. Dexter was surrounded by a circle of *somnerri*. He fought desperately, barely managing to avoid the talons that slashed at his flesh. Volleying spells so quickly there was no way to discern where one bit of magic ended and another began.

But the other fight was larger, more vicious than Jacob could have imagined.

Aunt Iz stood in the center of the yard surrounded by more than a dozen *somnerri*. Some that she had enchanted to fight on her side were striking out at the other monsters, severing arms and legs mechanically with no hint of hatred or remorse.

But there were still too many. The *somnerri* Iz had enchanted were beginning to fall to the ground, hurt so badly they could no longer defend her. And more monsters were running to join the fight. All the beasts that had been in the corridor a moment before were joining the attack on Aunt Iz.

"Stop them!" Emilia screamed, chasing the *somnerri* as they charged Aunt Iz. "Stop them! *Fulguratus!*" Lightning shot from her palm, hitting a beast in the back.

"*Talahm delasc!*" The whip blossomed from the tip of Jacob's wand, and with a jerk of his wrist, the streak of red wrapped around a beast, pulling him deep into the ground with a sickening crunch.

More spells came from behind them. Molly shot bright flashes of magic over their shoulders. More voices Jacob didn't recognize were trying to help.

But the pack had closed in on Aunt Iz. Any thought for staying away from her spells apparently gone as they tried to overwhelm her.

"*Conarde,*" Samuel shouted.

But he couldn't send the spell close enough to halt the terrible attack. The monsters shrouded Aunt Iz in their shining black armor.

A red light flashed from deep within the hoard of beasts, but none of them were thrown away.

"Aunt Iz!" Emilia screamed. But the monsters had piled in on the place where Aunt Iz had fought. "Get off of her."

"Emilia!" Jacob shouted as she dived into the *somnerri*, stabbing every one of them she could reach with the red bolt she had clutched in her hand.

"*Talahm delasc!*" Jacob used his whip, dragging monsters away from Aunt Iz, Samuel finishing each of them off in turn. Dexter was there, too, fighting through the beasts, who seemed to have lost the will to fight back.

In less than a minute, there was no one left to fight the Grays. Only bodies of fallen *somnerri* and thick, dark blood coating the ground.

"Iz!" Jacob shouted, his heart freezing in his chest as he waited to hear her call back to him. He searched the ground, but there was no sign of the long, grey hair in the darkness

"Aunt Iz." Emilia staggered forward.

She lay at the center of the fight. Covered in dirt and blood. The only parts of her unmarked by the battle were her eyes. Open to the sky. Blank and unseeing.

20

RED AND BLACK

"Aunt Iz," Emilia whispered, falling to her knees beside her. "Aunt Iz!" Her voice echoed through the silent grounds.

But Isadora Gray didn't answer.

"Wake up." Emilia pulled Aunt Iz's head onto her lap. "Maggie! Maggie, help her!" Emilia looked wildly around, but Maggie wasn't there. "Nurse Bracken. Jacob you have to find Nurse Bracken."

Jacob didn't move.

"Jacob, please!"

But he didn't turn and run for the Academy. He knelt down next to her, his hand trembling as he laid it on her shoulder.

"No." Emilia shoved him away. "No, we have to help her. Please someone, Samuel, fix her."

"I can't." Tears glistened on Samuel's cheeks.

"You don't know if you won't try!"

"She's gone, Em," Larkin said.

"She can't be." Emilia shook her head. "You don't understand. She just needs help."

"There were too many of them." Dexter collapsed to the

ground as though standing required strength he no longer possessed. "She fought. She fought better than any of us could have."

"Then help her!" Emilia screamed.

"We can't, Emi," Jacob whispered. "She's gone."

Pain surged through Jacob's chest and became Emilia's own. Isadora Gray was dead.

"No." Tears streamed down Emilia's cheeks and fell onto Aunt Iz's face, washing away the blood that coated her. Leaving streaks of pale skin that shone in the night. "Please, Aunt Iz." But there was nothing more Aunt Iz could do for her.

She was gone.

"What's going on? Did we win? We got stuck inside trying to help some kids." Claire gasped when her gaze found Emilia and Iz.

"No." Connor's face turned so white it glowed in the bright moonlight.

"We have to secure the grounds." Larkin pushed herself to her feet. "Find the wounded and make sure there are no more Nandi or *somnerri* left."

"We just finished off a *somnerri* near the cafeteria," Connor said, his voice low and old. "That's where most of the hurt kids have been taken. At least the ones who have been found."

"Dexter, help me sweep the perimeter." Samuel leaned heavily on his staff as he started toward the gate where a long row of giant holes littered the ground.

"Claire, Connor, help me with the students." Larkin looked toward the doors. Students had gathered on the steps, watching Emilia.

Their wide eyes and gaping mouths shot bile into her throat. She wanted to scream at them, to collapse the school on top of their heads. Punish them for staring at her, for not realizing the whole world had fallen apart on the grounds of their terrible school.

"We have to find out who betrayed us," Jacob said. "They knew. The *somnerri* knew Aunt Iz was here. Someone told them."

Larkin nodded silently and moved away toward the doors.

"Wait!" Emilia called as her family began to disappear into the night. "You can't leave. We can't leave her here."

"We aren't leaving her," Molly said gently. "We'll take her inside, where she'll be safe. But we have to keep the students here safe, too. Isadora Gray knew that better than anyone." Molly leaned forward and closed Aunt Iz's eyes, blocking the reflection of the moon, which had made them sparkle so brightly. "*Funus Motus.*"

Aunt Iz floated into the air, gliding as though supported by a dozen gentle hands.

Jacob wrapped his arm around Emilia's waist, lifting her to her feet, guiding her to follow as Molly led the way to the doors.

"What about them?" Emilia asked as she stepped over a dead *somnerri*.

Molly turned to face the dark lawn, Aunt Iz floating safely beside her. "*Terramotus.*" The ground shook, rending the air with terrible *cracks* as each of the *somnerri* fell into a hole in the earth, which snapped shut behind them.

"That's better than they deserve," Lee growled from the shadows of the entryway.

"I quite agree," Molly said.

The lights of the hall burned Emilia's eyes. Bright red blood smeared the walls, and the black of the fallen *somnerri* lay scattered on the floor. Red and black mixing together, destroying the pristine order of the Academy.

Aunt Iz, Mikey, and how many others dead in the attack?

The girls.

Aunt Iz, Mikey, and the girls the Nandi had killed. But how many was that in all?

Would someone count? Would she have to?

Lee led them down the hall. The silence that had blanketed

the grounds was gone. Sounds of fear and grief echoed from the cafeteria.

He didn't say a word to the four students who stood outside the door, guarding the cafeteria. Each of them looked sadly at Iz before stepping aside.

The inside of the cafeteria was chaos. Injured students lay on the tables on the boys' side of the room. Maggie ran between them, shouting instructions as other students attempted to assist her.

"Keep pressure here," she told an older boy, pointing to a long gash on a girl's arm before moving on to a boy who lay twitching on a table. "I don't know what to do for him." Maggie dragged her filthy and blood soaked hands desperately through her hair.

"Where's Bracken?" Lee asked.

Maggie pointed to the other side of the wall where unmoving victims had been laid out on the tables. Nurse Bracken, Essec, and Ms. Bildge were laid out amongst the students. Mikey had been placed near the center, seeming even smaller in death than he had in life.

"It's venom from the *somnerri*," Molly said. "I'll have a look at him. Jacob." Molly nodded, and Jacob slid his hand under Aunt Iz's head to support the spell. "I'll need your help, Emilia."

Molly ran toward the shaking boy.

For a moment, Emilia wanted to scream that she was not going to leave Aunt Iz. But Isadora Gray was gone, and this boy was fighting for his life.

For the good of the Clan. For the good of Magickind.

It was Emilia's job to protect, to fight and defend. Everyone now. Everyone here.

The weight of it threatened to overwhelm her as the room spun.

"Lee," Connor called from the doorway. He stood between Claire and Larkin. All three of them were supporting injured students. "Give us a hand."

There was menace in Connor's voice.

Lee nodded and ran over, Connor whispered to him for a second before they brought the students into the room, slamming the doors shut behind them.

"Emilia, now!" Molly called from the table.

Emilia ran over.

"Hold his leg down so I can get to the wound without being kicked."

Emilia pushed the boy's leg down on the table and muttered, "*Silva alescere.*" The polished wood of the table began to grow and shift, forming tentacles that wrapped around the boy's leg, pinning it in place on the hard surface.

"Not what I meant, but it will do," Molly said before murmuring a string of spells under her breath.

"What can I do to help?" Emilia turned to Maggie, who was running to another table. Emilia closed her eyes, not wanting to watch as Jacob carefully lay Aunt Iz down on a table in the corner of the room.

"You can do some basic healing?" Maggie asked, continuing as Emilia nodded. "Find everyone who has cuts. If there's no venom or spell damage, heal it."

Emilia nodded again and turned to the room, but before she could try and think of where to begin, Lee shouted, "Alice Chandler! Where is Alice Chandler!"

Heads turned to the corner where a girl with curly hair and dark eyes pressed herself into the grey wall. Fear filled her face, but other than that she seemed completely unhurt. No dirt or blood marked her perfect pajamas.

"Alice Chandler, you betrayed us all."

∾

*E*very conscious person glared at the dark-haired girl now.

"I-I what?" Alice stammered.

"You told the Dragons we were going to evacuate the Academy. You told them the head of the Gray Clan was here." Lee strode across the room toward Alice.

"I didn't." Alice shook her head as everyone around her scattered. "I didn't tell anyone anything."

"I saw you," Bonner said, walking only a step behind Lee.

Jacob glanced to Aunt Iz one last time before moving toward the low wall in the center of the room. He didn't want to leave Iz, but they couldn't afford a fight amongst the students.

"I saw you with a mirror," Bonner said, hate flaring in his eyes. "You had one outside the mirror room. I should have stopped you."

"She might not have done anything," Emilia said, stepping between Alice and Bonner.

"And even if I had," Alice said, "how do you know they came for the Grays? The Grays are the ones who have been saying that we were going to be attacked from the beginning."

"Because they came for Aunt Iz." Emilia slowly rounded on Alice, hand raised.

Jacob leaped over the wall and raced to Emilia's side.

"They came to kill Aunt Iz!"

"They were coming anyway." Alice tipped her chin up though fear flickered through her eyes.

"You idiot!" Lee shouted. "We could have gotten out! All of us, alive!"

"I didn't—"

"You've already as much as admitted it," Bonner growled, raising his wand and pointing it between Alice's eyes. "All of these people are dead because of you."

"They were going to come anyway," Alice said. "I asked to go home. I wanted to go, and they asked me questions."

"And you betrayed all of us." Emilia's voice was soft, dangerously soft. "They let Nandi and *somnerri* into the school. They killed your friends. They killed Aunt Iz."

"They said we would all be safe," Alice said.

"Never believe the Dragons." Magic crackled around Emilia's fists. "They will lie, and they will kill you."

"But they were going to come anyway," Alice begged. "I helped. I helped them so they would only kill the people who fought them."

"Nandi don't care who fights them," Jacob said. "*Somnerri* don't care who fights against them. All they want is blood."

"Isadora Gray was going to save us," Lee said. "She was going to take us in, give us a chance. You've just killed us all."

"No she hasn't." Claire raised her palm, her silver ring glistening. "She betrayed the Academy. Innocent people are dead because she's a spineless coward. But she hasn't destroyed the Gray Clan. The Gray Clan is bigger than one person. Bigger than Aunt Iz. The Gray Clan is still right here." She threaded her arm through Emilia's. "We are right here. And the Dragons didn't beat us. Not today. Not ever."

The room fell silent, every eye on Emilia.

"She's right." Emilia's voice rang around the room. "The Gray Clan is still very much alive. And we will honor our promise. Anyone who has said they will fight with us is still welcome to stand by our side. We will attack the Dragons. We will make them pay for what they've done. For sending monsters to fight children, for murdering without thought. For killing Isadora Gray, and little Mikey, and for every other life lost today, the Dragons will pay."

A cheer rose around the room. Emilia stepped back, looking at the people around her. Staring at her, looking to her for more words of wisdom and strength.

"What about her?" Bonner asked.

"Take her to the pit," Emilia said.

"What do we do with Dellard?" Lee asked, grabbing Alice and roughly pinning her arms behind her back while Bonner kept his wand to her temple.

Emilia paused for a moment.

"Let Dellard out," Molly said. "She can't argue with us being right about the Dragons attacking now. Let Alice stay with the other children of Dragon families."

"B-but what if they hurt me?" Alice stammered.

"Such is war," Connor said, standing next to his aunt, showing their resemblance more than ever.

Lee nodded and shoved Alice toward the door.

Jacob moved forward, standing close to Emilia while Claire still stood on her other side.

"What are we going to do?" a boy in the crowd asked. "What if they come back?"

"They won't come back tonight," Emilia said, her voice faltering. "They got what they came for. We'll all leave tomorrow. Get out of here during the daylight. Get you home to your families."

"And the ones without families?" a girl asked. "Where are we going to go?"

"The Mansion House," Emilia said without hesitation. "Tomorrow morning, the Gray Clan is going back to the Mansion House."

21

WRAPPED IN WHITE

*T*he sun had risen before preparations for their departure were complete. The bus would be there soon. A school bus would take them all home. Including Iz.

The others would go to the bus station in town. Samuel had arranged for the transportation of the bodies. They had all been wrapped in white sheets from the dorm. It didn't seem right. They had fought the Dragons and that was all they got—a white sheet.

Poor Mikey. So small.

Jacob hadn't been able to watch as Mikey was carried out the front doors. It seemed wrong not to take more time. But they would risk more lives by waiting.

The fifteen students who had chosen to join the Gray Clan would ride with them to the Mansion House.

Aunt Iz was loaded into the bus first. Laid gently in the back. With her face covered, there was nothing to show who was hidden by the white shroud.

Jacob wanted to scream, to demand better treatment for the woman who had taught him so much—who had saved him more than once—who now lay in the back of an old school bus.

"We should stay," Emilia said as she joined Jacob by the bus. "Make sure everyone else gets out of here safely."

"Dellard will help with the evacuation," Samuel said behind them. "And the sooner we get away from here, the safer they'll all be."

The rest of the students were lined up in the yard, waiting for the second bus to appear. The few who were too injured to stand lay on stretchers that floated in midair.

"Dellard is on our side now," Maggie said as she stepped onto the bus. "She doesn't want any more of her students murdered. She may be awful, but she's no killer."

"What about the Dragon kids?" Claire asked.

"We've given them food," Emilia said. "The Dragons will come looking for them before they run out."

Claire gave a half-laugh before climbing onto the bus.

Jacob tried not to think of the fallen students, of little Mikey. What if no one wanted to bury them? Who would make sure they were laid to rest?

But the living had to come before the dead. Staying still and waiting for answers wasn't a possibility. Jacob climbed the steps onto the school bus.

It smelled like Fairfield High School. Like cleaner, fake leather, and sweaty lockers. They should be riding in a sleek, black car, carrying Aunt Iz away in the finest vehicle money could buy. Samuel should be driving. But those days were over now.

Emilia sat in the second row of seats across from Connor and Claire, behind Molly and Samuel. Jacob sat beside Emilia, and she took his hand without even looking at him. Her heart was breaking, her pain palpable in Jacob's chest. He squeezed her hand, wanting to say something eloquent and comforting. Knowing that sitting silently next to her was enough.

Larkin stood at the front of the bus next to a stranger who sat behind the wheel. She did a quick head count before nodding to the bus driver. The man steered down the drive as though nothing were strange, pausing for only a second as the gate swung open before turning onto the road.

The dirt road was surrounded by trees. Barren and snow covered. Waiting for spring. Jacob looked down at Emilia's hand. She wore the silver ring Aunt Iz had given her to replace the one that was lost at Graylock. A silver band with the tree of life etched into it. The crest of the Gray Clan. The Clan Emilia was now the head of.

Trees and dirt soon gave way to houses and highways.

"Where are we?" Jacob asked after they passed the third city he didn't recognize.

"Delaware," Emilia said, still looking out the window. "The Academy is in Delaware."

"How long until we get"—Jacob paused on the verge of saying *home*—"to the Mansion House?"

"About eight hours," Molly said.

The driver nodded to her in the mirror. It wasn't until then that Jacob noticed how similar the driver looked to Molly and Connor.

"Who's the driver?" Jacob whispered across the aisle to Connor.

"Wainwright Black," Connor said. "He's from High Peaks like me. I think he's like my second cousin or twice uncle. I don't know."

"The others will meet us at the Mansion House," Molly said, looking out the window, the tip of her wand pressed to the glass as though poised for attack.

"Others?" Claire asked.

"The others from the Preserves, the Elis Tribe. Everyone who can come will be at the Mansion House," Samuel said. "They should all be there by tomorrow morning."

"Will there be enough room for everyone?" Connor asked.

"You would be amazed at how big the grounds really are,"

Claire said. "If you follow the garden wall all the way to the corner, you can find some amazing things."

"Why are they coming?" Jacob asked, hating himself the moment the words left his lips.

"To pay their final respects to the Elder of the Gray Clan," Wainwright said from the front of the bus, "and to greet the new Clan head."

~

*E*milia had waited tensely for an attack. Eight hours on the bus, watching out the window. Watching the mountains glide past and the rivers flow beneath them.

How would the centaurs reach the Mansion House? Would they run? They would have to do it at night. She should know. If she was going to be in charge, she should know how the centaurs moved in mass from place to place. But the only answer she had was *carefully.*

For a moment a smile crept to her lips before guilt overwhelmed her. It wasn't funny. The Gray Clan was at war. She, seventeen-year-old Emilia Gray, was supposed to lead her Clan against the Dragons and kill her father. And she didn't even know how the Elis would get to the Mansion House.

The streets became familiar as they neared home.

The sun had begun to dip below the horizon when they entered the tree-lined drive that led to the house.

"The *fortaceria*," Emilia gasped. "We have all these people. We won't be able to get through the gates." Emilia clamored across Jacob. "Samuel, we can't get all these people through the gates."

"They'll get through just fine," Samuel said. "We'll have to take it slow, but if they're loyal, the spell should let them pass."

He sounded so sure that Emilia sat back in her seat, though she still dug her nails into her palms as the end of the drive drew closer.

They had promised all these students refuge. How terrible would it be if they couldn't even get them into the house? The gate came into view beyond the trees, and all the breath disappeared from Emilia's body.

At least two-hundred people, wizards and centaurs alike, waited outside the gate. Proteus, the head of the Elis Tribe, stood at the front of the centaur herd, next to Sabbe, the old centaur whose white hair gleamed in the light of the setting sun.

Tears sprang into Emilia's eyes as Proteus bowed to the bus and the gates swung open. The movement passed like a ripple through the crowd. By the time the bus crept up to the gate, every head was lowered, welcoming Isadora Gray home for the last time.

The bus shuddered as it passed through the *fortaceria*. The spell was different than other shield charms. Stronger than the one that had failed to protect the Academy, this spell could sense each person who passed, knowing if they should be allowed onto the grounds or not.

Gasps and whimpers sounded in the bus as each student felt the spell.

Claire turned in her seat to watch Dexter a few rows behind.

"Pity." Claire sighed as Dexter's part of the bus passed through the gate. "I thought he might not make it in. Thought maybe he'd get pushed to the back of the bus, or disintegrated, or—"

"Claire," Emilia warned.

"Times may be dark, but a girl can still dream," Claire said, "and dreams of sweet vengeance can be fun."

Emilia opened her mouth to speak, but before she could, the bus stopped in front of the steps to the Mansion House.

They were home.

22

HOME AGAIN

*J*acob stood next to Emilia at the foot of the steps, nodding as each group in the long procession passed. Some bowed deeply to Emilia like Proteus and the other centaurs. Some nodded or offered condolences.

The end of the line was in sight when Connor finally came back out the front door. Jacob expected Connor to join himself and Emilia, but instead he ran to the very back of the line, throwing his arms around the neck of a woman who beamed at him.

"His mother," Emilia whispered to Jacob, though he didn't really need Emilia's words to help him figure out who the woman was.

She stood next to a man, tall and muscular with greying red hair. The man took Connor by the shoulders for a moment, examining him as though looking for damage before pulling Connor into a tight hug. From the sharp look in the man's eyes as he had searched his son for injuries, it was easy to tell he was Molly's brother, even without the red hair.

"His parents are here with the High Peaks Preserve group." Tears glinted in Emilia's eyes as Connor moved forward in the receiving line, walking between his parents. Jacob stepped closer to Emilia, letting the back of his hand press against hers, hoping the slight touch would give her a shred of comfort.

"Losing Isadora is a terrible blow," the next woman in line said. The woman was stooped, looking almost as old as Sabbe. She took Emilia's hand in her worn and wrinkled ones. "Losing her at a time like this is worse."

Jacob wanted to tell the woman to shut her mouth, but she continued.

"Isadora groomed you for leadership, to take her place at the head of the Clan. None of us thought it would happen so soon, but it has. Isadora chose you and taught you"—the woman patted Emilia's hand—"I never second-guessed a choice Isadora made when she was alive, and I won't start now she's gone. Isadora never led us astray. We're all following you now, Emilia Gray. We follow you into darkness. Don't forget to be the light."

Emilia nodded, and the woman tottered away.

Jacob wanted to still be angry with the woman, but she was right. Emilia had been his light for a long time, now she would be the light for the Gray Clan and all Magickind.

~

*E*milia lay in her bed in the Mansion House, staring up at the pale purple canopy above her.

It was past midnight. The house should have been silent, but there were too many people under the Mansion House roof. All the students that had come from the Academy had been given beds in the house. Cots had been added to all the student bedrooms but Claire's, Connor's, Jacob's, and Emilia's. Molly had insisted they all keep their rooms for themselves to *maintain a bit of normality.*

The Clan members had taken up residence on the grounds,

the Elis Tribe moving deep into the trees to set up their jewel-colored tents.

The breath of hundreds of people hummed within the *fortaceria* as though the air itself knew something large was happening.

Emilia rolled onto her side, willing herself to fall asleep. But there was an aching hole in her chest. She tried not to wonder where Aunt Iz was now. She wouldn't be buried until sundown the next day. She was safe. She had to be someplace safe.

But did safe matter when you were dead?

Tossing her sheets aside, Emilia sat up, sliding on her shoes before going to the window. Molly had insisted on Jacob and Emilia sleeping in different rooms. Emilia didn't argue with her. It wasn't the time to tell Molly she and Jacob had shared a bed the whole time they were locked in Elder's Keep.

She needed to sleep, and the ache in her chest wouldn't let her. She needed Jacob next to her. To feel she was not alone. To hear him promise he wouldn't let her fail her Clan.

"*Aperestra ab externum.*" The window flew open without Emilia touching it. She climbed up to sit on the windowsill. "*Scalaxum.*"

With a *scrape*, a shingle pulled itself loose from the roof and flew into the air, floating directly below Emilia's dangling feet. Emilia eased her weight onto the shingle as a second pulled itself free, giving her a place to step forward.

Another shingle came loose and another, each flying back into place as she moved past. Settling back onto the roof as though nothing strange or magical had happen.

Emilia glanced down at the ground two stories below. Her heart leaped into her throat at the distance between herself and the light dusting of snow covering the dead grass. She kept her gaze down, not allowing herself to look up, letting her head swim with the knowledge that there was nothing between herself and death.

A missed step and she would tumble down. Adrenaline

rushed through her veins. There were no Dragons or monsters to fight, but the open air was just as deadly.

Tipping her head up to the sky, Emilia laughed at the stars. At the absurdity of it all. But a sob caught in her throat, and air no longer came. Forcing a shuddering breath into her lungs, Emilia took a step forward, not looking to see if the shingle was waiting for her foot.

The cold night wind was beginning to blow with more strength, making the tears on Emilia's cheeks burn with cold.

Scrape, scrape, scrape. The sound marked her every step.

Slowly, the shingles began moving higher, bringing her level with the pitched windows that peeked through the roof. The boys lived on the top floor of the Mansion House. Emilia didn't need to count windows to know when she had reached Jacob's room.

He sat on the pitched roof wrapped in a blanket, silently watching Emilia's approach.

He didn't say anything as she stepped onto the roof. He simply unfurled the blanket to make room for her.

Emilia sat beside him, letting his warmth fill her as he wrapped his arm around her shoulder.

"How are you?" Jacob asked after a few long moments.

Emilia looked up at the sky. The stars shone brightly, and though the wind blew, there was no trace of clouds.

"I'm fine," Emilia said, knowing her lie was useless.

"No, you're not." Jacob kissed her hair. "You've lost a lot. And now people are looking to you to lead. You haven't even gotten a moment to get your head on straight. And hundreds of people are camped out on the lawn."

Emilia followed Jacob's gaze out into the trees. Lanterns peered through the branches, marking the places where tents had been pitched.

"You didn't get a chance to breathe either. After your dad died, I brought you straight here, and the crazy hasn't stopped."

Emilia nestled her head onto Jacob's shoulder. "I'm sorry I dragged you into all of this."

"I'm not." Jacob lifted Emilia's chin, looking into her eyes. "I'm not sorry for any of it. Being here, being with you, is worth every bit of pain and danger. Never be sorry for bringing me to the Mansion House, or for helping me become a wizard. You gave me a family, Emi."

"But our family is broken." Tears flowed freely down Emilia's cheeks. "We lost Aunt Iz and Rosalie and Professor Eames. And the Pendragon still wants to kill all of us. He'll keep picking us off one by one until there's none of us left. I can't keep losing people. I can't lose you. I just can't."

Emilia buried her face on Jacob's shoulder.

"You're right," Jacob whispered. "We can't keep losing people. We can't let the Pendragon call the shots. He's scared right now."

Emilia laughed, the sound of it muffled against Jacob's sweater.

"I'm serious." Jacob took a deep breath, as though steeling himself for something unpleasant. "The *somnerri* were sent to the Academy to kill Aunt Iz."

"And it worked. The Pendragon won." Emilia sat up and moved away from Jacob. She didn't deserve the comfort of his touch. Aunt Iz was dead. She hadn't protected the woman who had raised her, the head of her Clan, the only real parent she'd ever had.

"But at a huge cost," Jacob said, catching Emilia's hand before she could move farther away. The faint golden glow of their palms warmed the night. "The Pendragon lost, what, thirty men? All to get Aunt Iz. Which means he was scared of her. He was scared she would lead the Clan against him. Whether the *somnerri* knew what they were fighting for or not, the Pendragon wanted to murder the head of the Gray Clan to stop us from attacking."

"And it worked."

"It didn't." Jacob took Emilia's face in his hands. "We lost Aunt

Iz, but we didn't lose the Clan. Aunt Iz wanted to attack Graylock."

"Aunt Iz is gone."

"But you're not. You're the head of the Clan now, and you can lead us against the Dragons. We can go to Graylock and fight him."

Emilia gave a horrified laugh as panic shot through her chest.

"He wanted to break the Clan apart, but look"—Jacob pointed to the lawn—"look down there. He brought us all together. There are more people down there than Iz could have rallied when she was alive. We have an army to fight the Dragons with, and you, Emilia Gray, are their leader. This is it. This is our chance to fight him. He took Aunt Iz from us, so now we take everything from him."

Emilia stared into Jacob's bright blue eyes.

"I don't know if I can do it," Emilia said. "I'm not Aunt Iz. I'm not an Elder. I'm seventeen."

"It doesn't matter. You're the head of the Clan, and you can do this."

"What if they don't want to follow me?" Emilia asked, her voice rising in panic. "What if they don't want to fight?"

"They will. The Pendragon has done too many unforgivable things. They'll want to stop him. They'll want to end it."

Emilia swallowed, trying to force words past the lump in her throat. "What if they fight and we lose? What if he kills them all? What if I lead these people to their deaths for nothing?"

"It isn't for nothing, Emilia. The Dragons are murderers. They kill innocent people. Magickind, humans, they don't care. They just kill. Fighting against something that evil is never for nothing."

"But what if"—Emilia held tightly onto Jacob's hand—"what if I lose you? I can't survive that. I know I can't."

Jacob brushed the hair away from Emilia's face. "You won't lose me, because we'll fight together. And if they get us, they'll get us both. If we die in the fight, it'll be together. And we'll take out the Pendragon and as many of his murderers as we can on our way."

Emilia nodded. It was true. They would fight together. They would die together. There was no other path left for either of them. "We're too far gone, aren't we?"

"What do you mean?"

"Too far gone for a happy ending." Emilia brushed the tears from her cheeks. The time for crying was over. "We've lost too much, been through too much. We don't get to come back to a happy ending."

"Don't say that. There's always a chance we'll make it to the other side of this mess."

"Is there?"

"Yes. We're going to have to fight for it, and maybe we won't make it that far. And it won't be the ending we wanted."

"Not everyone will be there."

"They won't. But there's a chance. For everyone who's still breathing, there's a chance. For us, there's a chance."

"To sit in the trees and not be afraid?" Emilia asked. "To eat in the kitchen with Molly and laugh?"

"All of it." Jacob leaned in and gently kissed Emilia. "We've got a shot at a happy ending, and I'm going to fight like hell to get us there."

"We'll fight together." Emilia laced her fingers through Jacob's, letting his strength and hope fill her chest.

"It's how we belong."

Emilia pulled herself close, pressing her lips to Jacob's. Sparks flew through her veins, and hope dazzled her senses. Fire, flood, blood, death. They had survived it all. Now all they had to do was make it through one last battle.

"*I* want to go to Graylock," Emilia said as soon as the family had convened in the kitchen.

Samuel and Dexter sat at the table with Larkin while Molly hovered by the stove and Connor and Claire perched on the counter. Jacob stood next to Emilia, his silent force giving her the courage to press on.

"I want us to attack the caves and end this once and for all." Emilia waited for Molly or Samuel to protest, but Connor was the first to speak.

"Sounds great. I mean, I'd like to finish my breakfast first, but then I'm game."

"It isn't a game," Larkin said, not sounding angry as much as tired.

"It was a metaphor," Claire said.

"I know you want revenge," Larkin said. "We all do. But this was a huge blow to the Clan. We need time to recover. Then we can start planning a strategic attack."

"I know the caves," Dexter said. "I drew up the map to find Samuel. I can make another one. Highlight weak points where we might be able to break through. If we aren't looking for stealth, we could break in at a few different points and flush them out."

"It'll take a while to plan and coordinate, but I think it might be our best chance," Molly said. "We can ask Proteus to stay with some of his people. They can help us plan and when the time is right—"

"The time is right now," Claire said. "We can plan today, and go in tomorrow."

"It's not that simple." Larkin shook her head.

"I didn't say it was simple." Claire jumped off the counter and crossed to the table. "But it has to be done. We have to attack."

"And we will," Molly said. "But we have to be careful. People will be risking their lives."

"They're risking their lives just by being here," Connor said.

"We'll only get one chance at this," Larkin said. "We can't risk wasting it."

"Which is why we attack now," Samuel said, not looking up from his balled fists on the scrubbed wooden table.

"We can't just—" Molly began.

"We have more people out there than we could have hoped for," Samuel pressed on. "If we let them leave the gates without a plan of attack, they might not want to come back to fight for us. They'll get home and realize what they're risking. Or find Dragons on their front steps, waiting to slaughter them. We will never be stronger than we are right now. The Dragons just took a huge hit at the Academy. We have to use that to our advantage."

"But we took a huge hit, too," Larkin said. "And the students we've brought back don't know how to fight."

"They know how to spar," Connor said. "We fought them, and they're pretty good. It would take months to get them in better shape, and we don't have that kind of time."

"But we don't have a plan either," Dexter said. "I know we have people, and we do need a lot of people for this to work, but we can't just run screaming at the caves and hope enough people make it inside to find and kill the Pendragon. It won't work."

"I didn't know we were allowing scum to have an opinion," Claire said.

"I know I don't deserve to have a say in anything," Dexter said, "but I've seen this family go through enough—"

"Because you caused it."

"—and I don't want to see anyone else get hurt," Dexter continued. "We can't go charging at the caves without a plan."

"But there is a plan," Emilia said, her nails biting into her palms as she steeled herself to continue. "I know we can't go running at the entrance. And even if we could find a way to dig into the tunnels from the top, we'd still be running through tunnels looking for the Pendragon. No matter how much we study a map, we won't know the caves as well as the people who live there."

Dexter nodded his agreement.

"So we draw the Pendragon out," Emilia said. "We fight him in the open."

"But how?" Larkin said. "He's completely unpredictable. We could set a hundred traps and there would be no guarantee he would show up for any of them."

"There is if I'm the bait." Before the words had fully left Emilia's lips the kitchen was in an uproar.

"I'll be the bait." Dexter pounded his fists on the table and stood up. "I'm a traitor. He wants me dead."

"It should be someone else. You're the Elder," Larkin said.

"I will not allow—"

"I'm his daughter!" Emilia shouted above the din. "He wants to get to me more than any of you. If I show up at the caves, he'll come out. To kill me or capture me, he'll show up. And once he's in the open, we attack with everything we have."

"He could kill you," Larkin said. "What if we can't get to you in time?"

"Then you make sure he doesn't get back into the caves," Jacob said quietly. "We know it's a risk, but it's one we're willing to take."

"Oh, both of you are the bait?" Molly snorted derisively. "Well, that changes things. You'll just walk up hand in hand and ask the Pendragon for an appointment."

"We aren't just going to walk up," Emilia said. "And Jacob has to be with me for this to work."

"What do you mean?" Samuel leaned across the table, as though sensing what Emilia didn't want to say.

"There's a spell," Emilia began slowly. "I don't know how it works, but we can transport ourselves, and we can take people with us."

"Transport?" Larkin said, one blond eyebrow climbing high on her forehead.

Jacob stepped forward and took Emilia's hand.

"*Retivanesco.*"

With a flash of purple light, the air was knocked from Emilia's lungs as the world went momentarily black. By the time she realized everything had gone dark, she was standing on the other side of the kitchen and Molly was screaming.

"How the hell did you do that?" Larkin asked, her face paler than usual.

"The Hag gave us the spell," Jacob said.

"And you thought she was a good one to take advice from?" Molly asked.

"We didn't really have any other choice the first time we tried it," Jacob said.

"Or the second," Connor added. "That's how they got us to the Academy."

"Jacob and I can use the spell to appear right outside the cave entrance," Emilia said. "And we can each take a person with us. We'll find a way to hide them, and then they can attack once we draw the Pendragon out."

"So the plan is to use a spell from someone we don't trust, transport into a shield spell that's damn near impossible to break through, and hide two people who are supposed to be your back ups in a way you really haven't come up with?" Claire asked.

"We hide the others with a little flash bang magic," Jacob said.

"But the shield," Dexter said. "It all depends on you being able to get through the shield."

"You won't know if it'll work until you try it, and that's just too risky," Larkin said. "I know you want to attack, but being stuck on the other side of that shield would be a death sentence, if the spell doesn't get you killed trying to break through. It's too risky to chance it without knowing for sure."

"Then we'll just have to find out," Jacob said.

"How?" Samuel asked.

"We ask the one who gave us the spell."

24

OLD FRIEND

*a*unt Iz's office looked exactly the same as it had when they left a few weeks ago. Jacob had expected dust to be coating the surface of the gleaming cherry wood desk that matched the intricately carved office door. But everything was pristine.

Whether Iz had placed a spell on the room to keep it tidy, or too little time had passed, Jacob didn't know. It was as though Iz could walk through the door at any moment and playfully scold Jacob for sitting in her chair.

But Jacob lowered himself into the chair without interruption. Emilia was with Molly and Samuel, planning the transportation to Graylock. It seemed strange that in a world of magic, carpooling to battle was a concern.

A full-length mirror was positioned in an alcove next to the desk. Jacob had skryed before, but did the Hag skry? And if she did, would she even answer his call?

He would never know until he tried.

"*Volavertus* Hag," Jacob said. The Hag had been stripped of her proper name when she chose to become immortal. But since she didn't have a real name, would *Hag* be enough for the spell to work?

The mirror on the wall glowed brightly for a moment. Jacob held his breath, waiting for the Hag's perfect face to appear. But instead, the mirror returned to a dull reflection of Jacob sitting in Aunt Iz's chair.

Jacob dug his fists into his eyes, making white spots dance before them. They needed to know if the spell would get them through the shield. If skrying wouldn't work, maybe he and Emilia could use the spell to go to Newport, and then what? Hope the Hag would give them a real answer? He laughed darkly.

"*Volavertus* Hag of the Gray Clan." Jacob opened his eyes to see the mirror shine for a moment before showing his tired face. Jacob cursed before gasping and falling out of his chair as the reflection showed a woman standing behind his shoulder.

Jacob scrambled backward on the ground as the Hag sauntered toward him.

Her bright red lips curved in a smile, the color as startling as always against her alabaster skin. Dark curls hung around her shoulders. Her usual white dress had been replaced by a sheath of black fabric that clung to the curves of her body, and tall black heels clacked against the wooden floor as she stepped forward.

"Skrying, Jacob Gray?" the Hag said, her voice dripping with sarcasm. "You really thought you could call me through your little mirror and ask for my help?"

"Well, it got you here, didn't it?" Jacob scrambled to his feet as gracefully as he could, wedged between the desk and chair.

"I'm here because I choose to be," the Hag said.

"And I called for you because I want to speak to you," Jacob said, refusing to give the Hag an inch. They had been through enough because of her. He might need her to answer a question, but he didn't want to prolong the conversation.

"Oh you little wizards, always in such a hurry." The Hag sat in Iz's chair.

"We have to be." Jacob balled his hands into fists. "Life moves more quickly for us."

"And death comes racing around the corner. Have you reconsidered my offer, Jacob Gray? Now that you've seen your *family* covered in blood, does an eternity of peaceful safety sound more appealing?"

"No."

"Good." The Hag smiled sadly. "Because the time for that has passed. You are too deep in this mess to have any way out but through fire and blood. And who knows which of you might fall when the next battle comes?"

"That's why I called you." Jacob knelt in front of the Hag, staring into her eyes. "I need your help."

"I've told you before, Jacob Gray, I have no power to fight or kill." The Hag shook her head, sending her curls bouncing around her shoulders. "One who cannot die cannot kill. I offered you my protection, and that was the most I could do."

"I know you can't fight with us," Jacob said, searching for each word to make sure he didn't push the Hag too far, "but we are going to Graylock. We are going to fight the Dragons on the mountain."

"And many will die." The Hag stated it like a simple fact.

"But fewer could die if you help us," Jacob said. "All we need is a little information. And it could make the difference between victory and defeat."

"What do you want to know? Who will run out of the caves first? Which way the wind will be blowing? I've told you before, I don't watch the future like a program on your silly televisions. It's all too vague to be of any use to you."

"It's not the future we need to know about, it's magic." Jacob took a breath and pressed on. "The spell you gave Emilia and me—"

"I'm surprised the two of you used such *dangerous* magic." The Hag gave a tinkling laugh that didn't seem to match the power and magic she exuded. "Let alone twice, and bringing your friends with you?"

"We didn't have a choice," Jacob said, trying to keep his anger at her amusement out of his voice.

"It's amazing what becomes a possibility when there is no other choice. How far one is willing to push magic suddenly changes so drastically."

"We want to use the spell again," Jacob began.

"By all means, use it as much as you like."

"And we want to use it to transport into the Dragons' shield."

The Hag froze, her dark eyes scanning Jacob's face.

"You are genuinely serious aren't you?" The Hag leaned forward. "And what are you going to do? Magic your way into the Pendragon's bedroom and kill him in his sleep? I wouldn't blame you, but it doesn't seem like a very Gray thing to do. And then who knows which head might begin to control the monster?"

"We don't want to go all the way into the tunnels," Jacob said. "There's a shield spell that covers the entrance to the cave. There's a group of chanters who keep the spell going all the time, so breaking into it is really hard."

"You've done it." The Hag shrugged.

"But am I really going to be able to find a Dragon wandering in the woods so I can knock him out again?"

"Come now, little Gray, have a bit of faith in yourself."

"But if Emilia and I could use the spell to get through the shield, we could surprise them, draw the Pendragon out and break the circle that keeps the shield spell going." Jacob waited, his words hanging in the air as the Hag considered him.

She placed her red painted nails under her chin.

"I didn't make their shield," the Hag said. "I might have done a few favors for the Gray Clan in the past century in a fit of misplaced sentimentalism, but I've never made a shield for the Dragons."

"So you're saying you don't know." Jacob slumped against the desk, allowing himself the luxury of feeling defeated for a moment.

"I'm saying the spell would never cut through one of my shields." The Hag put a finger under Jacob's chin, tilting his face to meet her gaze. "I know much more about the ways of old magic than the Pendragon ever will. Fortunately for you, he doesn't seem to have ever figured that out."

"So it'll work?" Excitement flared in Jacob's chest.

"If by *work* you mean the spell won't care if the Dragons' pathetic excuse for a shield spell is between you and your desired destination, then of course. I would hate for you to think my sort of magic could be disrupted by such a tiny thing. But if by *work* you mean will you die instantly upon arrival, then perhaps, the Dragons could easily kill you as soon as you appear. The spell is for transportation, not fighting. It will not win you the battle against the Dragons. There will be a battle, and more Gray blood will be spilled."

The Hag strode over to the window, hiding her face behind the veil of her hair. "But I've warned you. I've tried to save you, and you want none of it. So go, Jacob Gray, take the magic I've given you and try to fight the monsters. Perhaps your death will be my great contribution to the cause."

"We won't go down without a fight," Jacob said, his voice tight.

"I've no doubt you will fight, little Gray. You've shown me that often enough."

"And it won't be your fault," Jacob said as the Hag crossed the room. "I know you've tried to stop me. You've even tried to save me. Staying with Emilia is my choice. Fighting the Dragons is my choice. And if I die, it will be because I chose to fight."

The Hag turned to face Jacob with a sadness in her eyes so complete, it looked as though she might have cried if it had been a thing she were capable of.

"The Pendragon tethered Emilia and me together, he forced us into that." Jacob took a step forward, reaching out for the Hag's hand. Her skin was cold to the touch, not like ice, but marble. Hard and lifeless. "You gave us a chance to choose a different life, and we didn't. We want to stay together, to fight together. You gave us the chance to find that out. I don't like what you did to us in the tunnels, but I know why. And I am grateful. No matter how this whole mess turns out, I will stay grateful."

"I will have to keep that in mind if I ever need comfort as the centuries pass." The Hag slipped her hand from Jacob's. "We could have had such fun. At least I will have the luxury of knowing that, if the world crumbles, it's not *my* fault. That's the problem with derring-dos. They are willing to risk everything. Sacrifice and nobility are their specialties.

"But the rest of us, the ones who have never seen the pleasure in giving all for those who will never care, we are the ones left standing in the ashes. Fight your battle, Jacob Gray, and if you have the chance, live. The world will be better for it. There are incredible things you could yet achieve."

Without another word, the Hag turned and vanished through the closed door.

25

THE BLOOD HEIR

*E*milia walked through the garden toward the shadowy trees. She was so used to the grounds being quiet—just the family and the students. When she was very little, there had been twenty students living in the house at a time. But then the rumblings of trouble had started, and families wanted to keep their children closer to home. And who could blame them? When the world proved it could be evil, why chance sending your children out into it?

But even when the Mansion House had been packed full of students, it was still possible to feel utterly alone in the garden. Now the place buzzed with life. Wizards bowed as she passed, and conversations halted when she came into view.

She didn't need an eavesdropping spell to know what they were all saying. Everyone had the same questions. Was Emilia ready to lead the Gray Clan, and now that she was in charge, what would she do?

Emilia walked into the trees and down the wide path to where the centaurs had pitched their many tents. She only had a half-an-hour to speak to Proteus and make sure he would agree to the plan. The centaurs were considered a part of the Gray

Clan, but the Elis Tribe might not be willing to take her orders. And if the Elis decided not to fight at Graylock, the plan would be hopeless.

"Emilia Gray." Raven, a centaur with a jet-black coat and hair approached, his hooves thumping softly on the frozen ground.

"Raven." Emilia nodded. She opened her mouth to ask where Proteus was, but there was something in the young centaur's face that made her pause.

"You have had the mantle of power thrust upon you," Raven said. "It does not run in your veins, and yet you were chosen and now must feel the weight too soon."

"It always would have been too soon." Emilia blinked away the stinging in her eyes.

No more tears.

"It would," Raven said, his low voice rumbling. "It will be for me."

"For you?" Emilia asked, trying too late to hide the confusion in her voice.

"Proteus's daughter was killed by the Dragons." Raven looked down at his palms, examining them as though studying the map that had led him to stand in the Mansion House trees with Emilia. "Willow was to be Proteus's heir. Now that she is gone, I have been chosen to stand in her place."

Emilia wavered on the edge of saying congratulations before, "I'm sorry," slipped from her lips.

"I am not a leader." Raven shook his long, dark hair. "I am a warrior. I will defend the Elis Tribe with my life, but to lead…"

"I know."

"With the battle coming, I may never have to lead." Raven straightened up, going back to his usual hard demeanor. "I assume you are coming to discuss attack plans with Proteus. With the battle we have upon us, it would be unwise to worry about what we shall do with our lives afterward. If the shadows take us, there will be no future to worry about."

Emilia nodded and turned to walk the rest of the way to the centaurs' tents, Raven's hooffalls following her.

The tents were every jewel tone imaginable. The inks were dark and rich, as though the warmth of the sun had been mixed into every color. Textures in the canvas were shown deeply in the shadows, each with a design as unique as the centaur it housed.

A young, bright-white centaur, Loblolly, stood outside a deep green tent in the far corner. He bowed to Emilia as she came into view but didn't leave his place at the tent opening.

The largest tent was in the center of the group. Ruby red with an intricate pattern woven into it that Emilia didn't understand. She stood outside the tent flap, wishing it had a wooden door so she could knock. She was the head of the Gray Clan. She needed to look authoritative. But it was Proteus's tent, and he was much older and more experienced than she was. Or might ever be if Raven was right about the shadows taking them in battle.

The other centaurs had moved outside their tents and were beginning to stare.

"Proteus," Emilia called in the most calm and mature voice she could muster, "may I enter and speak with you?"

A second later, the flap was pushed aside to reveal Proteus, who bowed Emilia into his tent.

Emilia was grateful Raven followed her in. Standing alone in Proteus's tent would have felt too much like being called to the principle's office, even though Emilia was supposed to be the one in charge.

"What can I do for you, Emilia Gray?" Proteus asked.

"You can tell me that when I lead the clan into battle at Gray-lock tomorrow, the Elis Tribe will stand with us."

"Tomorrow?" Proteus asked.

The light in the tent was dim. A lantern with an unnaturally bright flame had been placed in the center, but the red of the tent seemed to mute its glow. Redden it. Making it seem as though sunset had already arrived.

"Tomorrow," Emilia said. "The Dragons took a huge loss at the Academy."

"And our hesitation will only give them more time to rebuild their strength." Proteus stared deep into Emilia's eyes.

It took every bit of willpower she had not to look away from his gaze.

"We will fight with you," Proteus said. "We must, and not only because it is our duty as members of the Gray Clan. The Dragons have hunted and killed us. They have attacked our home and our elders. We cannot allow such evil to fester. It is time to kill the Dragons once and for all."

"That's what we're going to Graylock to do," Emilia said, feeling Raven move closer behind her as though ready to charge immediately into battle.

"How?" Proteus asked. "How do you plan to attack the Dragons in the dark den they seem to be so happy to hide in?"

"We lure them out," Emilia said, feeling more confident about the plan now than she had in the kitchen. In the house she was a little girl waiting for treats from Molly. But here, it was easy to pretend that little girl was someone else entirely. A child from a different life who would never know pain or death. The Emilia standing in the tent wasn't afraid to fight or to die. "Jacob and I will be the bait."

Proteus considered her for a moment. "If the Elis are going to be used in the attack, I want a hand in planning it. I know where my warriors are most valuable. We are willing to die, but I will not have my whole Tribe slaughtered in a battle that cannot be won."

"I agree." Emilia bowed. "We would be grateful for your help and advice. Molly, Samuel, and Larkin are in the kitchen, planning. If you would like to join them, I'm sure they would be more than happy to move outside."

"As you wish." Proteus stepped toward the tent flap.

Raven looked from Proteus to Emilia before stepping away from the entrance.

"Raven can go with you if you want," Emilia said quickly as Proteus began to exit. "He's your heir now. He should be there."

"I thank you." Proteus turned to face Emilia. "In times of war it is more important than ever that the young ones learn quickly. Before the old ones are no longer there and their knowledge is lost to the shadows."

Emilia nodded stiffly.

"Sabbe is here," Proteus continued. "She would like to see you. Perhaps she has some wisdom for the head of the Gray Clan."

"Thank you." Emilia's stomach twisted at the thought of seeing Sabbe. "I have to speak to the wizards. Claire and Connor are rounding them up. And now that I know the Elis will fight with us, it's time to make sure the wizards will come, too."

"They will," Raven said. "She made you stronger than you know."

"Do not let night fall without seeing Sabbe." Proteus turned and walked away, Raven only a step behind.

She wanted to follow them. To make plans and prepare for the fight ahead. But she was the leader of the Gray Clan. It was time to make sure they would follow her.

26

BEFORE

*I*t was the night of Emilia's eleventh birthday. Dinner had been eaten and Jacob had gone home. As the cake was being cleared away, Aunt Iz sat Emilia down on the couch, took both her hands, and spoke solemnly.

"People believe being in charge is entirely made up of forming grand plans and making hard decisions. And you do have to do both those things. You have to make decisions when others refuse to. You have to plan for the Clan's future. You have to be smart and wise, and yes, my Emilia, they are two very different things.

"But the hardest task is convincing people to follow you. When things are going well, they won't see why they need you. They are doing fine on their own, why should they listen to the old lady in the big house? Why should she be allowed to teach their children when they can do it themselves? Why follow her rules when they've always done fine on their own? And they will continue to wonder why they need you until they need you. Until things go badly."

Iz smiled sadly, understanding the fear on Emilia's face. But still she pushed on.

"Until the humans have discovered them or another settlement is trying to steal their land. Then they will come to you. Angry sometimes, *but nearly always more afraid than anything else. And it will be up to you to comfort them. To tell them everything will be all right, even when you're not sure of it. When you are in charge, the most important thing is to keep your head held high and push forward. Keep fighting no matter how useless it may seem. Because the very moment you stop believing that you will win, that you will survive, they'll see the crack in your armor. As soon as they see that crack, they will stop believing. And once they think the Clan won't survive, all will be lost.*

"Always remember to believe in the strength of the Clan. For if you believe in it hard enough, the strength of the wizards will follow you. I wish I could lay out an easier path for you, Emilia, but I know you are strong enough for the road that lies ahead."

27

WE FEW

*J*acob leaned against the wall near the front door, pressing himself out of sight of the windows that flanked it. The Gray Clan had begun assembling outside a few minutes ago. Preserve-wizards stood in groups while the other wizards wandered among them. Centaurs filed into the back, standing in one silent line.

Jacob glanced out the window. He had never really considered the difference between settlement wizards, who lived on the preserves, and wizards who chose to live in houses amongst humans.

The settlement wizards stayed in their little clumps, presumably with the others from their homes. Jacob had never been to a wizard settlement before. He knew that was where Connor was born and where Molly had come from. Groups of wizards who lived deep in the woods, out of reach of humans, where they were able to use their magic without fear of being seen.

Jacob had been to the home of the Elis Tribe, and he imagined it would be much the same for wizards. Clusters of tents and lots of magic out in the open. The settlement wizards looked more rustic than the city wizards. Not dirty or poor, just much more practical. Like they were ready for a very long and rather cold camping trip. Which seemed to be accurate, all things considered.

The city wizards looked like the families of the people Jacob had gone to school with. Completely normal, though notably more comfortable moving between groups than the preserve wizards.

Jacob didn't fit in with either group. Last year at this time he had been a normal junior in a normal high school, trying to figure out which college might give him a scholarship.

His biggest worry had been finding enough money to keep the lights on and buy food. But then Emilia had come back for him, and his old life had melted away. He had gotten the only thing he had ever truly wanted. To be with her, to spend his days with her. And if fighting, if dying was the price he had to pay for these months by her side, it was worth it. To protect her and protect the family she had brought him into.

But those people on the lawn, the ones who had chosen to spend their lives quietly in the woods or blending in with normal humans, was it worth it for them? If he and Emilia led these people into battle and the terrible moment came when they knew their lives were about to end, would they hate the people who had led them there or find comfort in knowing they were giving their lives for something more?

He had the horrible feeling it would be the former.

"You all right?" Maggie walked down the stairs with Lee and the others from the Academy.

"Fine." Jacob nodded. "Just fine."

Maggie narrowed her eyes at him, appraising him for a moment before speaking. "You're not fine. Of course you're not fine. If you were, you'd be insane."

"Are we going to fight?" Lee asked.

Jacob answered with a nod, not sure how much he was allowed to say.

"Good." Lee drew his shoulders back as though ready to turn his wand against the Dragons on the spot. "Because none of us are going to be fine until we know the Dragons can't hurt the people we care about anymore. And the sooner they're gone, the better."

"We have to fight," Dexter said, coming up the hall from the kitchen followed by Connor and a glaring Claire. "We can't let things stay as they are. If we sit by, innocent people will keep dying. The only way out is forward."

"And that means a fight," Maggie said, moving aside so Dexter could stand next to her.

Dexter gave her the slightest look of appreciation.

"So are we going to hide in the hallway?" Claire said slowly. "Or go outside and hear Emilia's grand and impassioned speech that will lead us all into battle?"

Jacob took a deep breath and opened the front door.

As soon as the door moved, the crowd on the lawn fell silent. Jacob felt for a moment as though he had cheated them or maybe Emilia. The crowd had been expecting her to come out of the house. Instead, a group of students filed down the steps to stand at the front of the crowd.

"Where is she?" Connor whispered to Jacob.

Emilia was close. He could feel that. She was nervous, anxious even. A deep thread of fear and grief ran through her every breath. But she was all right.

"Should you say something to them?" Claire asked, turning to Jacob as the crowd began to grumble.

"Why me?" Jacob asked.

"You're Emilia's *coniunx*," Connor muttered out of the corner of his mouth. "That makes you important by proxy."

"Umm." As Jacob realized he had no idea what he should say to these people, Emilia appeared around the side of the house followed closely by Molly, Samuel, Larkin, Proteus, and Raven.

Emilia's gaze found Jacob's before she scanned the crowd, as though checking to make sure everyone was there.

She climbed to the top of the steps, Molly, Larkin, and Samuel standing behind her while Raven and Proteus flanked the stairs.

"Gray Clan"—Emilia's voice carried over the crowd as if by some unseen magic—"we have gathered here to mourn the loss of Isadora Gray." Emilia paused for a moment, her eyes flicking back down to Jacob's before she continued. "Great Elder of our Clan, loving protector to us all."

Murmurs of ascent rose from the crowd. And that little bit of sound bolstered Jacob. They might not have been there, might not have seen the horribleness of her end, but each of these people standing behind him, listening to Emilia, mourned the loss of Aunt Iz.

"She was killed as she fought bravely to defend the students of the Academy, the children of all the Clans." Emilia tipped her chin up. "And we, the Gray Clan, were the only ones to fight to protect those children!"

A roar of pride soared through the crowd.

"The Grays fought at the Academy! We lost our leader." Emilia's face grew somber, and Jacob felt the massive pull of grief that clawed through her chest. "But we saved the students."

A faint sniffle came from one of the Academy girls behind Jacob.

"Other Clans have tried to stand with us, and have been slaughtered," Emilia said. "Many have lost their lives. Humans, wizards, centaurs. The Dragons kill without mercy. Without care or defense. They are murderers and monsters."

A murmur of agreement shuddered through the crowd.

"And those who murder innocents without any regard for the worth of a life cannot be allowed to kill without consequence. We cannot allow the Dragons one more day to gain power. If we let them continue to murder and terrorize without retribution, the damage to the magical community will be astronomical and beyond the point of repair. The life for which Magickind has fought for centuries will be lost forever."

There was no sound from the crowd this time. Only terrified, unrelenting quiet.

"There are only two choices." The composed demeanor Emilia had begun with shifted, and the real Emilia, Jacob's Emilia, showed through. "We can hide. Take those we love and the knowledge we possess and run. Hope the Dragons will lose track of us and allow us to live in peace. Hope we can ignore reports of broken dams and innocent people massacred at concerts. Hope our conscience will scream *we let those people die* quietly enough that we can pretend not to hear.

"Or we can fight. We can fight the Dragons with every last bit of strength the Gray Clan has. We can attack them in their den. In the dark place where they breed monsters. We can attack the Dragons and end this once and for all!"

A bellow of approval rose from the back of the crowd where the centaurs stood. Raven's face morphed from impassive stone to pride for a split second before all emotion drained away as Emilia continued.

"We must attack the Dragons at Graylock. We have to hit them with everything the Gray Clan has. And we can't do that unless you"—Emilia looked toward the groups from the preserves—"unless each of your settlements"—she turned to the city wizards—"and families agree to fight with us. We can't live in fear waiting for the Pendragon to decide where and when he wants to murder us. We have to strike back, and we have to do it now. I am leading an attack against Graylock tomorrow. And I am asking each of you to fight by my side. Fight for a future without fear. Stand with me, and we can finally end this war."

A cheer so loud it seemed to echo off the *forteceria* itself sprung from the crowd.

Emilia raised a hand, and silence fell. "But there's one thing you need to know. One thing you have the right to know." She looked down to Jacob and stretched her hand out to him.

Feeling the eyes of everyone in the crowd boring into the back of his neck, Jacob walked up the steps and stood by Emilia. She slipped her hand into his, and warmth spread up his arm.

"You all know I am not Isadora Gray's natural born daughter," Emilia began, holding tight to Jacob's hand. "She raised me as her own. Chose me to be her heir. But I can't ask you to fight the Dragons without knowing the whole truth. The Pendragon, Emile LeFay, is my father."

Rumbles came from the crowd, but Emilia pressed on.

"I had never met him, never even heard his name until he kidnapped me last summer. He took me to the caves and tried to make me one of them, tried to convince me that murder was the only way for wizards to survive. But he failed. All he did was show me how cruel and impossibly evil the Dragons are. But the Pendragon will come after me, he will attack Jacob and me before any of you."

"And we will protect you!" The shout came from Connor's father. "You are the head of our Clan."

"Thank you," Emilia said, her voice faltering for the briefest moment. "But I will not be standing at the back of this battle watching my Clan fight. Jacob and I will be at the front. The Pendragon wants us, he can come out and get us."

"And when he does come," Jacob said, "he'll find all of you fighting with us."

There was a silence that could have lasted a hundred years before the crowd cheered louder than ever. Bellowing that they would fight with Emilia, stand next to her when the battle came.

The energy pouring from the crowd was palpable. The power and fierceness of the Gray Clan, united as one, determined to destroy the enemy that had so damaged their family.

The din continued for a few minutes before Emilia raised a hand, gesturing for Larkin, Molly, and Samuel to step forward.

"We have little time to prepare," Molly said. "At sunset, we bury Isadora Gray. Then we leave for Graylock and attack just after Sunrise."

Everything dissolved into groupings and orders. Molly, Samuel, and Larkin divided the fighters into sections. Maps of the Graylock Preserve and rough sketches of the caves appeared as plans began to form within the groups.

"Wouldn't it be better to attack at night?" Connor's father asked. "I don't mean to contradict Mol, but then we could hide our numbers."

"We'll be going in toward the end of the last night watch," Dexter said, keeping his eyes firmly on the map in front of him as though afraid someone might ask how he knew. "The chanters will be tired, most of their magic drained. Guards will have been standing for hours as well. And the new shift won't be ready to come out yet."

"Besides, Billy," Molly said, swatting her brother on the shoulder, "if they know their preserve half so well as you know yours, trying to fight them in the dark would give them a huge advantage. They'd know the ground while we stumbled blind."

"Best to hit them at dawn when they think the danger from the night is gone," another preserve wizard with a long, greying beard said.

The man's words made Jacob's insides squirm. They were going to be the danger. They were going to attack. But they weren't the bad guys. They weren't the ones who needed to be stopped.

With a gentle pressure on his hand, Emilia led him away from Molly's group. Together they wove through the clusters of fighters. Proteus had a map much larger than the others and had laid it out on the ground. Shimmering shapes danced on the map, showing Proteus's plans for the centaurs. At the center of the map was the entrance to the caves. Two golden, shining figures stood alone, facing the dark blot that was the cavern.

The other fighters looked so far away from where Jacob and Emilia would be. But that was for the best. They would deal with the Pendragon. The farther away everyone else was, the better.

Larkin was with the group of students from the Academy.

"The most important thing is to hold the perimeter," Larkin said, using her finger to trace a wide line around the caves. "When we get them out and fighting, we have to make sure we don't let them surround us and push us in toward the cave entrance. If we let them corral us—"

"We die," Claire said without any hint of sarcasm in her tone.

A pang flew through Jacob's heart as he felt Emilia's begin to race.

"Connor and Claire won't be fighting with you," Emilia said.

Larkin eyed Emilia for a moment before nodding.

"Are we going with you?" Claire asked. "'Cause I missed the first magical piggy back ride."

"No," Emilia said. "I have another job for you two."

All of the students from the Academy were staring at Emilia now. Jacob squeezed her hand, wishing there were something he could do to help.

"We can talk about it later. Just don't count those two for the perimeter." Emilia dropped Jacob's hand, turned, and walked toward the centaurs' tents.

Jacob jogged to catch up. "Are you okay?"

"I can't let them fight," Emilia said, her voice tight. "I won't do it. They'll have to stay somewhere else. I'm sorry, but I just can't."

"Okay."

"You don't think that makes me terrible?" Emilia spun toward him, desperately searching his eyes.

"No."

"You don't think it makes me a horribly weak and selfish person who has no right to be a leader or ask anyone else to fight for her?"

"No." Jacob kissed the back of Emilia's hand. "You were amazing. Talking to all those people. Making all of this happen"—Jacob made a sweeping motion toward the lawn where the groups were pouring over their maps—"was amazing."

"I just can't lose them, I don't want to see it. I can't bear the thought of it."

"We don't need another Mikey. You've lost enough. It's okay to want to protect them." He kissed Emilia's forehead. "It means you care."

"But Molly and Samuel and Larkin, they'll be with us."

"They're adults who have been trained for this. Larkin was a MAGI, for God's sake."

"What about you?" Emilia twined her fingers through Jacob's. "You'll be fighting with me. I should make you stay back."

"You need me to make the travel spell work."

"I could find another plan."

"And I would follow you anyway." Jacob leaned in and kissed her. Her scent of lilacs drifted over him. Her lips were soft and warm against his. He held her close, and every nerve in his body seemed to rejoice *this is right! This is home!*

"My place is with you Emi," Jacob said when reason finally told him they couldn't stay intertwined on the lawn forever. "I fight with you. I win with you, or I die with you."

"I don't want anything to happen to you."

"Losing you is the worst thing I can imagine. I have to be there to protect you, to do everything I can to make sure my worst nightmare doesn't come true. I can't lose you, Emi." It was true. Losing her would tear his soul in two. He had suffered too much already. There was no way he could survive that final and most terrible blow. "I love you."

She kissed him, winding her fingers through his hair. She shifted so her cheek pressed against his and whispered in his ear, "I love you, too. Through everything that comes, I will always love you."

Too soon the moment was over. The people around them

were planning for battle, and Aunt Iz's funeral was in a few short hours.

"Where are we going?" Jacob asked.

"To see Sabbe."

Jacob didn't follow as Emilia moved to lead him forward.

"You want me to come?"

Emilia had always spoken to Sabbe alone. Their words meant only for them.

"I've never understood anything she's said to me." Pain crept into Emilia's voice. "I've done all the wrong things, and people have died."

The words didn't need to be spoken to know that Rosalie's death hung heavy in the air.

"If she wants to see me, maybe it's better if you talk to her." Emilia ran her free hand through her dark hair, sending it flying around her shoulders as though a sudden wind had blown. "Maybe you can understand her. If she's going to tell me something about Graylock, I can't risk misunderstanding, not with this many people entrusting me with their lives."

"But what if she won't tell you in front of me?"

"We're tethered." Emilia smiled, a tired but true smile. "As far as magic is concerned, we're the same person. We'll just have to make sure Sabbe sees it that way."

She strode off through the trees to the centaurs' tents, and Jacob followed. Hoping Emilia was right and Sabbe would share whatever she had to say with both of them, and terrified it was something neither of them would want to hear.

28

WRITTEN IN THE SHADOWS

*L*oblolly stood outside the emerald green tent. Emilia hadn't seen him with the rest of the centaurs, but she hadn't questioned why. The centaurs protected their elders as they did their children, both precious resources the future and survival of the Tribe depended on.

"Emilia Gray." Loblolly bowed deeply, every trace of his old twinkling smile gone. "I am glad you have come. And Jacob Gray." He bowed again. "It is good to see you again."

"You too," Jacob said, giving his own small bow.

"Can we see her now?" Emilia asked.

"We?" Loblolly's gaze moved between Jacob and Emilia.

"I'm taking Jacob with me to speak to her."

Loblolly considered for a moment before bowing and turning to open the tent flap.

"You are lucky to have someone who is a part of your soul to walk into battle by your side. May the rest of us be as strong when the darkness comes."

Emilia nodded, tightening her grip on Jacob's hand as they walked into the tent.

The air in the tent was cooler than she had expected. Not

with the cold of winter that blustered outside, but with the chill air that filled the woods with the first breath of spring. The scent of earth and new life came from the ground, which was soft beneath Emilia's feet. Emilia glanced down to find deep green moss and lichen covering the ground. A strange contrast to the frost they had just left.

Sabbe stood at the back of the tent, the green light reflecting off her bright white coat and hair, making her appear not of this world. Not dead or alive, but other. The green made Emilia shiver, her mind racing back to the mist of the Siren, but this green was different. A green of earth and pure magic.

Sabbe turned to them, fixing Emilia with her good, pale blue eye, the white of the other hidden in shadow.

"You've come to see me, Emilia Gray?" Sabbe said.

Although Emilia doubted it was meant to be a real question, she answered anyway. "I have."

Sabbe's gaze moved to Jacob. "And you've brought your *coniunx*."

Emilia's chest tightened as she struggled to keep her voice calm. "We've spoken before, and I've gotten everything wrong. People have died because I was foolish enough to believe I understood what you were saying. I won't take that chance again."

The lines on Sabbe's forehead grew even deeper as she furrowed her brow. "You believe you failed to understand my words?"

"I have failed," Emilia said, the nails of her free hand biting deep into her palm as she pushed away tears, "and I've lost people. People died because I was too stupid to understand. I wanted finding my mother to be the thing that would save us. I wanted her to be special and brilliant. For her to teach me how to stop the Pendragon. But she wasn't brilliant. And now she's dead because of me."

"And Isadora Gray?" Sabbe tipped her head to the side.

Ice shot through Emilia's heart. "I won't take the blame for

Aunt Iz. She would have fought no matter what. She would have stood at the middle of the battle. She died fighting. It's the Pendragon's fault, and I will have revenge."

"And in all this—blame, revenge, blood, murder—did you never once think that perhaps I was wrong?" Sabbe stepped forward so the green light shifted on her coat. "That I led you astray? That I wanted these terrible things to happen?"

"No," Emilia said.

"Why?" Sabbe stepped forward again so she was close enough for Emilia to reach out and touch her flank.

"Because I can't. Because if you had been plotting against me, trying to make the people I care about die…"

Emilia's voice faded away, and Jacob finished the impossible thought for her. "Then we would have lost much more than we understood. And this would be a fight we couldn't win."

"Your mother made you the warrior you needed to be to fight the Pendragon." Sabbe's voice was low. "The lesson was there to be learned, the manner of teaching yet to be decided."

"But she didn't teach me anything," Emilia said. "I didn't learn any magic from her. She didn't teach me to fight. I learned more magic from the Hag than from Rosalie."

"She didn't teach you magic." Sabbe reached out to Emilia.

Emilia stared at the old and weathered hand. A very childish and angry part of her wanted to bat it away. But if there was a lesson to learn, a reason for it all…

"She gave you the strength you need to defeat the Pendragon." Sabbe gripped Emilia's hand.

"But she didn't make me strong." Emilia shook her head, sending her dark hair flying.

"She did," Jacob whispered. "She made us stronger. Because we went after her, the Hag made us stronger together."

"And people died at that concert," Emilia said. "It was our fault."

"You cannot be blamed for murder done by a madman," Sabbe said.

"And Rosalie killed herself," Jacob pressed on, "to protect you, to keep the Pendragon from hurting you. Emi, you lost your mom because of him."

"I know that!"

"Which means you won't hesitate to kill him," Jacob said. "Don't you get it? Someone is going to have to get near him in order to end this. The people who have the best chance of stopping him are us. Would you have been able to do it? Would you really have been able to kill him? Not try and disable him or capture him, but kill him?

"I know you, Emi. Before, you would have tried to stop him without hurting him. But now"—Jacob took Emilia's face in his hands—"your mother died to stop him. More than Claire getting hurt or the murders at the Academy. Even more than Aunt Iz. He loved her, in his own twisted way, he did. She was the other half of his soul. And she knew him well enough to be willing to die rather than let him near you."

"Your hand will not waver when the moment comes," Sabbe said. "When the end is near, you will fight to kill until your last breath is gone."

Emilia felt as though her last breath had already left her.

"So we won't make it through the fight." There was no trace of fear in his voice as Jacob spoke.

"There is too much blood to see the faces buried beneath," Sabbe said, a single tear escaping from her good eye.

"Then should we not go?" Jacob asked. "If we're going to lose everyone, then what are we fighting for?"

"For the sunrise on the next morning," Sabbe said, "because some will live through the day and night. And for them, there will be a new beginning. If there is no battle, there will be nothing but darkness and pain for all. The shadows would take longer to come, but they would swallow the world. You must fight, Jacob Gray. All must fight."

"Not all," Emilia said, finally finding her voice. "I'll be there, but not everyone can fight. Some"—Emilia swallowed, searching for words that would not betray her selfishness—"some will have to stay behind."

Sabbe focused her pale blue eye on Emilia for a moment before nodding. "You will lead the fight, and when the moment comes, you must deal the final blow to the Pendragon. Blood will rain blood, and fire will scorch fire. It is the only way the world can begin anew."

Sabbe backed away. Emilia hadn't noticed that Sabbe was still holding her hand until she let go and turned her back to them, their time apparently over.

Jacob walked to the tent flap and held it open for Emilia.

"I want to thank you," Emilia said, her feet frozen to the ground as though they had become a part of the moss. "I wish I could thank you. For leading me down the right path. For showing me a path to strength. But my mother is dead because you told me to look for her. Finding Rosalie made everything worse, and so many people have died."

A tear fought its way from Emilia's eye. She hated the tear for betraying her even if Sabbe didn't turn to see it.

"But I can't be grateful for the blood on my hands."

"I did not decree what was to come," Sabbe said. "What is written in the shadows is written in the shadows. I should not be blamed for being able to see."

"But if you hadn't told me to find her, I would have left Rosalie alone." Emilia's voice shook.

"No," Sabbe said, "you wouldn't. You would have found her name and the way to bring her back. You would have fought with everything you have because she was your mother. I only gave purpose to the return. The blood is on other hands, not yours nor mine. Neither of us is to blame."

Emilia opened her mouth to argue again, wanting to scream and shout. To tear down the green tent and burn all of it. But there was something in the sadness of Sabbe's tone. A sadness that could only come from indisputable truth.

"Come on, Emi," Jacob whispered.

Emilia gave the bright white aging centaur one last look. "Goodbye, Sabbe."

A feeling of finality sunk into Emilia's chest as Jacob led her back to the Mansion House. She would never see Sabbe again. Whether by Sabbe's death or her own, those were the last words they would speak to each other. It was written in the shadows.

29

DRESSED IN BLACK

*E*milia stood alone in her room. It was time to change. She needed to get ready for Aunt Iz's funeral. But she caught a glimpse of herself in the mirror. There was a scar on her ribs right under her bra. It looked new, but she couldn't remember when she had gotten it. Or who had given it to her. Bruises marked her bare arms and back. Her legs were probably worse, but she hadn't gotten that far in undressing. She looked so different than she had a few months ago. And it wasn't just the marks of battle or the pale and worn color of her face.

She had grown up. It had happened so quickly, and it could never be undone. The bruises would heal and the scars would fade, but nothing could ever change all she had been through. Her eyes drifted down to her left palm, to the golden streak that was the sign of her connection with Jacob. Rubbing her fingers across it, the mark didn't feel like anything. Yet it meant more than the rest of the scars put together. She would never let that mark go.

Voices from the ground floor pulled Emilia back to the task at hand. The sun was beginning to sink, and in less than an hour it would be time for the funeral.

Her closet was full of clothes. A black dress Aunt Iz had bought to take her to the opera in Manhattan. A thick, black sweater Larkin had given her for Christmas the year before. But neither seemed right.

And as soon as the funeral was over, they would need to begin sending people to Graylock. Some by broom, others by car. They would have to leave in waves. There would be no time for sleeping or changing shoes.

It seemed wrong to mar Aunt Iz's funeral with preparations for battle. The world should be silent. Even humans who had never heard of the Gray Clan should feel the loss of the woman who had tried so hard to protect them from the evil of the Pendragon. But the battle needed to be fought. Anyone who was left at the end would have time to grieve.

Emilia reached into the closet and pulled out a long-sleeved, black shirt. Too plain for a funeral, but comfortable enough to fight in.

"You can't wear that," Claire said from the door to Emilia's room.

"You shouldn't sneak into people's rooms." Emilia pushed down the panic that had surged in her chest.

"I guess not when the world has been flushed down the toilet." Claire walked over to Emilia's bed and laid down an armful of clothes. "But some things can't wait. I'm glad I caught you in time."

"In time for what?" Emilia began pulling on the black shirt.

"In time to stop you from wearing that." Claire made a face and waved a hand at Emilia's shirt. "You're picking out an outfit for Aunt Iz's funeral and the battle for the future of Magickind. You can't wear something off the rack."

"Well, I don't really have time to make a trip to the tailor." Emilia yanked the shirt roughly over her head.

"No one's asking you to go anywhere, just to do as you're told. And don't try and go all high and mighty Clan Elder on me—"

"I'm not an Elder—"

"If we still had a Council of Elders, you'd be sitting on it, and once you went grey, they'd even start giving you the title. And you know what?" Claire strode over to Emilia and began tugging her shirt off. "I'd be dressing you for the meetings, too. The Gray Clan has an image to uphold, and I will not let it falter in these dark and terrible times. Now take the shirt off before I have to magic it off. I'm too short to reach over your head."

"Fine," Emilia said, feeling her mouth pull into the tiniest smile. "You can be my official dresser, but we still don't have time—"

"I have everything right here." Claire presented the pile of black clothing on the bed. "The pants and shirt are fairly generic, but have great lines and will be super easy to move in for the impending battle of doom. Undershirt is the same—your waist will look fantastic—but the jacket is the real treasure, see?"

Claire held up the jacket. It was made of fine black leather, smooth and supple, but the thing that caught Emilia's eye was the tree of life embossed in gold on the left breast.

"The Clan crest." Emilia ran her fingers over the tree. "The Dragons have dragons like this on their uniforms."

"I know. That's why I decided to go with this concept," Claire said. "Like old-school armies going into battle bearing their insignias. I wanted to make jackets for everyone, but there's only so much leather magic a girl can work in an hour, so only you and Jacob got the cool Clan jackets. I wanted to make them for Connor and me, but since I don't know what our part of the plan is yet, I didn't know if we should blend in with the others a bit more."

"Right." Emilia pulled on the black shirt Claire handed her. The fabric was smooth and soft. Something in it made her aching arms feel less tired as the cool material lay against her skin. "I still need to talk to you and Connor about that."

"Well, now that you're not standing around in your bra, the

boys can come in. Connor, Jacob," Claire called over her shoulder, and a moment later the bedroom door opened. Connor was wearing a dark coat and jeans, but Jacob had already changed into his Claire-made uniform.

Jacob followed Emilia's gaze to the golden tree of life on his chest before shrugging.

"Emilia is ready to tell us our part of the plan," Claire said, moving to stand next to Connor.

"Good." Connor nodded "We're running out of time, and if there's any preparation we need to do, we'll have to get started."

"There's nothing to prepare," Emilia said, taking a deep breath before pushing on, "because neither of you is going to be fighting."

The uproar was predictably instantaneous.

"Of course we're fighting!"

"My whole family is going to be there!"

"We've fought the Pendragon before!"

"And his monsters!"

"We trained with the centaurs for longer than you did!"

"Enough! This isn't about you. I need you to do this for me." Emilia's voice broke. "We've all lost a lot, and I don't want to lose anyone else. I know I can't keep Larkin, or Samuel, or Molly from fighting."

"Or my parents," Connor added.

"But you two are kids," Emilia said. "I don't want to see another Mikey. We almost lost you once, Claire. I won't do it again."

"So none of the Academy kids are going?" Connor asked, anger rumbling in his voice.

"They're older than you two," Jacob said.

"So you're in on this, too?" Claire turned to Connor. "I should have known he'd be in on this, too."

"Those *kids* haven't fought or trained like we have," Connor said. "Jacob and I beat them in sparring so easily it was embarrassing."

"I don't care," Emilia said. "You two aren't going."

"Yes, we are," Claire said. "You gave us the *everyone has to fight* speech. Well, we're a part of that everyone. I will not sit here while all the people I love most are risking their lives to save the whole freakin' world with only the thought of *Well, I made them cool jackets* to comfort me."

"I just need to know that someone will survive!" Emilia squeezed her head in her hands, trying to find a way to make them understand. "I need to know that if we die doing this, there will be someone left who was worth fighting for."

"So you want us to stay behind and then bury all the bodies!" Claire shrieked.

"If we're really lucky, we might have time to give everyone I know a proper funeral before the Pendragon comes to kill us." Connor's voice was so low, it was nearly lost in the echo of Claire's scream. "He won't let us live."

He said it in such a simple tone Emilia's heart seemed to disappear from her chest.

"If we don't win this thing, the Pendragon will come for us," Connor said. "He'll find us here or wherever we try to hide. And then what? He'll take his time killing us himself, or maybe send a dozen *somnerri* to do it for him?"

"He knows we're a part of this family," Claire said. "We fought him at the concert. He's not going to let us run happily into the sunset."

"It's win or die for all of us, Emilia," Connor said. "And if I'm going to die, I'd rather die fighting with everyone else than spend my last few days running from Dragons."

"You can find a place to hide," Emilia said. "Claire can build you a whole new life. You can move to another country."

"You just want us to abandon everything?" Claire laughed.

"Well, now I understand. Just live the rest of our lives checking over our shoulders for Dragons."

"It won't matter where we go," Connor said. "We're too deep in this. They won't let us run away."

"He's right," Jacob said after a long moment. "They both are. He'll come for them."

"But then they're right about being targets, too," Emilia said. "If he sees them, he'll go after them."

"Aren't you the ones being used as bait?" Claire asked.

"That's different," Emilia said.

"How?" Connor asked.

"Because I need you to survive." Emilia paced her bedroom, the familiar feel of the pale purple carpet under her feet making her want to scream. "I don't want you at the front."

"Then we can lead the Academy students," Connor offered. "You've given them perimeter watchdog duty. Don't you think there should be people there who can really fight?"

"There will be fighters right in front of them," Jacob said.

"Then give them two more."

"No." Emilia spun to face them. "If you're coming you're staying at the back."

"Should we wait in the car with the doors locked?" Claire asked.

"You should go where I tell you since I'm the head of your Clan." The words flew from Emilia's mouth before she knew she was saying them. Claire looked as though she had been slapped. But it didn't matter. Emilia needed to keep them alive, she didn't need to be liked. "You stay at the very back of the fight behind the Academy students. If someone comes up from behind, stop them from breaking our lines. But you do not move into the fight unless there is no other option."

"Yes, ma'am," Claire said through gritted teeth. "We'll stand at the back. And when some Dragons make it that far, we'll dispose of them. I'm not just some thirteen-year-old in pink, Emilia. I can fight." Claire spun toward the door. "Come on, Connor, we're going to the corner of the garden wall."

"Why?" Connor asked, his confusion mixing with the anger etched on his face.

"I'd like to introduce you to some friends of mine." Claire flung open the door, only stopping to say, "you're welcome for the jackets," before leaving.

"You did the right thing," Jacob said after Connor had slammed the door.

"Did I," Emilia said, "or am I just selfish for wanting them to survive while everyone else dies?"

"They're the closest thing to a new generation for the Gray Clan we have," Jacob said, drawing her in to lay her head on his shoulder.

Instinctively, her head found the place where it fit so perfectly.

"What if I never get to be here again?" Emilia whispered. "What if I don't get to kiss you again?"

Jacob lifted Emilia's chin up so her lips were nearly touching his. "You will."

"What if I don't?" Emilia gripped the front of his jacket. "We've seen too much and been through too much darkness. We're buried too deep. What if we can't find a way back out?"

"Emi, I have you. You're here, and I'm here. As long as we have each other, we have hope."

"Promise?"

"With everything I have, Emilia Gray." And he kissed her. His arms wrapping around her, holding her close to his chest. Emilia's breath caught in her lungs as his heartbeat flowed through her.

Lacing her fingers through his hair, she willed time to stand still and let them stay there in each other's arms forever.

Too soon the horn sounded on the lawn.

The time for the funeral had come.

30

LIFE IN A TREE

The centaurs led the procession into the trees behind the garden, their hooves thumping as one on the snow-dusted ground. The wizards filed in behind, not keeping to their groups. Who lived where didn't matter tonight. They were each of the Gray Clan.

Jacob stood next to Emilia on the front steps with the family. Connor and Claire were missing from the group, but Jacob didn't dare ask where they might be. The air around the Mansion House felt muted, like a blanket had been laid out over everything. He didn't want even a few murmured words to disturb the solemn silence.

When it was the families' turn to join the long line, Jacob moved to let go of Emilia's hand so she could go first. But she held on tight, keeping him by her side.

Jacob tightened his fingers through hers, telling her without words that he wouldn't let go as long as she wanted him next to her.

The sky was turning from orange to grey as they reached the trees. Giving the bare branches a ghostly and skeletal look that made Jacob's heart quicken as they entered the darkening shadows.

They weren't traveling on a path he had ever been on before. Or perhaps it wasn't a path at all. But they followed the line deep into the trees toward the high stone wall that surrounded the Mansion House grounds.

The walk wasn't very long, much shorter than when Jacob had once before followed mourning centaurs into the trees at the Green Mountain Preserve.

When they finally reached the wall at the edge of the garden, the centaurs had formed a half-circle, letting the wizards fill in in front of them.

Emilia took a shuddering breath as they walked through the crowd toward a fresh patch of earth ten feet in front of the wall. The square of newly turned dirt was all that marked Isadora Gray's grave.

Jacob wanted to shout that there must have been some sort of a mistake. They had forgotten to make her a headstone. But Emilia was staring straight ahead. Molly, Larkin, Samuel, all stood flanking them, Connor and Claire joining only a moment later. As soon as they stopped moving, the night fell silent. There was no wind in the air or leaves on the trees to make a sound.

Emilia took a breath before letting go of Jacob's hand and stepping forward. Molly and Larkin followed her. Jacob wanted to stay near Emilia, but there was something in the way she moved that told him this was not a thing to be disturbed. His place was only as an observer.

Emilia walked forward until her toes were nearly touching the edge of Aunt Iz's grave.

Jacob's heart thudded in his chest as Emilia's grief and fear matched his own.

"*Terra factunum*," Emilia began. "*Sinolvo navis*," Molly joined her. "*Sumellis pacsium*," Larkin added her voice to the spell.

Jacob stared at the ground in front of Emilia's feet, waiting for something to happen. But a loud *crack* five feet ahead of the grave pulled Jacob's gaze forward to a place where the frozen ground had split. Something bright green rose from the earth.

"Milkawa Prorsus."

The green grew quickly like a time-lapse video. Leaves formed from the blur, and a brown trunk began to show between them.

"Requiam bellusera."

The tree was ten feet high now with a trunk four feet wide. Before Jacob could take another breath, the tree was fifteen feet high, then twenty.

He heard Iz's voice in his mind as though she stood right behind, just tricking him and slipping out of sight as she had the first time she had shown him magic. *"We don't make them grow. We supply the energy, and they do the growing."*

Aunt Iz herself had said that to him in the garden what seemed like two lifetimes ago. Her time with them had ended. The tree was her last gift to them all, a living reminder that she would never truly be gone.

"Valarens." Emilia finished the spell alone.

A tree twenty-five feet tall with fresh new leaves rose above Isadora Gray's grave, a living headstone for the fallen Elder of the Gray Clan. The leaves on the tree stirred as though the last words of the spell were whispering through their branches.

And then all was still.

Jacob rubbed the tears from his cheeks, wishing he could talk to Aunt Iz one more time. To have her gaze at him with her penetrating eyes and feel that she was reading his soul. But she was gone.

Proteus was the first to move, stepping forward past the lines of wizards.

"Isadora Gray was a great leader," Proteus began. "She was killed by a coward who would not face her himself. The shadowing for her cannot take place until her murder is avenged. We fight tomorrow to lay Isadora Gray's soul to rest."

"Till she runs with the shadows," the centaurs murmured from the back of the group as though it was a solemn promise they were all now bound to keep.

"Thank you," Emilia said, looking at the tree for a moment longer before turning to face her Clan. "We have work to do and a battle to fight. Mourning is a luxury the Dragons have stolen from us. You all know what you have to do."

There was no roar of approval or shout of triumph at her words. An understanding had settled over them all. There would be more funerals before there was time to mourn.

"I'll take the brooms with me," Dexter said. The Academy students and a handful of others turned and followed him down the new path to the Mansion House.

Slowly they filed out. The centaurs following Proteus. They faced the hardest travel. Even with centaur magic, the way to Graylock was a long run through the dark.

Molly and Billy took their groups last, Connor and Claire following to ride in the cars. Claire throwing one last hurt look over her shoulder before disappearing into the trees.

"You did the right thing," Larkin said to Emilia as soon as she and Samuel were the only ones left. "It's what I would have done for you."

"Does it make me a bad leader?" Emilia asked.

"No, it means you have a heart and love people," Samuel said. "It's what separates us from the Dragons."

"Are you sure you want to go into the shield with us?" Jacob asked, knowing the answer but needing to ask the question.

"We aren't sending you in there alone," Larkin said. "Besides, I have a debt to repay. Stone is mine."

"They tortured us, they tried to take away my humanity," Samuel said, the scars on his face growing more apparent as he spoke. "We have a right to the first spells aimed."

"You do," Emilia said. "I know you do."

"What do we do until it's time?" Jacob asked, feeling as though it would have been easier to go to Graylock right then. The waiting would be worse than just going, but the others had to be in place and they would need time to get there.

"We make sure the others get off safely, guard the gate while they leave, then practice the Hag's spell so we know we can pull this thing off," Larkin said.

"It'll work," Samuel said. "We've got no choice but to make it."

RETURN TO GRAYLOCK

*D*arkness pressed in on Jacob, stealing the air from his lungs. But before he even had time to panic, dim light replaced the stifling blackness. A flash of bright purple threw his new surroundings into strange relief. Before he could look at the rocks, trees, or people in front of him, a flash of orange light and a billow of smoke lit the dim morning, blocking Jacob's view entirely.

Screams of fright echoed in front of them as a hand pulled quickly away from his and Emilia shouted, *"Primurgo!"*

The shield shook almost instantly as a spell struck the barrier, sending veins of red lightning dancing across it.

Someone shouted orders through the smoke. "Maintain the shield! Do not let the chanters be stopped!"

Footsteps moved toward them as another spell shook their shield.

"My name is Emilia Gray." Emilia's voice rose above the chaos. "I have come to demand an audience with the Pendragon."

The footsteps stopped as the smoke began to clear, and the chanting grew stronger as the circle refocused.

For a moment, Jacob wanted to attack the chanters, to break

the Dragons' shield spell and bring the Gray Clan in to stop them. But that wasn't the plan. They needed to get the Pendragon out into the open first.

"Stop," a voice shouted. A low, calm voice Jacob recognized.

Tall, dark MAGI Stone was the first face to appear out of the smoke, his shaved head reflecting the glow of the fading orange light. His gaze shifted slowly from Jacob to Emilia. He had been terrifying to look at when they thought he was on their side. But now that he had betrayed them, Jacob wanted nothing more than to attack.

"Emilia Gray," Stone rumbled, "why have you come here to see the Pendragon?"

"Why did you betray us?" Emilia growled.

"Answer me," Stone said without flinching.

"Oh, were you trying to get an answer?" Emilia said. "I thought we were just exchanging unpleasantries."

"Answer me."

They hadn't counted on meeting Stone so soon. Jacob willed Emilia to stay calm. To follow the plan.

"I'm surprised the Pendragon lets someone with such a history of betrayal guard the tunnels," Emilia said. "I'll speak to the Pendragon. No one else."

"Then please, come inside," a man called.

Jacob looked to the dark cave entrance. A man stood in the opening. He wasn't someone Jacob had ever seen before, but he held himself with an undeniable air of authority.

A look of anger settled onto Stone's face as he stepped aside for the stranger.

"The Pendragon has told you many times he would be willing to accept his daughter with open arms," the man continued.

"As long as he gets to kill Jacob?" Emilia asked. "I have heard that one from him before."

"We demand an audience with the Pendragon," Jacob said, stepping sideways toward Emilia, his muscles tense and ready to fight. "He'll want to see us, but he's going to have to come out here to do it."

"And what if he refuses?" the man said. "Perhaps he's not even here. Wouldn't it be a shame if you went through all the trouble of sneaking into our shield and your father wasn't even here?"

Jacob pressed his arm against Emilia's, feeling her tense at the hateful word *father*.

"We didn't sneak," Emilia said. "We broke right through. And if you don't bring the Pendragon out, we'll leave the same way."

The man studied Emilia for a moment.

"We aren't going to tell you how we broke through your fancy shield, so don't bother asking," Jacob said, luring the man's gaze from Emilia to himself.

"You'd be surprised what you'll tell me." The man smiled, an expression that did not reach his eyes. "But the Pendragon will decide what you will tell us in the end."

"I will decide all things." The Pendragon's voice came from the shadows by the entrance. "Obedience is something Isadora Gray never managed to instill in my daughter."

"How dare you say her name," Emilia spat.

"But no matter," the Pendragon continued. "Obedience can be taught."

"I didn't come here for you to teach me anything," Emilia said.

"Then why have you come?" The Pendragon stepped out of the shadowed opening of the caves. He looked different, like he had aged a decade in the week since he had flown away on a fiery dragon, leaving them with Rosalie's lifeless body. His hair had greyed, and lines marred his handsome face. His movement was no longer smooth and daring. There was a mark of age in the way he walked now. "Why has my daughter appeared to me after all this time? I suppose that is the real question, my Emilia."

"I am not *your* anything," Emilia said.

Jacob willed the Pendragon forward. Just keep walking forward. Ten more steps, that was all they needed.

"You are my daughter," the Pendragon said. "Blood knows blood, never forget that. You are made of your mother and me. You have never been a Gray."

"I am a Gray," Emilia said. "That is my family and my Clan."

"And now you're their leader, aren't you?" The Pendragon moved a step closer. "Such a mantle of power to be thrust upon one so young. She should have left a proxy to fill your place until you had reached a suitable age. She should have protected you."

"Aunt Iz did protect me. She loved me, she raised me, and you had her killed."

"It was necessary," the Pendragon said without a hint of remorse. "She was trying to turn all the children of Magickind against me as she had turned my own daughter."

"I would have been against you with or without her," Emilia said. "You're nothing but a murderer."

"I am a leader." The Pendragon stepped forward again. He was three feet in front of the entrance to the caves now, and seven from the circle of chanters. "I am bringing Magickind into a bright and wonderful future. And you, *you*, my sweet Emilia, are now the head of a powerful Clan. A Clan that could help me rule—"

"I will never help you!"

"And with magic such as yours, it is clear that you belong by my side." The Pendragon smiled. "Breaking through my shield spell...I will admit I had thought that impossible."

"It wasn't even that hard," Emilia said. "And it's only the beginning. I will fight you. The Gray Clan will fight you."

"Is that why you've come here?" the Pendragon asked. "To warn me that you'll fight me? That hardly seems worth it."

He was still too far from the circle. He needed to step forward, they were running out of time.

"We didn't come here to warn you. We came because I asked her to," Jacob said, his mind racing so quickly it took him a second to realize he had actually said the words. "You lost Rosalie. You lost your *coniunx*."

Pain surged onto the Pendragon's face as though Jacob had driven a dagger into his heart. "The Siren took her from me years ago. I could not save her from herself."

"Is that really what you think?" Jacob said, genuine fury rising in his chest. "It's not your fault that Rosalie is dead? She did it because she hated you, hated feeling your heart beat in her chest."

"How dare you." Magic crackled around the Pendragon's gloved fingers.

Jacob wanted to send a spell at him, anything to keep him from getting an inch closer to Emilia. But he was still too far from the chanters.

"She died to keep you from taking Emilia," Jacob said.

"And yet you've delivered her to me!" The Pendragon bellowed, stepping forward, magic dancing in his grey eyes. "And why? Are you tired of her?"

"I love Emilia." Jacob clutched his wand. The time had almost come. "I will always protect her."

"Then why ask her to come here?"

Jacob's mind raced, searching for an answer other than *to help me kill you.*

"We've come for the traitor Stone!" Jacob shouted.

BLOOD FROM A STONE

"*H*e betrayed the Gray Clan, and we want our justice," Jacob spat the words, hoping they sounded firm.

Stone stepped toward the Pendragon, a sneer twisting his lips. "The Dragons care nothing for the justice of the Gray Clan."

"You will when you hear what we have to offer," Jacob said. "A traitor for a traitor. You give us Stone, we'll give you Dexter Wayland."

"An interesting proposal," the Pendragon said, the anger slipping from his voice.

"Pendragon, you cannot possibly consider—"

"I may consider what I wish." The Pendragon took a step forward, appraising Jacob. "They must know Dexter Wayland could be dangerous to us or they wouldn't have bothered to come." He was at the circle, in position, but nothing happened.

"I have followed your orders, Pendragon. I have served the Dragons' cause," Stone said.

"And sometimes the most valuable service that can be given is sacrifice," the Pendragon said. "Much could be gained by retrieving the Wayland boy."

"I will not be handed over like some pawn." Stone strode forward, planting himself in front of the Pendragon.

And then it happened.

A blast of white-hot light shot from the far left of the shield, striking the circle of chanters. At the exact same moment, two fiery bolts came from the right, heading for the Pendragon and Stone.

Jacob shouted, reaching out for Emilia as the blast from the circle knocked them off their feet. Even with Emilia's shield protecting them, the heat made Jacob's skin prickle like he was standing too close to a bonfire.

Jacob rolled over to see if Emilia was all right, but something else caught his eye. The Pendragon had been too quick. The blast had knocked him back, toward the stone by the opening of the caves, but the lightning shard meant for him had missed its mark. Stone lay gasping on the ground, clutching his chest. And the chanters were still, sprawled on the rocky earth, their black uniforms singed, eyes wide open and afraid, pointing to the lightening sky.

"Emilia, are you all—" But before the words had fully left Jacob's mouth, shouts echoed in the distance as the Gray Clan charged into battle.

The Pendragon pushed himself off the stone wall and moved toward the entrance to the caves.

"*Terraminis!*" Emilia shouted, letting go of her shield to block the Pendragon's path. As though a giant had stomped on the opening, the entryway collapsed with a resounding *crack* that shook the earth.

The four guards that had been standing by the entrance surrounded the Pendragon, but Samuel had let go of the spell that had been hiding him and charged forward.

Two of the Dragon guards lunged toward him, wands raised.

Jacob started forward, but a hand grabbed his shoulder,

pulling him back. Jacob whipped around in time to see a streak of blond rush past him.

"Stone!" Larkin shouted, a ball of crackling light forming in her hands. She leaped, tossing the ball into the air and smacking it with her palm, sending it blazing toward Stone. The spell struck the ground where Stone's head had been only a second before, scorching the fallen branches and leaves.

A scream from his left pulled Jacob's attention back to Samuel's fight. The two Dragons from before lay at his feet, but the other two guards had joined the fray, sending spell after spell at Samuel, who battled with blurring speed.

Samuel leaped over the fallen Dragons, swinging his stone staff at the nearest guard and missing by mere inches. The fourth Dragon shot a spell, which whizzed by Samuel's right ear.

"Samuel, watch out!" Emilia screamed.

The two guards Samuel had leaped over had struggled to their feet. He was surrounded.

Dread shook Jacob's spine. The four guards raised their wands in unison.

"*Recora!*" the Dragons cried, muffling Samuel's yell of, "*Festigo!*"

It was over in a flash of red and grey.

The four Dragons swayed for a moment, then crumpled to the ground. Samuel stood between them covered in blood but seemingly unharmed.

Jacob's relief lasted only a moment. He started toward Samuel as Emilia screamed, "Larkin! Behind you!"

The scene was something out of a nightmare.

Larkin stood directly over Stone, another ball of light held overhead, oblivious to the pulsing mound of earth racing toward her.

In one fluid movement, Larkin spun around, threw the crackling sphere of light at the wriggling mound, and leaped aside as a dozen *somnerri* exploded out of it.

Jacob felt Emilia's fear as he ran toward the mass of black. "*Fulguratus!*" he screamed, sending shard after shard of lightning at the monsters.

The *rumble* of breaking earth sounded behind him. A sharp talon raked across Jacob's back. He shouted as pain shot through him and turned to face his attacker. But too slowly. The beast's claws were already coming down for another blow.

A crunching *thud* sounded, and the *somnerri* looked down at his own chest. An arrow had pierced his armor, and with a shudder, the beast fell.

A surge of fear shot through Jacob, and he spun to find Emilia. Two Dragons lay at her feet but three *somnerri* had surrounded her.

"Emilia!" Jacob shouted. "*Fulguratus!*" The bolt formed in his hand, and he threw it at the nearest *somnerri* as he charged toward her.

It wasn't enough to break through the monster's armor, but the beast turned to face Jacob.

Centaurs galloped into the clearing, and before Jacob could think of how to get past the monster and get to Emilia, a centaur had charged in front of him, taking off the monster's head in one quick blow.

Jacob was running again before the *somnerri*'s head hit the ground. His heart nearly stopped as the talons of one of the beasts still battling Emilia swept past her throat.

"*Fulguratus!*" Jacob screamed. He reared his hand back, but before he could release his magic, a blinding light flashed to his right, sending him flying. He slammed into the ground, feeling the air vanish from his lungs.

Gasping for breath, he pushed himself back to his feet, searching for his new attacker.

Chaos swam before his eyes.

The wizards from the settlements were scattered across the clearing, battling the *somnerri* and Dragons. The smoke of smoldering spells surrounded Jacob. Pain pulsed through his chest. He couldn't breathe. He was being choked, but not by the smoke.

Someone's arm had found his throat. The someone spoke, and Jacob recognized the deep voice of Jeremy Stone.

"I will not be traded to you for that worthless shit Wayland." Stone's words came in short spurts.

Jacob struggled uselessly against Stone's grip. He had to get to Emilia. She was still alive. He could feel it. But she was afraid. Horribly afraid.

He let his magic burn within him, rising up like a storm of fire. He had survived the spell once. Visions of trees and bodies on fire flashed through his mind. If he let the magic go, how many would he hurt? Could he control it enough to keep from killing the preserve wizards?

There was no other choice. He closed his eyes, ready for the fire.

At that moment, the grip around his neck slackened, and Jacob lunged forward, breaking free of Stone's grasp.

Without taking the time to look back, Jacob pelted to where he had last seen Emilia. But something was wrong.

The *crackle* and *whoosh* of a spell raced toward him. He turned in time to see a streak of blue, a bolt of red, and a blur of black cross his path.

The whirling light of the blue spell struck Dexter in the stomach, lifting him into the air and knocking him off his feet. The battle seemed to slow for a moment before Dexter crumpled to the ground.

"Dexter!" Jacob shouted.

But Dexter didn't shout back, or leap to his feet.

Jacob dove toward Dexter, narrowly avoiding a crackling orange spell that stung his face as it passed. Grabbing Dexter under the arms, he dragged him backward. It wasn't until he heard Dexter moan in pain that Jacob knew he was alive.

Jacob dragged him to two large trees, laying him down on the thin patch of frozen grass that lay between them.

"Dexter, you're going to be all right." Jacob knelt beside him, but when he looked at Dexter's face he knew he was wrong. Dexter's skin was pale, paler than a corpse. Blood touched the corners of his mouth, and the veins beneath his white skin throbbed. A sizzling wound marked his stomach.

"You need help," Jacob said. "I'll get help."

"No help," Dexter said, his voice coming out in a strained gurgle. "There is no help."

"I can find someone," Jacob said as Dexter grabbed his hand. "I can find Samuel."

An ear-piercing scream came from the clearing.

"Find Emilia. Keep her safe." Dexter seemed to be running out of air, his eyes glassing over as he looked up into the branches.

"No," Jacob said, desperately trying to think of a way to fix this, to fix him. "*Pelluere.*" The spell shimmered for a moment, but the ragged wound did not heal. "You saved me. I have to help you."

"I didn't do it for you." Dexter gasped, his chest shuddering. "Protect her. Go."

Jacob didn't want to leave Dexter lying between the trees to die. He didn't deserve that. No one deserved that.

But the earth began to shake. A tree nearby groaned as one of its branches fell with a screeching *snap*. The ground was still shaking, and Samuel shouted, "Fall back! Everyone move back!"

"Thank you," Jacob whispered before running back into the battle.

INTO THE EARTH

*T*he ground split open, rumbling and shaking as chasms appeared in the earth just as they had at the concert.

The Pendragon stood at the center of it all on a boulder that seemed to grow from the destruction around it. Emilia searched for a way forward, but the ground under her feet was crumbling too fast.

"Emilia, we have to move!" a voice shouted from behind her as a strong hand grabbed her arm, dragging her back.

Emilia turned to see Connor's father dragging her away.

"But we've nearly got him," Emilia shouted.

The *somnerri* had been killed in the attack, and the few that were left had fallen into the cracks in the earth.

"We have to regroup," Billy shouted as the rubble that had covered the opening of the caves was blasted aside and a hoard of Dragons appeared at the entryway, talismans ready to fight.

"Where's Jacob?" Emilia shouted, panic rushing through her as the first of the Dragon's spells hit the retreating Gray Clan. "Where is he?"

Emilia searched the crowd as she ran. The caves were still in sight, but he wasn't behind her. If he was hurt, she would know.

She would be able to feel it. "Jacob!" she screamed so loud it felt as though her throat would tear.

"Emilia!" Jacob sprinted toward her, parallel to the clearing. He was running fast, his wand gripped in his hand, still ready to fight.

The Pendragon's voice rose over the crowd as he shouted a spell. The earth shook so violently, Emilia was thrown from her feet as the clearing disappeared into the earth, leaving a bottomless hole where the ground had been.

The Pendragon looked down into its depths from his perch high above and smiled as dirt began to rise, forming a narrow bridge leading from the entrance of the caves to the Gray Clan.

The cries of the Dragons rent the air as they charged forward. Emilia scrambled to her feet, preparing to meet the Dragons, but Proteus was already at the bridge, his centaur legs carrying him faster than any human could run.

Swinging his sword with his powerful arms, three Dragons were lifted into the air, dead before their feet ever touched solid ground. But the fourth had time to prepare.

"*Immospatha!*"

The spell hit Proteus in the flank, and magic crackled along his skin as he howled in pain, still swinging his sword at his attacker. His blade found the Dragon's skin, but too slowly.

The Dragon behind him had already raised his wand.

"No!" Emilia ran forward a moment too late.

"*Pavicula velloras!*" Long tentacles of darkness wrapped around Proteus's torso, jerking him forward.

An arrow flew past Emilia, striking the Dragon in the chest, but the Dragon's spell had already done its work. Proteus's sword fell from his hands as his hooves slipped over the edge and, without a sound, he fell into nothingness.

"Proteus!" Raven charged forward, but there was nothing to be done. He had been swallowed by the blackness. There was no coming back.

"Emilia." Jacob reached her side.

"We have to break the bridge," Emilia said.

Jacob nodded, and they ran forward. But a scream made Emilia look back. The students the Academy were running toward them, chased by Nandi. A man in a black suit rode in a bubble behind them, herding them on. Mr. Wayland had joined the fray.

"*Oscutio!*" Lee shouted, wheeling around and tossing his spell at a Nandi a moment before its claws would have sunk into Maggie's flesh.

The animal's back leg cracked, breaking instantly, but the thing still lunged forward.

"Move!" a centaur shouted, thrusting his sword into the Nandi's skull.

"You!" Molly shouted at Wayland. "How dare you send monsters after children!"

Wayland spun toward Molly.

"He never did like kids," Larkin said. "Not even his own."

"How dare you," Wayland growled. He swept his arms through the air, as though beckoning the wind, and the remaining Nandi all turned to Molly and Larkin.

"Want to play with the big kids?" Larkin asked, pushing her bloody hair from her eyes.

"Attack!" Wayland screamed, and the Nandi ran forward as one.

"No!" Emilia shouted, switching directions from the bridge to Larkin and Molly. There were too many Nandi. They couldn't defend themselves from that many vicious claws.

But shards of lightning rained down on the Nandi from above. Claire and Connor stood perched on what looked like a glistening pillar of newly grown wood. Bright lights danced around them as Connor and Claire threw shard after shard of lightning at the Nandi.

"Claire?" Emilia shouted. "What are you doing?"

"Saving people!" Claire shouted. "I do have a life while you're not in the room. Go and end this, Emilia!"

But Wayland's bubble was floating closer to Connor and Claire's perch.

"You vile little—"

"Don't you dare touch them." Samuel charged forward to stand at the bottom of Claire's pillar of shimmering light. "You may have tortured me, but I will not let you lay a hand on these kids." Samuel planted his staff into the earth and shouted, "*Crevexo!*"

A line of explosions flew toward the pack of Nandi, sending them lurching and tumbling toward the ground.

"*Recora!*" Wayland shouted, sending a light of pure gold directly toward Samuel. It soared right at his heart but vanished an inch before it would have struck as tiny lights surrounded Samuel

With a great heave, Claire launched a pink stone at Wayland, which elongated and caught fire mid-flight. It pierced the bubble surrounding Wayland, striking him in the shoulder and sending him toppling, alight with fuchsia flames, toward the earth.

Emilia didn't want to look away. She wanted to help her family.

"Emilia, go!" Larkin shouted as she threw a ball of orange light at a Nandi, which turned to ashes where it stood.

Emilia spun to face the cave entrance and the chasm and knew instantly that something was wrong.

More than twenty Dragons had made it onto solid ground, and the Gray Clan was fighting them. But everything had gone eerily silent. Shadows laced in green mist rose from the darkness, their faces terrified.

The Dragons that were on the bridge had frozen, unwilling to move forward, toward the floating figures. A centaur's arrow flew past the specters, striking a Dragon and knocking him backward into the chasm, and still they did not run.

"How dare you!" The Pendragon screamed at the figures. "You have no place here."

Emilia ran forward to see the faces. *Ghosts.* A centaur drifted among them, his long, dark hair laced with green. Rosalie stood at the center of them all, her gaze finding Emilia for a moment before turning on the Pendragon who screamed in terror.

"Dexter, move!" Maggie ran forward. Her arm hung limply at her side, and blood drenched her shoulder. "Dexter, watch out!" She reached for the phantom Dexter, but the moment she touched him, she disappeared in a flash of green.

"Maggie!" Lee screamed, but he didn't run forward.

"It's the Siren," Jacob whispered.

All of the figures turned to face the Pendragon.

"Dexter." Emilia shook her head. "He's dead." It wasn't a question. It was the only reason Dexter would be standing with Proteus, Rosalie, and—Emilia's heart caught in her chest —Aunt Iz.

"There is another way," a rich female voice emanated from the shadows, filling the air around them as though her words had tangible substance. "You have longed for peace. I offer salvation. I will give you worlds to rule."

Tendrils of green mist rose from the chasm, lapping at the Pendragon's feet.

"No," the Pendragon said. "I will rule this world."

"I have much to offer—an eternity of pleasure." Rosalie's figure floated forward, reaching for the Pendragon. "You are powerful, the magic you have—"

"Never!" Emilia shouted, breaking free of the spell of the Siren's voice. "There will be no eternity for him. This ends today!"

The figures turned toward Emilia. "I could end it for you, if one will come. Only one, and I shall leave this world to its own fate."

"Not gonna happen," Jacob said, taking Emilia's hand.

"I am more powerful than you can imagine," the Siren's voice called. "I will have one."

The face that looked like Rosalie's broke into a twisted smile as she floated forward, her hands now reaching toward Emilia.

Emilia's scream was barely past her lips when an explosion shook the trees, reverberating with such force that all other sound disappeared. Emilia covered her face as dirt and rocks flew through the air. Jacob pulled her in close, shielding her body with his own.

In less than three seconds, the noise had disappeared, leaving only the ringing in Emilia's ears. She spun to face the chasm, but it had vanished. Replaced with one solid sheet of polished stone. A flicker of a white dress and dark hair disappeared into the trees as the green figures dissolved in the sunlight.

34

BLOOD KNOWS BLOOD

a group of Dragons stood on top of the polished stone, gazing around as though unsure of what to do.

Raven was the first to move, charging forward and plunging his spear into the nearest Dragon, piercing him through the red emblem on his chest.

The rest of the Elis Tribe followed Raven, running at the remaining Dragons, arrows nocked and spears raised.

Before the Tribe had reached the center of the stone, a rolling *crash* pounded through the clearing as all of the charging centaurs were lifted into the air, each surrounded by a shimmering bubble that muffled their screams of rage and pain.

"No!" Emilia's cry was covered by the torrent of spells shouted by the wizards of the Gray Clan.

Lightning flashed in the bubbles as they began to contract. Two of the bubbles burst, sending ash tumbling through the air.

A flash of purple light cut through the charging Grays toward the Pendragon.

The rest of the bubbles disappeared with a pop, and the trapped centaurs fell to the ground.

Two centaurs had been turned to ash, but there was no time

to find out who. Arrows flew, and whips flashed through the air as the centaurs surged forward.

More Dragons appeared from the caves, charging the centaurs and pushing them back. Spells flew freely. Reds, greens, and gold lit the canopied sky.

One of the green spells slipped through the red of Raven's whip, cutting a deep gash into his shoulder. He bellowed in pain but kept fighting as another centaur was struck in the chest by a golden light and crumpled lifeless to the ground.

A golden streak of light flashed towards Jacob's chest. He parried it with his own bolt, catching the Dragon under his outstretched arm.

Samuel ran limping into sight, Mr. Wayland gaining on him with every step.

"Samuel, behind you!" Emilia screamed as Mr. Wayland dashed forward, seemingly unnoticed by Samuel.

It was over in a flash of grey.

Samuel stood panting over Mr. Wayland's body, his stone staff protruding from Wayland's stomach.

An unbearable heat flared behind Emilia, and she turned in time to see a cone of fire, with the Pendragon at its center.

Trees ignited. The centaurs and preserve wizards, who had all moved toward the Pendragon, were flung away from him.

Just as the flames roared an inch from Emilia's face, a deep voice shouted, "*Talahm sciath uisce!*"

A sphere of raging water blossomed in front of them, hissing as it devoured the flames.

Raven stepped up to Jacob's right, staring directly at the Pendragon.

The Pendragon stood before the three of them. Blood, dirt, and ash coated his face.

Emilia glanced at Jacob, holding his gaze for a moment.

"So touching," the Pendragon said, his voice coming out a thick rasp. "The two of you, fighting side by side. I suppose nothing could seem more meaningful to children than dying together."

"That's not the plan." Jacob raised the tip of his wand, pointing it at the Pendragon's chest.

"You can't actually believe you can kill me," the Pendragon laughed.

"We've destroyed your men," Raven said.

The Pendragon ignored him, keeping his gaze fixed on Jacob and Emilia.

"Or perhaps I've misjudged you, Jacob Evans. Perhaps you've realized the best thing for Emilia would be to stand with her father. That the best thing for Magickind would be to toss aside the veil that has kept us living in darkness out of sight of the humans." The Pendragon's voice dropped as he spoke slowly, seductively. "Let her live, Jacob. Let Emilia see the dawn of a new world."

"He's not going to *let* me do anything," Emilia said. "This ends today."

The Pendragon tossed his head back and laughed.

"If you are so determined to die, my Emilia, I will not stand in your way. *Leferio.*" The spell flew from the Pendragon's wand.

"*Recora!*" Emilia shouted, leaping aside as the Pendragon's spell scorched the place where she had stood not a second before. But Emilia's spell missed its mark.

"*Fulgurmortus!*" Jacob shouted.

The Pendragon batted his spell aside.

"Do you think two children could defeat me?" the Pendragon asked.

"*Talahm mharú!*" Raven's spell hit the Pendragon in the chest, and he smiled as the waves of magic coursed through him.

"None of you are strong enough," the Pendragon sneered, stepping toward Jacob and Emilia.

"*Manuvis!*" Jacob shouted, and a ball of fire flew from his hands.

"*Impetaura*," the Pendragon laughed. The wind from his wand blew Jacob's fireball off-course, sending it toward Emilia.

She threw herself sideways, feeling the spell burn her back as she rolled away.

"Emilia!" Jacob shouted as she leaped to her feet.

Something sharp sliced deep into her left palm, and she fell back to the ground as pain like a surge of electricity cut through her hand.

"Emilia!" Jacob's voice was closer.

She turned in time to see a spell from the Pendragon knock Jacob and Raven backwards.

"Jacob! Raven!" Emilia pushed herself up again, and again her hand found something hard on the ground.

"You could never kill me, my Emilia." The Pendragon's voice carried over another *bang* that sent trees crashing to the ground around her.

Emilia rolled to the side as a tree limb came smashing toward her head. Instinctively, she held onto the hard thing on the ground. The weight of it tore at her arm as she rolled, and bright silver flashed in the sunlight. She gripped the hilt of Proteus's sword tight in her hand. It was coated in blood, but the blade was whole, unbroken by the battle.

"You don't have the strength to kill your own blood. It is not in you, Emilia LeFay."

"My name is Emilia Gray." Emilia stood, hoisting the sword in her grip. "And you know nothing about me."

The Pendragon tipped his head back and laughed. "A little girl with a sword. Is this what the great Gray Clan has been reduced to? *Fulgur mortel—*"

"*Solentus!*" Jacob screamed, cutting through the Pendragon's words. Air flew from his wand, visible in its thickness. It wrapped around the Pendragon, coating his body and muffling his cry of rage.

"*Talahm delascar ó cuíg!*" Raven shouted. A whip with five tails appeared in his hand. With a flick of his arm, the bright red veins of light wrapped around Jacob's spell.

The Pendragon's cry changed from rage to pain as Raven's whip burned him.

The Pendragon turned his gaze to Jacob, his lips forming a spell.

Emilia charged forward, her sword held high. Jacob's spell was shattering. The Pendragon was fighting his way through.

"*Rospina!*" the Pendragon screamed.

Before the magic could leave the Pendragon's body, Emilia stabbed him through the chest.

His grey eyes turned to Emilia, filled not with fear or anger, but surprise. His mouth opened to form a word, but a rattling gasp and trickle of blood came out instead. His gaze drifted down to the sword in his chest. He struggled to move his arms, trying to reach the hilt of the sword, but Raven's spell held him fast.

With a shudder and a cough, his head fell back, and his eyes went blank.

Raven released his spell, and the Pendragon sank to the ground. Emilia let go of the sword, letting it fall with the Pendragon's body.

"Emilia." Jacob was by her side, wrapping his arms around her waist as she swayed on the spot.

Raven stepped forward, staring down at the Pendragon.

Emile LeFay didn't look dark or frightening. Death had stolen his power. He was nothing but a shell now. A man who was nothing.

Raven reached down and pulled the sword from the Pedragon's chest. With one swing, he severed the Pendragon's head from his neck. Bile soared into Emilia's throat as she buried her head on Jacob's chest.

"It's over!" Raven roared over the last of the fighting. "The Pendragon is dead. Your leader is slain."

"No!" a cry came from the trees. Emilia turned to see a Dragon running forward, palm held high and aimed directly at her.

"*Aurictus!*" Claire shouted from her perch, and the Dragon crumpled to the ground.

A few Dragons tried to run toward the trees, but the Centaurs chased after them, stopping them before they could get out of sight.

Molly and Larkin were still fighting one Dragon who seemed determined to be killed in battle. Molly obliged.

"Shall we dispatch the rest?" Raven asked.

It took Emilia a moment to realize he was speaking to her.

"We'll take them to the dungeons after you question them," Emilia said. "We need to make sure there are no more traitors lurking within the Clans, or Dragons hiding in the shadows."

Raven nodded and began giving commands to the centaurs. Ropes flew from their palms, binding the living Dragons.

"What about the caves?" Samuel asked, walking slowly toward Emilia. His limp was worse than before, blood coated his torso, and burned skin shone brightly on his arm.

"There could be information in them," Jacob offered.

"Or traps," Samuel said.

Emilia stared down at the smooth stone that led up to the entrance to the caves. The opening was no longer neat and tidy. The rubble had been cast aside, and a jagged mouth led into the darkness.

"We've lost too many today," Emilia said. "I won't risk more death sending people in there. Destroy it."

Samuel nodded and moved toward the entrance, planting his staff on the ground. "*Finraco.*"

The ground rumbled, but the smooth stone didn't shake. A plume of dust flew from the entrance. Then the clearing was quiet.

"What do we do now?" Claire panted as she arrived at Emilia's side.

Emilia looked around. Everyone was staring at her, waiting for her to give instructions.

"Search the perimeter," Emilia told Larkin. "Make sure no Dragons have escaped. Molly, help the injured." Emilia turned to the crowd. "We need to collect the dead. Our people deserve a proper burial."

"What about the dead Dragons?" Lee asked.

"Burn them with the Pendragon."

35

UNTIL DAWN

*T*he sun had already sunk well past the center of the sky. It had taken hours to search the woods, first finding the wounded then collecting the dead.

Molly had healed the long gash on Jacob's back and his other wounds, but he still hurt. He hadn't slept in days. Every muscle ached from fighting. His arms burned every time he helped carry a fallen fighter to the clearing, as though death had added weight to the shell that was left behind.

They had won. The Dragons had been defeated. But the cost. The terrible cost in blood and death seemed to grow every time a new body was laid in the center of the clearing.

The injured had all been healed or moved away from the forest, Molly and Larkin taking the Academy students back to the Mansion House, each of the other groups claiming their own.

The dead had been left to be dealt with after the injured. Time mattered less for them.

Six centaurs had died in the battle, but only three bodies were laid out on the ground. Two had been turned to ash, and Proteus had fallen into the earth.

"We're going to take ours back to the preserve to be buried,"

Billy said, making Jacob jump as he spoke from behind his shoulder.

Jacob followed Billy's gaze down to a line of seven bodies. He searched the faces, glad that Connor's mother wasn't among them, knowing someone else had probably lost a parent.

That was the problem with fighting. He and Emilia, Claire, Connor, Larkin, Samuel, Molly—they had all survived. But others had died.

"Everyone's been claiming their own." Samuel limped up to Jacob, leaning heavily on his staff. "There are a few kids from the Academy. I don't know where they should go."

Jacob couldn't bring himself to look at the row of Academy dead. They had all been so young.

"Ask Lee," Jacob said. "He'll know if they have any family we should give the bodies to."

"And if they have no family?" Billy asked.

"They'll come with us," Emilia said. "I promised they would be members of the Gray Clan if they fought with us. The least we can do is give them proper burials."

Emilia took Jacob's hand, and warmth spread up his arm like a healing balm, soothing his heart, and giving new strength to his limbs.

"What about him?" Connor asked, walking over hand in hand with Claire.

Connor pointed to the one body that lay alone on the shining stone, separated from both the Dragon and the Gray Clan dead.

Jacob hadn't seen Dexter being carried back into the clearing. He looked as though he had been tossed onto the stone, his arms splayed at his sides.

It could have been Jacob lying there. Should have been.

Jacob swallowed the lump in his throat, forcing out the words. "He's a Gray. He should be buried with the Grays."

Emilia nodded.

"We'll take him with the others." Samuel walked away, giving orders to those left standing to help him move the bodies again.

Jacob tried not to think of how the bodies would be moved. Ambulances couldn't be called to Graylock. Sirens did not solve the problems of wizards.

"Emilia Gray." Raven bowed to Emilia, making the new scar on his shoulder twist and shine in the fading light. "You have avenged Isadora Gray."

Jacob felt a fist clench around Emilia's heart.

"You have avenged the lives of the Elis lost in this battle."

"They died fighting." Emilia's voice was strained.

"They died fighting so we might all live safe." Raven bowed again.

"I'm so"—Emilia began, swallowing before she continued—"so sorry Proteus was killed."

"It seems we've both been pressed into leading too soon." For the first time, a hint of sadness showed in Raven's dark eyes.

"So what do we do?" Emilia asked.

The clearing was almost empty now. Only the dead centaurs and Dragons were left lying on the ground.

"We bring the dead into the shadows," Raven said. "We honor them and look for sunrise tomorrow."

"And when dawn comes?"

"We keep living, Emi," Jacob said softly. "That's what we've been fighting for. A chance to live."

"Run with us, Emilia and Jacob Gray," Raven said. "Run through the darkness, and set the shadows free."

Jacob looked to Emilia, not sure what to say. He was certain being asked to run with the centaurs was an honor, but just as certain his two legs could not keep up with their four.

"Thank you." Tears shone in Emilia's eyes.

"Come," Raven said.

The sun had dipped below the horizon. The woods were falling into night. He led them to the bodies of the three centaurs, where the remaining Elis had begun to gather.

For a long while they stood silently, Raven looking up at the sky as though waiting for a sign.

Soon the only light came from the dim stars above and the warm golden glow that shone from Jacob and Emilia's hands. Jacob looked down at the light, letting it dazzle him for a moment before Raven began to chant in a low voice. Loblolly stepped up to his side and joined the incantation.

The words were guttural in the centaur's language that Jacob did not understand. *"Talahm siúl i scáth éineacht i lán."*

Emilia tensed beside Jacob, and he glanced at her. Her eyes were wide with confusion. Jacob followed her gaze to the bodies of the fallen centaurs.

They were each slowly disappearing into nothing. Not turning to dust or fading away, but becoming shadows, joining seamlessly with the darkness that filled the night.

"It is time," Raven said, turning to Jacob and Emilia. "Run with us."

Jacob nodded, wondering for a moment if he would be expected to ride on Raven's back. They'd ridden on centaurs before, but none offered to carry them.

Cold pulled at Jacob's toes. He looked down, studying his feet in the starlight, but there was nothing to see. His ankles went cold, then his legs. It wasn't until the chill had reached Jacob's waist that he realized darkness had come with the cold. He clung to Emilia's hand, willing the shadow spell not to separate them.

Jacob turned to Emilia. She met his eyes and didn't look afraid as the shadow engulfed her. Jacob studied her shadow. There was nothing left, even the grey eyes were black. But where their palms met, a glow still shone. A smile touched Jacob's lips. Even the shadows knew they were meant to be together.

The centaurs-made-shadow turned to face down the mountain. Each of them was covered in darkness ready to run with those lost in the final battle.

"Stay with me." Emilia's voice came as a whisper, not from her shadow, but floating on the cold night air. "Stay with me, Jacob."

"Forever."

The centaurs began to run, and Jacob flew after them, Emilia's hand clutched tightly in his. The cold that had poured through him with the shadowing seemed to have lightened him, too. His feet barely touched the ground. He could smell the deep scents of the woods in the air, but his breath didn't burn his lungs. The coldness wasn't of death but of a flying, freeing wind.

There were figures in front, beyond the centaurs, running just out of reach of the fastest of the living. Somehow familiar, but unrecognizable. Bigger and smaller than the living had been.

But his heart knew who they were. The ones who were lost. The ones who would run forever.

Jacob wanted to call after them, *Thank you. For all you gave and all you have given me! Thank you!*

But the words wouldn't come. So instead he ran, knowing he would never catch them, but determined to try.

On and on they ran. Through forests and fields. Never growing weary, just running.

Until the sun began to rise. And the shadows in front of them began to blur, fading in the unforgiving light of dawn. Jacob wanted to shout for the shadows to stay, that he would keep running with them forever. But the freedom of the darkness was for the dead. He still needed to live in the light.

His legs became heavy as the shadow that coated him faded, but he still ran on, determined to watch the shadows until the end.

They were in another forest. Flat land that seemed more forgiving and kind than Graylock had ever been.

With a bright flash of sun, the shadows vanished. The centaurs at the front stopped, and their color returned as they stood and watched the sun creep up over the trees.

Jacob wrapped his arms around Emilia, joy fluttering in his stomach as she leaned her head back onto his shoulder.

"It is done," Raven said, turning to Jacob and Emilia.

"Thank you," Emilia said. "Come and rest."

Raven nodded and turned.

Taking Jacob by the hand, Emilia led him and the others through the woods.

Jacob didn't question where they were going. Having Emilia's hand in his was enough to know that everything would be all right.

They walked through the woods as the sun rose, making the frost that covered the ground sparkle in the dawn of a dazzling new day. A stone wall appeared through the trees, and Emilia turned to follow it. Soon they had reached the high iron gate of the Mansion House. The gate swung open as Emilia approached, and the shudder in Jacob's chest didn't frighten him as he stepped onto the grounds. It was the Hag protecting them after all.

The centaurs all filed off into the trees while Jacob and Emilia walked toward the house.

They were almost to the front door when Jacob stopped, staring up at the Mansion House.

"We're safe," Jacob said.

"We are." Emilia nodded. "I didn't think we'd make it this far."

Jacob pulled Emilia to him, reveling in the feel of her in his arms.

"But we did," Jacob whispered. "We made it, and now we keep pushing forward. It's the only way to honor the people who can't. We rebuild what was lost, and we live our lives."

Tears sparkled in the corners of Emilia's eyes. "I love you, Jacob Evans."

Jacob pressed his lips to her forehead, breathing in her scent of fresh lilac. "I love you too, Emi."

Hand in hand, they walked into the Mansion House, ready to meet whatever would come next together.

AFTER

TWO YEARS LATER

*T*he Mansion House was silent, but Jacob knew it wouldn't last long. Soon Claire would be singing in the hall again, then Molly would be calling everyone down to lunch. With the house full of students, the quiet was strange. A rare gift on a bright summer afternoon.

Jacob sat at the window, looking out over the trees, waiting for Emilia to come back. The pull in his chest said she was nearby, but it was hard to feel over the joy that thrummed in his own heart. There was so much to be done, but Jacob couldn't bring himself to move away from the window.

An inevitable *clatter* came from the floor below. "Don't drop the dress, you swore you wouldn't drop the dress!"

Connor's retort was covered by Lee's laughter.

What did the dress matter anyway? It had really all been decided two years ago. Or maybe nine.

Jacob smiled to himself. The dress mattered plenty to Claire.

Larkin joined the fray, and the boys' footsteps pounded up the stairs as they were banished from the girls' wing on the floor below.

The family—*his* family—were all running around, trying to

make everything perfect. They didn't understand that the noise and chaos were perfection.

Jacob pressed his palm to the sun-warmed window, beaming as Emilia ran out of the woods, dark hair flying behind her.

"Emilia Gray!" Claire shouted out of a second story window. "You're late! Brides are not supposed to be late!"

Emilia stopped in the middle of the lawn, shaking her head at Claire before looking up to Jacob, smiling as their eyes met, knowing he would be waiting at the window for her to come home.

MAGGIE TRENT'S JOURNEY DIDN'T END AT
THE BATTLE OF GRAYLOCK

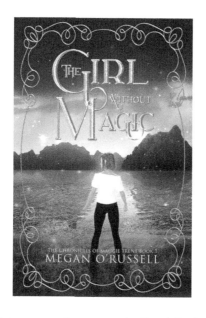

Enter a new adventure in the Siren's Realm.

Read on for a sneak peek of *The Girl Without Magic*.

CHAPTER ONE

*D*eath wasn't all that bad. Living had been harder. Dying hadn't even been painful. Every pain from the battle had stopped as soon as the world had gone black. Now there was nothing left but darkness and quiet.

The screams of her friends echoed in her mind with nothing in the silence to block out the unending wails. Were they lying in the dark, too? Free from pain and fear? Were they still fighting, alive and in danger?

Maybe they'd won. Maybe there was someone left to know she had died.

Did they leave her in the woods? Had there been a funeral? A hearse and a casket? Flowers with bright blooms? Did it matter?

She knew only darkness. Unrelenting black.

It did seem a little unfair that death should be so boring. If this was how it was going to be, perhaps existing wasn't worth it. Being alone with nothing but her own thoughts forever? Maggie had never expected much from death, but oblivion would have been better than knowledgeable nothingness.

Days passed in the darkness, or perhaps it was centuries.

There was no way to know without anything to measure the passing of time.

The blackness was maddening. It wasn't until Maggie clenched her fist in frustration at the absolute endlessness of it all that she realized she had a hand. Two hands actually. And a back, which was pressed into a hard floor.

Slowly unclenching her hands, Maggie ran her fingers across the ground. It was cool. How had she not noticed how cold the floor was? Carefully, Maggie rolled onto her stomach, feeling the darkness in all directions, stretching her toes out to see if the ground encased her or if she was lying on the precipice of a deeper blackness.

But there were no walls to run into or holes to tumble through. Pushing herself onto her knees, Maggie crawled a little ways forward, expecting to find something to tell her the size of her dark prison.

But still, there was nothing. Only endless darkness she could crawl around.

"Why?" Maggie asked the darkness, finding her voice as she pushed herself to her feet. "Why should I be able to move if there is nothing to see!" She had expected an echo, but her voice drifted away as though her cage were endless.

Recklessness surged through her. She was already dead—what was the worst that could happen?

Maggie took off at a run. Sprinting through the darkness. After a few minutes, her legs burned, and her breathing came in quick gasps.

"Couldn't get a nice breeze for the running dead girl, huh?" Maggie shouted.

Before the words had fully left her lips, a breeze whispered past her, cooling the back of her neck, kissing her face, and pushing her to run faster. The air even had a scent, like the ocean right before a rainstorm. The tang of salt filled her lungs. She could be running on a beach, an endless beach, but the floor was hard and maddeningly flat. And there was no sound of crashing waves.

"I wish I could see," Maggie whispered.

With a scream, she dropped to her knees, covering her face with her hands. Her heart racing in her chest, Maggie slowly opened her eyes, blinking at the dazzling light that surrounded her.

It was as bright as the sun but didn't come from a fixed point in the sky. Rather, it was like the air itself contained light.

The ground wasn't the hard stone Maggie had imagined. The floor shone a bright, pale color, like it was made of pure platinum.

"It's better than darkness," Maggie muttered.

Now that there was light to see by, the idea that this place went on forever seemed absurd. The floor had to lead somewhere. There had to be an end to it.

"Right." Maggie ran her hands through her hair. It was gritty with dirt and ashes and caked with blood at her temple. "Gross." Maggie moved to wipe her hands on her jeans, but they too were covered with dirt and blood. "I couldn't have clean clothes for eternity? All I want is a hot bath."

As though the air had heard her words, the light around her began to shimmer, twisting and folding into a hundred different colors. Coming closer, and growing solid, until, as quickly as it began, the air stopped moving.

Maggie swallowed the bile that had risen into her throat as the world twisted, blinking to adjust her eyes to the dim light of the tent. Her arms tingled like she had just tried to do a very long spell. Maggie gripped her hands together, willing the feeling to stop as she looked around the tent. And she *was* standing in a tent. It was small, only large enough for the little cot that stood at one end and the tub at the other.

The tent was made of deep blue fabric, which colored the light that streamed in from outside.

"Spiced Ale for sale!" a voice bellowed right outside Maggie's tent. She covered her mouth to keep from screaming. Slowly, she crept toward the flap of the tent.

Voices answered the ale seller's call. Bargaining and shouting came from off in the distance, too.

She pulled back the flap of the tent just far enough to be able to peer outside with one eye.

In the bright sunlight outside her tent, a street teemed with people. And not just wizards. There was a centaur at the end of the road, laughing with a group of witches. A troll sat not fifteen feet away, drinking from a mug the size of Maggie's head.

Maggie took a breath. Centaurs and trolls existed—she had known that for years. If she were dead, then why shouldn't she be with other members of Magickind? She gripped the tent flap, willing herself to walk onto the street and ask someone what was going on. How had death shifted from eternal darkness to a crowded street?

But everyone on the street looked whole and healthy, happy even. She was covered in blood and dirt. She glanced back at the tub in the corner. Thin wisps of steam rose from the water. If she was going to spend the rest of eternity here, she shouldn't scare the locals looking like she had just come from a blood bath.

The dried blood on her shirt crackled as she fumbled the mud-caked plastic buttons. The water burned as she slipped into the tub.

"At least a dead girl can still get a bath." Maggie sighed, leaning back into the water, running her fingers through her hair.

Her blood was in her hair—that much she knew for sure—and coating her sleeve, along with the blood of one of the wizard boys she had been fighting with. If he had died, maybe he would be here, too. But there was more blood.

She tried to think back through the fight, to remember what had happened before she had fallen into darkness. But the more she thought, the more disgusted she became. There could be dozens of people's blood on her.

"I wish I had some soap." No sooner had she said it than a bar of soap was floating in the tub, right next to her hand. A tingle in her chest made her pause as she reached for the soap. It felt like she had done magic. Like a little bit of her power had drained away.

That part was normal, but the tiny little space the magic had left behind wasn't refilling itself. It was just...empty.

Maggie scrubbed her hair and under her nails, washing her arms so hard they were bright red by the time she finally felt clean.

A soft towel waited for her next to the tub. It smelled of flowers and fresh air. Maggie breathed in the scent. Her clothes wouldn't smell like that. They would never be clean again.

"I wish," Maggie began, looking around the tent to see if anyone was even there to listen, "I wish for a clean set of clothes." Her stomach rumbled. "And some food."

Instantly, clothes appeared at the foot of the cot, and a platter of food sat on the table, filling the tent with the scent of roasted meat.

A sharp tingling shot through Maggie's fingers for the briefest moment. If she hadn't been thinking about it, she might not have noticed the tiny drain on the magic inside her. Her magic had always felt like a bottomless well before. She could feel it leaving when she did a spell, could feel her body channeling the energy, but it never seemed as though she might run out—as though there were a finite amount of magic she could access.

The scent of the food was enough to lure her from the warmth of the bath. Maggie took a shuddering breath and stood, wobbling on her shaking legs for a moment before stepping out of the tub. Maybe she wasn't using up her magic. Maybe she was just hungry.

Dripping on the grass that was the floor of the tent, Maggie sat in the spindly chair at the wooden table to eat.

She had always assumed, wrongly it seemed, that once you died you didn't have to bother with things like feeling like you hadn't eaten in a month. She had died only a little while ago. Or maybe it had been a hundred years. She wasn't sure it mattered.

A fresh loaf of bread sat on the carved wooden tray along with a hunk of roasted meat and a bowl of fruit. There was fruit that looked like an apple-sized blueberry that had grown spikes, bright orange berries, and a lavender thing the size of her fist that had a peel like an orange.

Maggie tore off a hunk of bread and stared at the bowl of fruit. Those weren't normal. They weren't real. But then maybe she wasn't real anymore either. Her head started to spin. Not knowing what was happening was beginning to feel worse than being trapped in the darkness. Her stomach turned, and she pushed the tray of food away.

"A trip toward the sea." A woman spoke outside the tent.

With a squeak, Maggie tipped out of her chair and fell to the ground.

"I'm tired of the streets," the woman continued, sounding so close Maggie could have reached out and touched her if the canvas hadn't been in the way.

"It's too crowded. I want to see the Endless Sea!"

Another woman giggled something Maggie couldn't understand, and then the two voices faded into the clatter.

Maggie lay on the ground, staring up at the blue fabric above her.

"Maggie Trent, you cannot lay here for the rest of your afterlife." She dug the heels of her hands into her eyes so hard spots danced in front of them. "You are going to go out there and ask someone what's going on." She let her arms fall to her sides. "Because talking to a troll isn't nearly as bad as lying naked in a tent talking to yourself. At least the grass is soft." Maggie laughed.

It started as a chuckle then turned quickly into a tearful laugh as panic crept into her.

She had charged into the woods knowing she might die. She had fought and killed. And then her life had ended. But being in a tent where food magically appeared was somehow more terrifying than fighting.

Maggie lifted her right hand, looking at the bracelet that wrapped around her wrist. It was only a bit of leather cord attached to a silver pendant. A crescent moon and three stars, the crest of the Virginia Clan. The last thing that tied her to her family. Funny it should follow her into death.

Reaching up onto the cot, she pulled down the new clothes. A loose-fitting pale top, dark pants, and a wide, sapphire-colored belt were all she had been given. Maggie pulled the clothes on, feeling a little like she was playing dress up. Not that she really remembered playing dress up. That had stopped when she was five.

Twelve years before I died.

Maggie ran her fingers through her short hair and, squaring her shoulders, pulled back the flap of the tent.

CHAPTER TWO

The light outside the tent was brighter than Maggie had expected it to be. The sun beat down on her, and she swayed as a centaur brushed past her. This wasn't Earth—it definitely wasn't. There was a wizard juggling balls of bright blue flames and a woman selling pastries shaped like dragon claws. There was nowhere like this on Earth.

Maggie took a deep, shuddering breath. The air smelled like spices, carried on a wind chased by a storm. She scanned the crowd, searching for a person she could talk to. Someone who might be willing to tell her why it felt like her magic was disappearing.

The troll was still sitting on her own at a table in front of a large red tent. Her table was laden with food, and she ate with abandon. Everyone else on the street seemed busy, either meandering to someplace or talking to the people around them.

Pushing her shoulders back, Maggie headed toward the troll. The red tent behind the troll seemed to be a restaurant of some sort. Empty tables sat in the shade inside the tent. There was only one man lurking deep in the shadows—a large man who looked angry as he held a cloth over his nose.

Three feet away from the troll, Maggie opened her mouth to speak, but before she could say, "Excuse me, ma'am," a foul stench filled her nose and flooded her mouth. Gagging, Maggie turned away, hoping the troll hadn't noticed her.

"Watch yourself," a man said when Maggie nearly backed into him.

"I'm sorry," Maggie said. "Actually, could you—"

The man walked away without listening to Maggie's question.

"Excuse me." Maggie stepped in front of a passing woman.

The woman was one of the most beautiful people Maggie had ever seen. She had silvery blond hair that hung down to her waist, lips the color of raspberries, and bright green eyes.

The woman looked at Maggie, her gaze drifting from Maggie's short brown hair to her plain boots. A coy smile floated across the woman's face before she spoke. "Whatever you are looking for, little girl, you aren't ready for me." She turned to walk away, but Maggie caught the woman's arm.

"Please," Maggie said, "I just need some answers. I don't even know where I am."

The woman laughed a slow, deep laugh.

"And I am not a little girl." Maggie let go of the woman's arm, fighting the urge to ball her hands into fists. "I'm seventeen. Or I was before I died. And it doesn't matter what I'm ready for. I'm here."

"You died?" the woman said with a fresh peal of laughter. "Poor child. Bertrand," the woman called over Maggie's shoulder.

Maggie spun to see who the beautiful woman might be calling. The street was full of people, none of whom seemed to be responding.

"Please just help me." Maggie turned back toward the woman.

The woman stood staring at her for a long moment before a man appeared over her shoulder.

"Did I interrupt something, Bertrand?" the woman asked, not bothering to look at the man.

"You are never an interruption, Lena." Bertrand gave a bow Lena didn't turn to see.

"This one *died*," Lena said.

"It's really not funny," Maggie said, wishing she had stayed back in her tent. "I was in a battle, and I got killed. I was fighting for the good guys when I died, so you could be a little nicer about it."

"Fighting for the good guys?" Lena laughed. "She thinks there are good guys. Oh, Bertrand, I just had to call for you."

"I can see why." Bertrand eyed Maggie as though examining a moderately interesting rock. "I shall do my best to help her."

Lena nodded and disappeared into the crowd.

Maggie warred with herself, not sure if she should shout a thank you after Lena or a string of curses.

"May I introduce myself?" Bertrand asked, the wrinkle of his brow showing his awareness that Maggie was considering saying no.

There was something about the man. He didn't seem to be much older than herself, probably only a little over twenty. But something in his eyes made Maggie wonder if he was two-hundred instead.

His long, dark hair was pulled back in a ponytail, and instead of the light clothing most of the others on the street wore, he sported a finely-made coat and vest, which matched his deep blue knickers, long white socks, and silver buckled shoes. Maggie had only ever seen clothing like that in old paintings. But she was dead, and if he had died a long time before she had ever been born, maybe those clothes were normal to him.

"Please do." Maggie's words came out a little angrier than she had meant them to.

"Very well." Bertrand smiled. "I am Bertrand Wayland."

"Wayland?" Maggie asked, her hands balling instinctively into fists.

"Yes. Wayland." Bertrand bowed. "Have you heard of my family?"

"I knew a Wayland." Maggie nodded. "Before I...well, you know...died."

"In battle?" Bertrand asked.

Maggie nodded.

Bertrand tented his fingers under his chin. "How very interesting, Miss?"

"Maggie Trent." Manners told her to reach out and shake his hand. Experience told her not to.

"Well, Miss Trent," Bertrand said, "I have the happy pleasure of telling you you are not, in fact, dead."

"What?" Relief flooded Maggie for only a moment before confusion washed it away.

"You are very much alive," Bertrand said, "but judging from your firm belief in your demise, I now have the unhappy duty of telling you that you are far from home. Very far from home, Miss Trent, and you are in a place I doubt you've ever heard of."

"So where are we?"

"The Siren's Realm." Bertrand spread his arms wide. "Welcome. It's not often we have arrivals who haven't meant to end up here, so I suppose you'll be more confused than most."

"Do people arrive here often?"

"I'm not really sure. If you'll follow me." Bertrand bowed before turning and striding down the street. "You see, time here is a bit funny. A day can feel like an hour or a year. It is all done by the will of the Siren."

"And you're the welcoming committee?" Maggie asked, having to run a few steps to catch up to Bertrand. The sights around her were enough to make her forget to wonder where he was leading her. A centaur smoking a pipe that puffed purple haze stood beside a woman selling jewels of every color Maggie had ever imagined.

"Oh no." Bertrand laughed. "I have simply been here for a

while without losing my love for the outside and those who dwell there."

"So who is the Siren?" Maggie asked. "And what do you mean *outside*?"

They had turned off the street where the red tent was and onto a tiny lane. The tents here were short like the one she had bathed in. There were no food vendors here or nearly as many people. A woman sipping wine sat outside the flap of her tent.

"Afternoon." The woman smiled.

Bertrand nodded to the woman as they passed, whispering to Maggie as soon as they were out of earshot, "Never trust that one. She'll cheat you every time."

"Cheat you at what?" Maggie asked. "Look, can you help me get out of here? If I'm not dead, then I might still be able to get"—Maggie stumbled on the word *home*—"back to where I belong. My friends could still be fighting. They might need me."

"Ah." Bertrand stopped so quickly Maggie ran into him. He took her by both shoulders to steady her. "Leaving the Siren's Realm is possible."

"Then how—"

"But getting back to the battle you left…I am afraid, Miss Trent, that might well be impossible." He strode down the lane, once again leaving Maggie running to catch up.

He led her onto a street so wide, centaurs walked down it four across. A line of people waited outside a vivid green tent trimmed with purple silk and embroidered with golden patterns. It was so beautiful Maggie wanted to stop and take a closer look, but Bertrand was still moving, and she didn't want to risk being left behind.

"Why couldn't I get back to the battle?" Maggie asked when she finally managed to get next to Bertrand. "How did I even get here? Why was I stuck in the dark?"

"All from the beginning." Bertrand turned left into a large square packed with people. "It's the best way forward."

He weaved through the crowd toward a fountain at the center of the square. A woman formed of the same shining metal the bright floor had been made of stood at the center of the fountain, her body draped in thin fabric. Her face was beautiful, but in a terrible way that made Maggie's chest tighten just looking at her. In one hand the woman held a goblet, which rained down bright, golden liquid. The other hand was encrusted with jewels of every color and reached toward the bright sky.

The golden liquid from the goblet filled a pool at the woman's feet, and people swam in the bright water.

"Here you are, Miss Trent." Bertrand bowed, gesturing toward the fountain.

"This is the beginning?" Maggie asked.

"The Siren is the beginning and the end. Knowing her rules is vital to living in her realm." He gestured to the fountain again, and this time Maggie found what he was showing her.

Inscribed in the side of the fountain was a verse.

> *In the Siren's Realm a wish need only be made.*
> *Her desire to please shall never be swayed.*
> *But should those around you wish you ill,*
> *the Siren's love shall protect you still.*
> *No two blessings shall contradict,*
> *so be sure your requests are carefully picked.*
> *Wish for joyful pleasure to be shared by all*
> *of the good and the brave who have risked the fall.*
> *But a warning to you once the wish is made,*
> *the Siren's price must always be paid.*

Maggie read through the verse three times without stopping. "What is that?" she asked when her eyes moved up to read a fourth time. "Some kind of demented nursery rhyme?"

"It is the Siren's Decree," Bertrand said, his tone giving a gentle reprimand for Maggie's remark. "It is the most basic rule we live under within her realm. Whether you meant to or not, Maggie Trent, you have become one of the brave who chanced the fall. You have arrived in the Siren's Realm where her greatest wish is for us all to live lives of pleasure and joy. You have, in short, arrived in paradise."

Order The Girl Without Magic *to continue Maggie's Adventure.*

ESCAPE INTO ADVENTURE

Thank you for reading *The Blood Heir*. If you enjoyed the series, please consider leaving a review to help other readers find Jacob and Emilia's story.

As always, thanks for reading,

Megan O'Russell

Never miss a moment of the magic and romance.

Join the Megan O'Russell mailing list to stay up to date on all the action by visiting https://www.meganorussell.com/book-signup.

ABOUT THE AUTHOR

 Megan O'Russell is the author of several Young Adult series that invite readers to escape into worlds of adventure. From *Girl of Glass*, which blends dystopian darkness with the heart-pounding danger of vampires, to *Ena of Ilbrea*, which draws readers into an epic world of magic and assassins.

With the *Girl of Glass* series, *The Tethering* series, *The Chronicles of Maggie Trent*, *The Tale of Bryant Adams*, the *Ena of Ilbrea* series, and several more projects planned for 2020, there are always exciting new books on the horizon. To be the first to hear about new releases, free short stories, and giveaways, sign up for Megan's newsletter by visiting the following:

https://www.meganorussell.com/book-signup.

Originally from Upstate New York, Megan is a professional musical theatre performer whose work has taken her across North America. Her chronic wanderlust has led her from Alaska to Thailand and many places in between. Wanting to travel has fostered Megan's love of books that allow her to visit countless new worlds from her favorite reading nook. Megan is also a lyricist and playwright. Information on her theatrical works can be found at RussellCompositions.com.

She would be thrilled to chat with you on Facebook or

Twitter @MeganORussell, elated if you'd visit her website MeganORussell.com, and over the moon if you'd like the pictures of her adventures on Instagram @ORussellMegan.

ALSO BY MEGAN O'RUSSELL

The Girl of Glass Series
Girl of Glass
Boy of Blood
Night of Never
Son of Sun

The Tale of Bryant Adams
How I Magically Messed Up My Life in Four Freakin' Days
Seven Things Not to Do When Everyone's Trying to Kill You
Three Simple Steps to Wizarding Domination
Five Spellbinding Laws of International Larceny

The Tethering Series
The Tethering
The Siren's Realm
The Dragon Unbound
The Blood Heir

The Chronicles of Maggie Trent
The Girl Without Magic
The Girl Locked With Gold
The Girl Cloaked in Shadow

Ena of Ilbrea
Wrath and Wing
Ember and Stone

Mountain and Ash

Ice and Sky

Feather and Flame

Guilds of Ilbrea

Inker and Crown

Myth and Storm

The Heart of Smoke Series

Heart of Smoke

Soul of Glass

Eye of Stone

Ash of Ages

Printed in Great Britain
by Amazon

16357199R00150